D1443122

LOVE BLOOMS IN WINTER

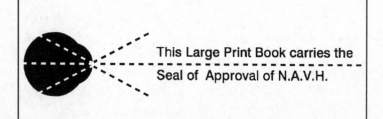

This Large Print Book carries the
Seal of Approval of N.A.V.H.

LOVE BLOOMS
IN WINTER

LORI COPELAND

THORNDIKE PRESS
A part of Gale, Cengage Learning

GALE
CENGAGE Learning®

Detroit • New York • San Francisco • New Haven, Conn • Waterville, Maine • London

GALE
CENGAGE Learning®

LIBRARY OF CONGRESS CATALOGING-IN-PUBLICATION DATA

Copeland, Lori.
  Love blooms in winter / by Lori Copeland.
    pages ; cm. — (Thorndike Press large print christian romance) (The Dakota diaries ; #1)
    ISBN-13: 978-1-4104-4765-4 (hardcover)
    ISBN-10: 1-4104-4765-0 (hardcover)
    1. Older people—Fiction. 2. Nephews—Fiction. 3. North Dakota—History—19th century—Fiction. 4. Large type books. I. Title.
  PS3553.O6336L74 2012b
  813'.54—dc23   2012009750

Published in 2012 by arrangement with Books & Such Literary Agency, Inc.

*To quote a famous person,
"It takes a village."*

*Writing a book takes
more than a village,
it takes a metropolis
and various minds,
hearts, and hands.
I dedicate this book
to three very special people
who helped me see this
book to completion:
Sharon Kizziah Holmes,
Kathy Garnesy, and my editor,
who is always at the head
of the helm, Kim Moore.*

ONE

Dwadlo, North Dakota, 1892

"The winter of '92 is gonna go down as one of the worst Dwadlo's ever seen," Hal Murphy grumbled as he dumped the sack of flour he got for his wife on the store counter. "Mark my words." He turned toward Mae Wilkey, the petite postmistress, who was stuffing mail in wooden slots.

"Spring can't come soon enough for me." She stepped back, straightening the row of letters and flyers. She didn't have to record Hal's prediction; it was the same every year. "I'd rather plant flowers than shovel snow any day of the week."

"Yes, ma'am." Hal nodded to the store owner, Dale Smith, who stood five foot seven inches with a rounded belly and salt-and-pepper hair swept to a wide front bang. "Add a couple of those dill pickles, will you?" Hal watched as Dale went over to the barrel and fished around inside, coming up

7

with two fat pickles.

"That'll fix me up." Hal turned his attention back to the mail cage, his eyes fixed on the lovely sight. "Can't understand why you're still single, Mae. You're as pretty as a raindrop on a lily pad." He sniffed the air. "And you smell as good."

Smiling, Mae moved from the letter boxes to the cash box. Icy weather may have delayed the train this morning, but she still had to count money and record the day's inventory. "Now, Hal, you know I'd marry you in a wink if you weren't already taken." Hal and Clara had been married forty-two years, but Mae's usual comeback never failed to put a sparkle in the farmer's eye. Truth be, she put a smile on every man's face, but she wasn't often aware of the flattering looks she received. Her heart belonged to Jake Mallory, Dwadlo's up-and-coming attorney.

Hal nodded. "I know. All the good ones are taken, aren't they?"

She nodded. "Every single one. Especially in Dwadlo."

The little prairie town was formed when the Chicago & North Western Railroad came through five years ago. Where abundant grass, wild flowers, and waterfalls had once flourished, hundreds of miles of steel rail crisscrossed the land, making way for big, black steam engines that hauled folks and supplies. Before the railroad came through, only three homesteads had dotted the rugged Dakota Territory: Mae's family's, Hal and Clara's, and Pauline Wilson's.

But in '87 life changed, and formerly platted sites became bustling towns. Pine Grove and Branch Springs followed, and Dwadlo suddenly thrived with immigrants, opportunists, and adventure-seeking folks staking claims out West. A new world opened when the Dakota Boom started.

Hal's gaze focused on Mae's left hand. "Jake still hasn't popped the question?"

Mae sighed. Hal was a pleasant sort, but she really wished the townspeople would occupy their thoughts with something other than her and Jake's pending engagement. True, they had been courting for six years and Jake still hadn't proposed, but she was confident he would. He'd said so, and he was a man of his word — though every holiday, when a ring would have been an appropriate gift, that special token of his intentions failed to materialize. Mae had more lockets than any one woman could wear, but Jake apparently thought that she could always use another one. What she could really use was his hand in marriage.

The bloom was swiftly fading from her youth, and it would be nice if her younger brother, Jeremy, had a man's presence in his life.

"Be patient, Hal. He's busy trying to establish a business."

"Good lands. How long does it take a man to open a law office?"

"Apparently six years and counting." She didn't like the uncertainty but she understood it, even if the town's population didn't. She had a good life, what with work, church, and the occasional social. Jake accompanied her to all public events, came over two or three times a week, and never failed to extend a hand when she needed something. It was almost as though they were already married.

"The man's a fool," Hal declared. "He'd better slap a ring on that finger before someone else comes along and does it for him."

"Not likely in Dwadlo," Mae mused. The town itself was made up of less than a hundred residents, but other folks lived in the surrounding areas and did their banking and shopping here. Main Street consisted of the General Store, Smith's Grain and Feed, the livery, the mortuary, the town hall and jail (which was almost always empty),

10

Doc Swede's office, Rosie's Café, and an empty building that had once housed the saloon. Mae hadn't spotted a sign on any business yet advertising "Husbands," but she was certain her patience would eventually win out.

With a final smile Hal moved off to pay for his goods. Mae hummed a little as she put the money box in the safe. Looking out the window, she noticed a stiff November wind snapping the red canvas awning that sheltered the store's porch. Across the square, a large gazebo absorbed the battering wind. The usually active gathering place was now empty under a gray sky. On summer nights music played, and the smell of popcorn and roasted peanuts filled the air. Today the structure looked as though it were bracing for another winter storm. Sighing, Mae realized she already longed for green grass, blooming flowers, and warm breezes.

After Hal left Mae finished up the last of the chores and then reached for her warm wool cape. She usually enjoyed the short walk home from work, but today she was tired — and her feet hurt because of the new boots she'd purchased from the Montgomery Ward catalog. On the page they had looked comfortable with their high tops and polished leather, but on her feet they felt like a vise.

Slipping the cape's hood over her hair, she said goodbye to Dale and then paused when her hand touched the doorknob. "Oh, dear. I really do need to check on Pauline again."

"How's she doing?" The store owner paused and leaned on his broom. "I noticed she hasn't been in church recently."

Dale always reminded Mae of an owl perching on a tree limb, his big, dark blue eyes swiveling here and there. He might not talk a body's leg off, but he kept up on town issues. She admired the quiet little man for what he did for the community and respected the way he preached to the congregation on Sundays.

How was Pauline doing? Mae worried the question over in her mind. Pauline lived alone, and she shouldn't. The elderly woman was Mae's neighbor, and she checked on her daily, but Pauline was steadily losing ground.

"She's getting more and more fragile, I'm afraid. Dale, have you ever heard Pauline speak of kin?"

The small man didn't take even a moment to ponder the question. "Never heard her

12

mention a single word about family of any kind."

"Hmm . . . me neither. But surely she must have some." Someone who should be here, in Dwadlo, looking after the frail soul. Mae didn't resent the extra work, but the post office and her brother kept her busy, and she really didn't have the right to make important decisions regarding the elderly woman's rapidly failing health.

Striding back to the bread rack, she picked up a fresh loaf. Dale had private rooms at the back of the store where he made his home, and he was often up before dawn baking bread, pies, and cakes for the community. Most folks in town baked their own goods, but there were a few, widowers and such, who depended on Dale's culinary skills. By this hour of the day the goods were usually gone, but a few remained. Placing a cherry pie in her basket as well, she called, "Add these things to my account, please, Dale. And pray for Pauline too."

Nodding, he continued sweeping, methodically running the stiff broomcorn bristles across the warped wood floor.

The numbing wind hit Mae full force when she stepped off the porch. Her hood flew off her head and an icy gust of air snatched away her breath. Putting down her

13

basket, she retied the hood before setting off for the brief walk home. Dwadlo was laid out in a rather strange pattern, a point everyone agreed on. Businesses and homes were built close together, partly as shelter from the howling prairie winds and partly because there wasn't much forethought given to town planning. Residents' homes sat not a hundred feet from the store. The whole community encompassed less than five acres.

Halfway to her house, snowflakes began swirling in the air. Huddling deeper into her wrap, Mae concentrated on the path as the flakes grew bigger.

She quickly covered the short distance to Pauline's. The dwelling was little more than a front room, tiny kitchen, and bedroom, but she was a small woman. Pauline pinned her yellow-white hair in a tight knot at the base of her skull, and she didn't have a tooth in her head. She chewed snuff, which she freely admitted was an awful habit, but Mae had never heard her speak of giving it up.

Her faded blue eyes were as round as buttons, and no matter what kind of day she was having, it was always a new one to her, filled with wonders. Her mind wasn't what it used to be. She had good and bad days, but mostly days when her moods changed as swift as summer lightning. She could be talking about tomatoes in the garden patch when suddenly she would be discussing how to spin wool.

Mae noted a soft wisp of smoke curling up from the chimney and smiled. Pauline had remembered to feed the fire this afternoon, so this was a good day.

Unlatching the gate, she followed the path to the front porch. In summertime the white railings hung heavy with red roses, and the scent of honeysuckle filled the air. This afternoon the wind howled across the barren flower beds Pauline carefully nurtured during warmer weather. Often she planted okra where petunias should be, but she enjoyed puttering in the soil and the earth loved her. She brought fresh tomatoes, corn, and beans to the store during spring and summer, and pumpkins and squash lined the railings in the fall.

In earlier days Pauline's quilts were known throughout the area. She and her quilting group had made quite a name for themselves when Dwadlo first became a town. Four women excelled in the craft. One had lived in Pine Grove, and two others came from as far away as Branch Springs once a month to break bread together and stitch quilts. But one by one the women had died

15

off, leaving Pauline to sew alone in her narrowing world.

Stomping her boots on the porch, Mae said under her breath, "I don't mind winter, Lord, but could we perhaps have a little less of it?" The only answer was the wind whipping her garments. Tapping lightly on the door, she called, "Pauline?"

Mae stepped back and waited to hear the shuffle of feet. Pauline used to answer the door in less than twenty seconds. It took longer now. Mae made a fist with her gloved hand and banged a little harder. The wind howled around the cottage eaves. She closed her eyes and prayed that Jeremy had remembered to stack sufficient firewood beside the kitchen door. The boy was generally responsible, and she thanked God every day that she had him to lean on. He had been injured by forceps during birth, which left him with special needs. He was a very happy fourteen-year-old with the reasoning power of a child of nine.

A full minute passed. Mae frowned and tried the doorknob. Pauline couldn't hear herself yell in a churn, but she might also be asleep. The door opened easily, and Mae peeked inside the small living quarters. She saw that a fire burned low in the woodstove, and Pauline's rocking chair sat empty.

Stepping inside, she closed the door and called again. "Pauline? It's Mae!"

The ticking of the mantle clock was the only sound that met her ears.

"Pauline?" She lowered her hood and walked through the living room. She paused in the kitchen doorway.

"Oh, Pauline!"

Two

Mae set the basket of bread and pie aside and rushed to the older woman, who was crumpled in a heap in front of her sink. Kneeling, she felt for a pulse and found a thready one. "Oh, you poor dear." How long had she been on the floor?

Mae had stopped by on her way to work this morning and Pauline had been fine. She was preparing to piece quilting scraps. Mae turned to look at Pauline's chair and saw a large box of squares. Perhaps she'd only just fallen. "Pauline?" When she didn't get a response, she stood, dampened a cloth, and then pressed it to the elderly woman's face. When the cold cloth touched her skin, Pauline's eyes flew open.

"Oh my! Did I faint again?"

"You did," Mae soothed. She slowly sat her friend upright.

Pauline brought both hands to her temples. "My head's spinning like a top."

Checking briefly for broken bones, Mae sighed. "This is the third time this month, Pauline."

"Goodness' sake." The elderly woman brushed her hand aside and struggled to stand up. "Anyone can fall. Why, I trip over my feet all the time."

Mae assisted her up and then helped the weaving woman to her chair. "How long have you been lying there?"

Pauline looked up. "Where?"

"On the floor."

"I don't know. Was I on the floor again?"

"You were. Do you hurt anywhere?"

She shook her head. "I never hurt anywhere."

Giving up for the moment, Mae fixed the woman a cup of hot tea and liberally laced it with honey. Kneeling beside Pauline's chair, she knew the moment she'd been dreading had come. Someone — some *kin* — must step up and take care of this woman. The poor thing might not make it through the winter if she didn't have help from family. Mae couldn't make decisions for Pauline that weren't hers to make. She racked her brain trying to recall if the woman had ever mentioned anyone. Brother? Sister? Cousin?

She was ninety-two. It was unlikely she'd

19

have kin close in age, but she might have distant nieces and nephews. Though Pauline was as poor as a church mouse, and her house, if sold, would bring next to nothing, the land she owned was valuable. At least that was something.

Mae recalled that years ago, when she was small and before the Dakotas had become separate states, there was some kind of ruckus over Pauline's property. The railroad was just beginning to come through the Dakota Territory, and if Mae's memory served, an official had offered to purchase a portion of Pauline's land.

Mae only recalled the incident because it had caused such a fuss when Pauline priced the land so high. Heated discussions ended abruptly when the official walked away from the uncompromising situation. He later purchased land from Dale that was not as well suited for a station and platform, but the price of it certainly fell within the railroad's offer.

The train station sat in a mud hole when it rained, and the track stopped there. Ideally, Pauline's property would have allowed the line to continue all the way to Pine Grove and possibly beyond, but Pauline could be as stubborn as a mule with a migraine, so Dale had been the one to benefit.

Mae's thoughts switched back to present. "Pauline, do you have any nieces or nephews?"

The older woman shook her head. "I did once, but they are all dead now."

"Cousins?"

"Yes." She nodded. "I had cousins."

"Are any of them still alive?"

She took a sip of tea, pondering the question. "Can't say for certain."

Mae noted that mentally she seemed fairly clear at the moment. "Think hard, Pauline. Are any of your cousins alive?"

Pauline thought. After a while she said, "Tom."

"Tom. You have a cousin whose name is Tom? Is he still alive?"

Pauline gave her a curt look. "I suppose he is. I haven't heard anything to the contrary."

"Oh, thank goodness." Some of the worry for her friend fell from Mae's shoulders. "Would you care if I wrote to Tom and told him he needs to visit you?"

"He wouldn't want to visit me."

"Why not?"

Pauline turned pensive. "Seems like we don't get along. He's a stubborn man."

Mae felt he was certainly a thoughtless man if he knew Pauline was alive and wasn't being cared for by family. "Do you have his address?"

Pauline turned blank. "Whose?"

"Tom . . . your kin. Do you have an address where I can reach him?"

Shaking her head, Pauline took another sip of tea. "It's all right, dear. They'll take care of everything."

"Who will take care of you, Pauline?"

"They will." She smiled. "They come around every night and I feed them. If I don't, they get in the biggest squabble you've ever heard."

Mae sat back. Pauline was gone again.

"They screech and take on until I go outside and feed them gravy."

"Really."

Pauline nodded. "I don't think they're my kin, but they tell me they are."

Mae settled a warm throw around the woman's thin frame and got up to put more wood on the fire. How was she going to find Pauline's relatives?

If only Mae's best friend, Lil, lived closer, she could talk to her, but it was sometimes hard for Lil to get into town in the winter. Her hog farm demanded her time.

Mae's eyes focused on the small writing

desk in the corner. She knew it wasn't her place to pilfer through Pauline's private papers, but how else would she find a clue to the woman's past? Pauline had lived in this house for as long as Mae could remember, and the only thing she'd ever heard about Pauline's past concerned the railroad ruckus. She never married. Therefore she had no children.

Settling in a chair across the room, Mae contemplated her choices. Her gaze shifted back to the desk, where late afternoon light highlighted a thick layer of dust. The house often smelled of pot roast or stew, but today it reeked of winter and neglect.

Getting out of her chair, she moved toward the desk, lightly wiping away a layer of dust with the hem of her dress. "Pauline?"

The elderly woman's mind came and went swiftly. Perhaps now that she had finished her tea her memory might be clearer.

"Yes, dear?"

"About Tom?"

The older woman smiled. "Yes?"

"Would you happen to have his address?"

Downing the last sip from her cup, Pauline gave her a dry look. "Cats don't have addresses, dear."

Cats? Cats. Tom cat. Mae's eyes focused on the bundle of fur curled up beside the stove. Giving her a wide yawn, the cat turned around and then settled back on the rug. The woman took in every stray that wandered her way. To date, she had a dozen or so dogs and several cats housed in a large shed beside her house. She allowed the one cat inside but barred the others except on warm days, when she left the front door open and the animals wandered in and out at will. They were pests to the whole town, but folks long ago decided they had to live with the fact because nobody else wanted them. Most of the animals had been dumped on her. An occasional guilty party would leave a sack of feed on Pauline's doorstep, but she depended on neighbors' scraps to nourish the pack.

Tom cat.

Mae's hopes faded. He'd be of no help.

Before leaving for the day, Mae fixed supper, tided up a bit, and then brought in enough wood to last until morning. When Pauline asked for prayer, Mae got down on her knees and the two held hands, thanking God for His favor yet another day. As Mae left for home, fingers of darkness laced the snow-laden sky. Soft snowflakes had turned into stinging sleet pellets.

Stomping her boots clean on her own

worn mat moments later, Mae reached for the doorknob and entered her warm kitchen, which was filled with the heavenly scent of baking bread. Jeremy turned from the stove, his cherubic features red from the heat. "Hi, sister."

"Hi, Jeremy." When she passed him to hang her cloak on the rack, she gave him a peck on the cheek. Their mother was in her late forties when she died giving birth to him, so Dad and Mae had raised the infant. He was the apple of both his father's and sister's eye. "God has sent this child," her father would say when they knelt to pray at night. "He's been sent to heal our grief." But Dad never got over his anguish. For years he struggled to overcome the loneliness that filled his waking hours. Long days crawled by as he dutifully set off each morning to perform his job as the town cobbler, but the light had gone from his eyes. The Gerald Wilkey everyone knew and loved became a shell of a man, aimlessly going about life, caring for Mae and his newborn but never caring for himself.

Mae watched as the father she adored withered on the vine. Five years ago he was thrown from a horse and suffered massive head injuries. He died fifty feet from the house. The responsibility to raise her nine-year-old brother had fallen on her.

"I love to come home to the smell of baking bread." She set the store-bought bread aside and gave Jeremy a tight squeeze. "It's scrumptious."

"You like my cooking."

Pride seeped through his voice. The one thing Dad never permitted was difference. Jeremy was treated like any other young boy his age, even though his limitations were many. Mae had always thought he understood more than he was given credit for. Jeremy's mind might be stunted, but his instincts were sound.

"I hope you weren't worried about me." She lifted the lid on a pot of beans and sniffed the bubbling contents.

"No. I looked out the window and saw you go into Miss Pauline's house."

"Yes, poor dear. She'd fallen again, so I helped her get her supper." She set the lid back on the pot. "Let's eat soon. I'm tired and want to go to bed early."

"Okay." Jeremy busied himself setting the table. The dishes were evenly spaced; fork on the left, knife and spoon on the right. Mae taught him basic manners and etiquette, and he was a quick learner. If only he'd remember to set the butter anywhere but on the woodstove. Removing the dish with its soupy contents, she said quietly, "The butter goes on the table, sweetie."

The meal was on the table a few minutes later, and Mae didn't realize how hungry she was until she bit into the warm bread. "You've done an excellent job, Jeremy."

A blush crept up the young man's cheeks. "Thank you, ma'am."

After dinner he cleared the dishes. He meticulously washed each bowl and plate and laid it on a tea towel-covered counter to dry. The small three-room house was neat and orderly. Not a spot of dust anywhere. He slept on a pallet, close to the cook-stove, on the kitchen floor.

When he'd finished, he tapped at Mae's bedroom door. "I'm going now."

Loosening her hair, Mae frowned when the long blond tresses escaped their pins. "It's snowing. Where are you going?"

"To feed the animals."

Of course. Meg's hand dropped to her side. She hadn't given Pauline's cats and dogs a thought today. Pauline paid Jeremy a small amount to feed and water her animals. Mae vividly recalled the day when Pauline humbled herself enough to ask a favor of Jeremy. "My mind isn't what it used to be," she'd said. "And I don't want my babies to suffer. Will you feed and water them?"

Her babies. During the day they roamed the town, digging up flower beds, loitering on the General Store porch, barking, and running everywhere in a pack. Pauline's dogs were the community's nuisances. And if Mae wasn't mistaken, she'd seen Elmer Hensley's mutt running with the bunch lately. Old Man Hensley apparently decided he didn't want the dog in the house anymore and dumped it in Pauline's yard. With her failing memory she'd never noticed that she'd acquired another "baby."

Ramming a pin back in her hair, Mae sighed. "I'll go with you." She could trust her brother to do his task, but with the worsening weather he might become confused and wander off. Jeremy had a good, if not better, sense of direction than she, but it was easy to get lost in a storm. The wrong path taken . . . one small misjudgment . . . She shuddered.

On the way out, she sliced off a large chunk of bread and wrapped it in a cloth. Taking a jar of apple butter from the pantry, she packed it in her basket and followed Jeremy out the back door into the cold.

The force of the wind surprised her. Mae huddled deep into her cloak and reached to tug Jeremy's hat down more firmly on his head. Warm lantern light bobbed a cheerful ray across the mounting drifts.

The two crossed the road and headed straight for the drafty shed. Weathered wood creaked against the heavy gale. Inside, the animals sent up an earsplitting ruckus.

Unlatching the door, Jeremy stood back and urged Mae inside. The racket was so loud she could barely think.

After hooking the lantern on a peg above his head, Jeremy waded through the pack of howls and meows with animals crowding his leg. Dogs leaped and the cats clung to his trousers as he lifted the large lid on a barrel and scooped out mash left by sympathetic neighbors. Rafters shook when the hungry animals made a beeline for supper. Mae braved the outdoors for the rain barrel and cracked the ice on the surface with a garden hoe in order to get enough water to fill two large buckets.

A little while later, she leaned against the heavy door as Jeremy fastened the lock. The howling wind made it impossible to hear one another, so Mae pointed at the basket containing Pauline's bread and apple butter sitting beside the barn and motioned for Jeremy to follow her.

Mellow lamplight spilled from the front window when Mae climbed the porch steps and knocked.

Pauline answered almost immediately. "Goodness' sake! Is that you making all that racket, Mae?"

She liked to think it wasn't her. "I came with Jeremy to help feed the animals."

"Oh, how nice. Come in and warm your-selves before you catch a chill."

After knocking snow off her boots, Mae stepped inside with her brother behind her.

"Hello, Jeremy."

"Hi, Miss Pauline."

"Would you like a cookie?"

Jeremy's face brightened.

"Oh, dear." She shook her head. "I haven't baked any in a while, but I have corn bread."

Mae extended the basket. "Thank you, but we've just eaten. Jeremy baked bread this afternoon, and I brought you some along with a jar of apple butter."

"Apple butter! My favorite sweet."

Mae's gaze fastened on the desk. The drawer was open, gleaming like a gold coin in the fading light. Big as you please, here was her chance to investigate Pauline's fam-ily . . . or lack thereof.

"Can I fix you a piece of bread and but-ter?" The older woman shuffled toward the kitchen carrying her treasures.

"No, thank you . . ." Mae's eyes traced the open drawer. Would there be a reference to Tom in there? Or a Jim — or Madge — or anyone? The odds were slim, but somewhere she must have a family album or journal with family contacts.

Pauline sniffed the air. "Fresh bread smells so good on a cold winter evening."

"Jeremy is quite the baker," Mae mused. "I see we've interrupted you." Her eyes pointedly fixed on the open drawer.

Seemingly unaware that she'd been doing anything, the woman's gaze followed Mae's. "Oh, yes. I was trying to tidy up a bit, but my goodness, I don't know what to throw away or to keep."

Mae seized the moment. "Why don't I help you?" She glanced at her little brother. "Warm yourself by the fire, Jeremy. I'll just be a minute."

It didn't take long to sort through the drawer's contents. Important papers were now in a neat pile and odds and ends in another. Old scraps and pieces of junk were thrown away, and the best part of all was that Mae had discovered one small clue. Tiny, but anything helped. In the very bottom of the drawer she found a slip of paper with the name "Tom Curtis" and a Chicago address scribbled on it. At the moment Pauline wasn't sure she even had family.

"I have three cats named Tom," she offered.

"It's okay. Perhaps this is the information
I need." At least it was a start. Now all Mae
had to do was hope this Tom was still alive
and living at the same address.

THREE

The snow was still falling in the fading light as Mae and Jeremy left the Wilson house. When they reached home, Mae stripped out of her cloak and hurried to the fire to warm her hands. She heard a knock at her door as realization of what day this was hit her. Monday. She froze. Jake came for supper on Monday and Thursday nights.

"Jake's here!" Jeremy called. "Want me to fix him a plate?"

How could she forget this was Monday? "Fix three plates!"

Frowning, Jeremy opened his mouth to speak.

"Do as I say! I'll explain later — and don't mention a word about us eating earlier." Where was her mind these days? She was getting as forgetful as Pauline.

Rushing to her room, she fussed with her hair, pushing stray locks into place. "Give me a few seconds and then tell him to come in." The mere mention of Jake's name used to send shivers up her spine, but after six years of waiting for a marriage proposal, the newness of their romance had faded a bit.

Mae had loved this man blindly, patiently waiting the hour when he'd finally slip a ring on her finger. At twenty-seven she was now at the age to be considered a spinster, and she didn't relish the thought, but spinsterhood didn't seem all that bad now. The community had become her family, and her best friend, Lil, was closer than a sister. Yet she still wanted toddlers at her feet giggling with her, learning to speak and walk. She wanted to bathe them at night and cradle their sweet-smelling warm bodies in her arms.

The sounds of Jake's entry reached her. She stole a final look in the mirror, smoothed her bodice into place, and went to greet her guest.

"Darling." An absent kiss landed between her eyes and hairline. Jake wasn't the mushy sort, but tonight's chicken peck seemed especially distant.

"Difficult day at work?" Two years ago Jake had opened Dwadlo's first law office. Business was slow at first, but it appeared to be picking up somewhat. Mostly land matters and plot issues, but he was making enough now to allow him to order his clothes from a Philadelphia haberdasher. She'd heard the whispers and snickers from some of Dwadlo's male population, but the women thought he was quite the catch.

Handing her his hat, he smiled. "Every day is difficult in my business, Mae." He sniffed the air appreciatively. "What has Jeremy prepared for us tonight?"

"Beans."

A wrinkle appeared in his forehead. "I was expecting chicken and dumplings."

"I'm sorry." She glanced at her brother. "Perhaps Thursday night?"

When Jeremy opened his mouth to speak, she urged him toward the kitchen. "Can you dish up supper, sweetie?"

"But, Mae —"

"Later, Jeremy."

Taking Jake's coat, she brushed snow off the collar and then hung it on a peg. He was like a pair of old shoes: comfortable. After dinner he would wipe his mouth on his napkin, push back from the table, and sit by the fire while she helped Jeremy with the dishes. Later, she would knit and Jake would doze until the mantle clock struck nine. Rising from the chair, he would place another brief kiss on her forehead, reach for his coat, and depart for home.

What did he do all day long in his office above the bank? There couldn't be that many legal problems in Dwadlo. Did he sit in his leather chair and peruse clothing ads from the latest men's magazines? The three-piece "ditto suits," the sack coat worn with contrasting color? Oh, dear. She studied his outline from the corner of her eye. What if he decided to cut his hair terribly short and grow a pointed beard and generous mustache like so many of the men in the pictures?

She wasn't supposed to look at people's mail and she didn't — except she occasionally succumbed to curiosity and took a peek between the pages of the new magazine, *Vogue.* Fashion was getting disgraceful. She was glad she lived in Dwadlo and didn't have to dress the way the women did in that magazine.

Tonight Jake remembered his manners when it was time to leave.

"Please stay seated. I'll clean the snow off my buggy."

Guilt washed over her. "I'm sorry, Jake. I'd forgotten about the storm." She and Jeremy always helped prepare the buggy in bad weather.

"Stay," he insisted. "There's no cause for both of us catching a chill." Nodding to

Jeremy, he said, "Fine supper, son, though you barely touched your food. Is it possible to have dumplings on Thursday?"

Jeremy glanced at Mae. "Yes, sir."

"Mae?"

"Yes?"

"I'll see you Thursday at six?"

She nodded. "And Sunday." When they would sit in church in the same row, knees barely touching, and sing from a shared hymnal. Jake's voice boomed over the other men's — quite pleasant to the ear. At the end of the service the pastor would dismiss in prayer, and then they would exit the row and shake as many hands as possible before they left the small church. Jeremy would fix fried chicken and mashed potatoes. After lunch Mae would knit, Jeremy would work a wooden puzzle, and Jake would doze. Around four he would get up, reach for his coat, give her a peck, and be gone until the next night, when Jeremy would serve pot roast. Mae was starting to wonder whether he loved her or her brother's cooking.

A gust of frigid wind filled the room when Jake opened the door and stepped out into the swirling snow. Purling a stitch, Mae fretted. Over the years they had come to live as though they were married. With the exception of the marriage bed, she imagined her life would be identical with his ring on her finger. She'd long ago given up the dream of an exciting, thrilling romance. Lil said that was only found in books. Jake was a godly man, a hard worker, and he loved Jeremy as though he was his own. She could do worse.

The dirty, uncivilized drovers who frequented the mercantile were a perfect example. Those men were rowdy, crude, and rude. Years ago Dwadlo closed the saloon in hopes of discouraging the cattlemen's business, but the move hurt the town's commerce, so last year a nearby farmer, with little concern for his community, opened a smaller version of the establishment on the outskirts of town and the drovers returned. Mae said that they were giving in to sin, but others argued that there was a penny to be made and why shouldn't Dwadlo reap the windfall?

Shaking her head, Mae's mind skipped to Pauline's dilemma. She would write a letter to Mr. Curtis before going to bed tonight and send it with the morning mail. What would she do if it never reached him? He could be elderly — or in worse shape than Pauline. Maybe even dead. Violence still reigned in these parts. Masked men robbed trains, and ruthless thieves overtook stagecoaches. Honestly. What was this world coming to? In order to err on the side of certainty, if she didn't hear anything in a month from Mr. Curtis, a second letter would definitely be in order.

She could only pray that Tom Curtis was a staunch man, and that his family's welfare would take precedence in this matter.

Yawning, she set her knitting needles aside and went to find pen and paper.

"Is there a Mr. Tom Curtis here?"

Tom glanced up to see the Chicago & North Western Railway mail clerk grinning at him.

"You back from your trip, Tom?"

"Just back."

"Good to see ya." The black boy dropped a letter on Tom's desk and walked on, whistling.

"Thanks, Harvey." Hopefully Tom would be able to stay home until spring. But with Christmas coming in a few weeks and with C&NW adding track at the rate of multiplying rabbits, he couldn't be sure.

In '79 they started a line from Minnesota and South Dakota, and then they platted the town sites in between. Every seven to ten miles tracks started to appear, and rival companies joined the march of railroad lines strung out like dominoes crisscrossing the states.

Tom reached for the letter and noted that the address was written in feminine cursive. He never received personal mail. Anything addressed to him came from the railroad office or was an occasional equipment sales notice. Glancing at the cancellation mark on the stamp, he saw that it came from Dwadlo, North Dakota. Probably someone wanting to sell the railroad land rights.

Dear Mr. Curtis,

I am writing in regards to your cousin or aunt Pauline Wilson — I presume she is a relation — and her immediate welfare. She is quite elderly now and needs family attention. While I check on her often, I cannot give her the care she needs. Please be advised that her mental state is not always clear. In spite of that, she is a wise and wonderful woman whom I am certain you care for very deeply.

Please come as soon as possible for your dear cousin — or possibly aunt. I'm sorry to have to inform you that she is rapidly failing.

Warmest regards,
Mae Wilkey

Wilkey. He mulled the name around in his mind. Pauline Wilson? Turning the fancy stationary over, he frowned. Aunt Pauline? Cousin Pauline? He shook his head. He'd been on his own for so long he'd lost track of family. His mother and father had died years ago. He'd had an older sister in Wyoming, but she passed last year. He glanced at the paper. Wilson. Pauline.

Great-Aunt Pauline Wilson?

Bringing his hand to his chin, he repeated out loud. "Aunt Pauline. Cousin Pauline. Seems like there was a cousin, Pearl, in the family. Or was it Prudence? Patricia?"

Picking up the envelope, he studied the writing. Who was Mae Wilkey? His eyes focused on the postmark again. Dwadlo. C&NW had track through there — he knew that because he'd seen the name on the roster over the years. Had he ever been there? The name didn't ring a bell, but then he didn't recall every town he'd visited in the sixteen years he'd been with the railroad. There'd been too many.

Setting the letter aside, he dismissed the matter. This Wilkey woman had her wires crossed. He certainly didn't have relatives in North Dakota.

Denial came easy in daylight. Work oc-cupied his time and thoughts for the rest of the day, but later that night it was harder to dismiss the odd inquiry. When he turned out the lantern and stared at the dark ceiling in his rented room at Bessie Hellman's Boarding Establishment, where he had a soft bed, meals, and laundry service for six dollars a week, the letter wasn't as easy to forget. Somehow someone must have come across his name and mistook him for distant kin to this Pauline. He mentally searched each side of the family again, and to his knowledge there wasn't a Curtis or Holland still alive.

The letter had to be a prank. That thought nearly made him slap his forehead. Of course. One of his fellow coworkers was playing a joke on him. The railroad crew was a crazy bunch — Harvey probably promoted the trick. Or Jack Billings. Jack was a real cutup, and his brain could easily come up with a plot that would make Tom run off to North Dakota in search of a mysterious aunt who didn't exist. Relief filled him. A trick. Jack was paying him back for the time he'd replaced roast beef sandwiches with tar-filled ones in his lunch bucket. Chuckling, Tom rolled on his back, plotting revenge.

Tomorrow morning, without Jack noticing, he was going to tape a sign on his back that said "Kick Me." The grin widened. He should know Jack would get him back. The crew was probably laughing, knowing Tom would be racking his brain to figure out where this mysterious "kin" came from.

Blockheads.

FOUR

When the boisterous Lil Jenkins came to town, everyone in Dwadlo heard her. Mae's best friend had a small spread north of town; nothing impressive except for her land. Her folks left her a hundred prime acres of fertile grass with deep springs and rolling countryside, but Lil didn't raise cattle. She raised hogs. Big black-and-red sows weighing upward of a thousand pounds brought a pretty market price. The animals provided Lil with more than ham and bacon. A place in Wisconsin bought her stock to render the fat into lard for baking and frying and to make lye soap for simple home cleaning tasks.

Lil worked hard to make her farm profitable as she was getting up in years. She'd be twenty-eight soon.

In fact, Dwadlo had two old maids, Lil being one and Mae the other. The former still had a ray of hope that she would find a man who loved the smell of hogs, but the latter was beginning to wonder if she would ever get a proposal from the man who was steadily seeing her.

Lil pulled her wagon to a stop in front of the General Store and set the hand brake.

Mae noted her arrival and stepped out of the store to meet her. The two embraced warmly. As usual, Lil smelled like her stock. "Where have you been?" Mae accused. "It's been three weeks since you were in."

"I had a couple of sows down. Had to stay around to keep 'em alive." Arms around each other's waists, the women went into the store to get out of the cold. "Got any mail for me?"

"Nary a thing." Lil always asked, and Mae always had the same response. Truth was, as long as Mae had worked at the post office there'd never been any correspondence for Lil. If Mae ever went on a trip, she'd write Lil a long letter and send pictures. Lots of pictures of foreign places. Lil would like that.

Lil opened the pickle barrel and helped herself.

"You'd better not let Dale see you," Mae warned. Lately the owner was getting persnickety. Winter was barely here and profits were down. Folks accustomed to raiding the barrel without paying were abruptly cut off last month from eating Dale's pickles for free.

Shrugging, Lil asked, "What's been going on?"

"Nothing much." Mae briefly explained about Pauline and how she'd managed to locate a Tom Curtis — Pauline's kin, she hoped. She had to admit that she was proud of her accomplishment and slept better lately knowing help would come.

"You wrote him a letter?"

Nodding, Mae took the list Lil handed her and moved about the store, filling the order. "You want Cooper's Best or regular flour?"

"You're carrying two kinds now?"

"Dale thought the women might enjoy having a choice."

"How is ol' Dale? Loud as ever?"

"Now, Lil. Dale is gifted, and you shouldn't make fun of him."

"If he's so 'gifted,' how come he never married?"

"How come we've never married?"

"I ain't ever been asked."

Mae sighed. "Me neither. I suppose Dale never found a woman he wanted to spend his life with." She glanced up and smiled. "Cooper's Best is a penny more a pound.

Comes from a new place in Humboldt, Nebraska. Supposed to be real fine."

"I'll take the usual. Flour's flour." Lil browsed the store as she finished her snack. "Have you heard anything back from this Curtis feller?"

"It's too soon." Mae closed the sugar bin. "I just sent the letter last week."

"Where's it going?"

"Chicago."

Lil whistled. "That far?"

"That's why I'm not concerned about hearing back yet."

"And if you don't?"

Pausing, Mae motioned to the sitting area in front of the mail cage. "Let's rest and chat a spell."

As the women settled on the small bench, Mae remembered her manners. "Would you like a root beer?"

Lil gaped at her. "You know I don't drink the likes."

"It's not saloon beer," Mae assured her. "And it's been around a long time, but we're just now getting some in. Remember when Dale went off to Philadelphia last year?"

"How could I forget? He couldn't talk about much else for months."

"Well, he was talking to a man there who

bottles the drink, and Dale told him it was delicious. The man promised he would send Dale a sample. Two weeks ago five cases of the stuff arrived, and I must say I love it. Tastes like sarsaparilla but better."

"Sarsaparilla's fine. Why mess with a good thing?"

"I don't know. Progress?"

"All right, I'll try a bottle."

Mae went to fetch two bottles from a cooler filled with chunked ice. "You're lucky that you've come today. This stuff is selling so quickly we'll be out soon."

Lil accepted the ice-cold bottle with Hires Root Beer written on the label. "This will never go over. Women won't buy anything that has the name 'beer' on it." She took a long swig. Then another, her eyes brightening. "Hot dog!" She burped.

"Isn't it lovely? I've had three already." Mae took a long drink of the refreshing beverage.

Lowering the bottle, Lil frowned. "What's in this stuff?"

Mae rose and scurried around the counter to locate the letter that arrived with the bottles. She read, "Allspice, birch bark, coriander, juniper, ginger, wintergreen, hops —"

"What's hops?"

"Um . . . not sure, but it's delicious." She continued. "Burdock root, dandelion root, spikenard, pipsissewa —"

"Don't have any idea what that is, but everyone knows what sarsaparilla is: spice-wood, wild cherry bark, yellow dock, prickly ash bark, sassafras root, vanilla bean, dog grass, molasses, and licorice." Lil paused and peered down the hole of her half empty bottle. "I think I'm going to be sick."

"Nonsense." Mae took another swig and then said, "Anyone who raises hogs can enjoy a root beer. Drink up! It's wonderful. Dale ordered ten more cases."

Setting her bottle aside, Lil stood up to stretch. "My hogs don't have stuff like 'pipsissewa' in them. I don't drink nothin' I cain't pronounce." She added a tin of salt to her order. "About Pauline's kin . . ."

"Tom Curtis."

"You're sure he's family? I never heard her speak about having relatives."

"As sure as I can be." Mae laid a tin of ointment on the counter. "But I wouldn't stake my life on it. I found Mr. Curtis' name and address in Pauline's desk drawer. I wouldn't think he would be anyone other than kin. Pauline has never been out of Dwadlo. I doubt she'd know anyone outside of here but family."

49

"Still . . ." Lil shook her head. "How do you know you're not inviting trouble into town? What if this Curtis fellow is someone we'd just as soon not have around?" She peered out the front window. "Mae?"

"Yes?

"Are Pauline's dogs supposed to have her couch cushion in the front yard?"

"No. Have they pulled one out of the house again?" Outside the window feathers spiraled like heavy snow. Heaving a sigh, Mae wiped her hands on a cloth. "Those animals. They are driving me nuts."

"Better she get herself a good hog. I keep a couple tied around my front door to scare off the varmints and mice."

"The last thing Pauline needs is a hog."

"Don't be so fast to criticize them. My old sows kill off the snakes, and that keeps me happy." Lil leaned closer to the window-pane. "Might as well forget about the cushion. There ain't anything left." She stepped away and looked through a pile of men's shirts. "What'd you say this Curtis fellow does?"

"I don't know. The scrap of paper just had his name and address on it. I don't expect he'll stay around long. I imagine he'll take Pauline and go."

"Go where?"

"Back to Chicago, I suppose. I know nothing about him." Mae finished boxing the order and turned to face her friend. "If Mr. Curtis arrives, Pauline will no longer be my concern."

"Maybe, but what if he doesn't want to take her? Ever consider that?"

"Of course I've thought of it." The news that he possibly had an ailing aunt who needed immediate care would most likely take him by surprise, but Mae was hoping for the best.

Leaning on the counter, Lil grew pensive. "I'd take her if I could."

"I know you would." Lil was a kind soul who would give anyone in need the shirt off her back, but her place had only one room and was miles from civilization. Pauline would die of loneliness.

The two returned to the bench and spent the next half hour catching up on news — of which there was very little.

"Guess Jake hasn't proposed yet."

"Not yet, but he will."

"You've been dating the man six years, Mae. How long does it take to set up a law firm?"

"The law firm is running fine now. Jake's rebuilding his finances. It won't take long." She smiled. "Are you going to wear a dress to my wedding?"

Lil shook her head. "I don't fancy up, missy, even for you."

"You'll have to. You're going to be my maid of honor."

"I'll wear overalls."

"No."

Lil flashed a mischievous grin. "I'd be willing to tie a pink ribbon in my hair."

"No." Leaning back, Mae closed her eyes. "You'll wear soft yellow. And I'll carry a bouquet of wild daisies. It'll be the finest day Dwadlo has ever celebrated."

"All we'll need is a willing groom."

Oh, Jake would be willing. Six years was beginning to stretch Mae's endurance, but she was sure God would reward her patience. "Rejoicing in hope; patient in tribulation; continuing instant in prayer." How many times over the years had she found comfort in that particular verse from the twelfth chapter of the book of Romans?

"What about you, my dear friend?" Mae sat up to study Lil. She was rough around the edges, but she had a heart of gold. Other than Jake, there was only one other eligible male in these parts, and that was Fisk Jester. However, he didn't like Lil for the simple fact that she enjoyed arguing with him. Fisk lost his wife some eight months ago, and

Isabelle Jester never said a bad word to anyone, least of all Fisk. He was also ten years older than Lil and independent as all get out, and he didn't appear to need anybody but his memorialized Isabelle.

"What about me?" Lil asked.

"You're always after me to marry. When do you intend to find the love of your life? I don't need to remind you that we both have a birthday coming up next summer, and neither of us is a spring chicken."

"Speak for yourself! Ain't nothing wrong with my chickenhood."

"That isn't a word."

"So? It is now."

Sniffing the air delicately, Mae said, "There is one thing you could do to better your chances of landing a man. You could use a good scrubbing. Dale has some lovely rose-scented soap you could purchase —"

"I ain't buying any of your rose-scented stuff with my hard-earned money, but what I could use less of are your opinions, Miss Mae Wilkey. I don't intend to go waltzing around here smelling like a flower, thank you."

"Don't know why not. It would suit your mood well." Mae stood up, brushing wrinkles out of her skirt. "I have a ton of work to do. Dale is feeling poorly, so he's resting in the back." The store owner ordinarily worked through any ache or pain, but today he'd taken to his bed.

Mae finished up Lil's order and then trailed the hog farmer on her way out of the store. "Do you plan to attend Joanne's tea this Saturday?"

"Way over in Pine Grove?"

"You'll be missing a lot of fun." Mae opened the door, smiling. "Fisk is planning on being there."

Lil's nose lifted. "All the more reason to skip the event." She walked through the door without a backward glance.

"Huh." Mae watched her friend store the goods in the back of the wagon with stiff, sharp movements. Mae's remarks had obviously riled her, but they were true. "She's never going to get a man with that attitude."

FIVE

A month later a second letter landed on Tom's desk. He saw the North Dakota stamp and snorted. This time he was ready for the pranksters. "Big laugh, Harvey. I'm on to you wiseacres. Who put you up to this? Jack?" Jack was still sore about the "Kick Me" sign Tom had taped on his back, yet it was worth the look on his face when someone had taken full advantage of the advice. He didn't discover why he'd had so many swift jars to his backside until almost noon that day.

Harvey turned to look over his shoulder on his way out of the office. "What's the joke? Is someone messin' with your mind, Tom?" The boy flashed a grin.

Tom reached for the envelope and read the return address. "Mae Wilkey. Oh, dear. My sweet senile aunt or cousin must be worse."

Lifting a shoulder, Harvey said, "Didn't

know you had an aunt or cousin. Hope she's feeling better real soon."

Sobering, Tom said, "That's just it, Harv. I don't have one."

Shrugging, the mail clerk moved on and Tom took out the single sheet.

Dear Mr. Curtis,
I am writing again in hopes that somehow my letter of last month failed to reach you. I am searching for Pauline Wilson's family. She is upwards in years and failing. I help all that I can, but I am unable to do enough to provide her with daily needs. If you are Pauline's kin, I would deeply appreciate your immediate attention to this weighty matter. She needs her family, and I am quite certain you would want to help in this dire time.
Warmest regards,
Mae Wilkey

He pitched the letter on the desk. The pranksters were taking this too far. Cousin. Aunt — he'd know if he had an aunt in Dwadlo.

"Tom?"

He glanced up to see Clive Letterman in his doorway, president of C&NW Railroad.

Tom pushed back from his desk and stood up.

"Keep your seat," Letterman said as he entered the office and sat down.

Tom did the same. Clive Letterman had been with the line since Tom went to work for the railroad in '76. He worked well with Clive, even serving as his confidant many a time. Every seven to ten years C&NW set up a new town site, and track was now being laid in Brookings, Minnesota. Tom didn't care for Minnesota weather in the winter. Too cold and too damp. He hoped Clive wasn't sending him there.

"How's the Brookings project coming along?" Letterman asked.

"Good. We signed the final papers yesterday. The new line should be up and running in a year."

"That's excellent."

Maybe Tom wouldn't be headed for Minnesota after all. He had one question he still needed an answer to. "Got a name yet?"

Often a town was named or renamed for a railroad tycoon. Tom wouldn't be surprised if Brookings would be called "Letterman." Or, more likely, Clive would want to name it after one of his daughters, Grace or Marylyn.

"The town's name will remain Brookings.

Marylyn wants a line closer to Savannah, and my dear Grace doesn't care a duck's feather about having a line named after her."

Tom smiled. He'd watched both daughters grow up and preferred Marylyn's spunkiness.

Letterman turned thoughtful. "Every Tom, Dick, and Harry in the state is vying for land rights now. I'm glad we had the foresight to buy early."

"There's still plenty of land left. I purchased five plots last week. Other routes will open to us soon." Tom grinned. "I saw the new poster."

"Which one is that?"

"The one advertising thirty acres of prime land in North Dakota — simply there for a man's taking."

"And we have the means to get them to it. We have immigrants coming from Europe. And they're coming with no money. Just the hope of owning their own piece of land. What if I tout the fact that the Dakotas have the best wetlands, best farming land, and best grazing land in the world, and they are free to all? An adult man can have a hundred and sixty acres. Single women can stake a claim. Think of it, Tom. The railways are going to break wide open. Why, if a man doesn't want land, he can make a tree claim.

Imagine that. Agree to plant ten acres of trees and keep them alive for eight years, and you're a landowner. The more people come, the more lines we open. With every new town settlers spread out, and then there's need for more towns, more track."

Chuckling, Tom marveled at the man's enthusiasm. Years of haggling with stubborn landowners, traveling long distances from home, derailments, and inept employees had somewhat dampened his own spirit, but the railroad was in his blood too.

Letterman pushed back to leave. "I'll see you later. I have a ten o'clock meeting."

Mae Wilkey's letter sat on the desk, its message drilling through Tom's mind. *"She needs her family, and I am quite certain you would want to help in this dire time."*

What if it wasn't a joke? The men knew he would eventually tell them to knock it off. It was very unlikely Pauline was his relative. This Mae Wilkey had the right to ask for his help if the elderly woman was family, but for the life of him he couldn't place her. If she wasn't someone from his mother's side, he had no idea who she was. Yet something gnawed at him about this situation, and he couldn't completely dismiss the matter. Heaving a mental sigh, he pushed the missive back. This wasn't going to stop until he checked into the matter. But heads would roll if this proved to be a wild goose chase.

"Clive?"

Letterman turned on his way out the door.

"I need a few days of personal leave time." He'd catch the Morganton line and take a few days to visit this Pauline. Perhaps they might discover a family connection. If she could prove that she was kin — then what? He personally couldn't assume her care. He was a single man living in a boardinghouse and working fourteen hours a day. How could he be responsible for an elderly woman?

"Got big plans?"

"Family matters. I shouldn't be gone but a few days."

His boss nodded. "Take all the time you need." He stepped back in the office and closed the door, lowering his voice. "I didn't want to mention this yet, but if you're going to be gone this week you'll miss the announcement."

"There's going to be an announcement?"

Letterman shrugged. "Nothing big. I just thought you might want to know that we've filled Horner's position."

"Sure." Tom's stomach tightened. He might have wanted the upper management job, but he hadn't applied for it. He liked what he did, and the last thing he needed was more headaches — not with the Populists raising cane. The railroads were thought to be part of the big business establishment, Republican and conservative, and only out to make a buck. The Populist movement was seen as liberal, reformist, and heroically trying to harness and control the railroads in the name of the people. Lately the matter was getting out of hand, and he'd welcome some help. "It's been a long time coming."

Earl Horner had suffered a heart attack six months earlier. His coworkers found him slumped over his desk. The man was overworked, and the constant haranguing over freight costs vs. profit was getting on everyone's nerves. Losing Earl had left a huge gap in the office staff and put important jobs on hold. "Who got it? Green?"

"Not Green. A younger man."

"Sanderson?" Even as he asked, Tom shook his head. Sanderson didn't know a railroad tie from a ball bat. Though he was well educated, graduating top of his class at Harvard, he was sadly lacking in common sense. Still, Tom thought he could work with him. He'd miss Horner's calm demeanor and sound judgment, but he was traveling most of the time anyway.

"There was some talk about Sanderson. He was close."

Tom tensed. "You can't be serious."

Letterman just smiled.

"It can't be Warton! You're giving *Warton* the promotion? He hasn't been here but a couple of years. He's still wet behind the ears!"

"True," Letterman conceded. "Actually, Tom, there wasn't a lot of debate about who would take Earl's place. Yours was the first and the last name considered."

Tom felt a silly grin break across his face. "Me? I didn't even apply for the job."

"No, but you're the only man who can fill it." Letterman smiled warmly and reached to shake his hand. "Welcome to a passel of more headaches, Mr. Curtis."

Tom pumped his hand, still grinning. He'd been kidding himself. He had wanted the job. A promotion like this meant more money, benefits, and credentials, but he hadn't pursued it because he feared he would be passed over in favor of a college graduate. His youthful mistake to leave formal schooling early came back to haunt him. When he was fourteen, he thought he had enough knowledge to conquer the world. "Thanks, Clive. I appreciate it."

His boss held up a restraining hand.

"Make that Mr. Letterman." Another quick grin. "Next promotion and I'll be out the front door."

Overwhelmed, Tom shook his head. "I never hoped to get the position." He lifted his gaze. "I won't forget this."

"Forget what? I didn't give you the job, Tom. You earned it. There's a big difference."

Six

January 1893

A shrill whistle shattered the air when the train pulled into the Dwadlo depot on an early Sunday morning. The track ran behind the town, with the back doors of businesses lined up in a row. The General Store sign stood out on the top of its building. Rubbing a clean spot on the dirty window, Tom studied the old station, faintly recalling the structure. It must have been one of the first depots in this part of North Dakota.

Travelers waited on the plank platform as the train pulled in and released a big plume of steam. Something clicked in Tom's mind when he stepped off the train and spotted the muddy sinkhole that contained the platform. An inch of half frozen water stood from melted snow. The ground sloped, and a thick row of bare-limbed oaks blocked the track's progression. This was the end of the line.

He'd been here before. Bursting with certainty, he gripped his satchel and waded through the crowd as though an anchor had dropped from around his neck. Nothing except the setting rang a faint bell, but he was certain it looked familiar. The Wilkey woman might be right. He must have visited Dwadlo when he was a boy.

Tom stopped for a moment to search for the stationmaster, finally spotting his cap in the small ticket office. When he had pushed past the emerging travelers, his gaze skimmed the run-down station and he winced. This depot needed renovation. He made a mental note to telegraph Jay Morgan about the matter immediately. The C&NW prided itself on having the cleanest route on line. After all, the company had a reputation to uphold.

The clerk glanced up as Tom approached the ticket cage. Showing his railroad credentials, he said, "Tom Curtis." The man's jaw dropped, and he nervously shuffled papers, smiling a friendly welcome.

"Mr. Curtis! What an honor! Ain't often that Dwadlo gets a big official passing through town."

"I'm happy to be here," Tom said with a friendly smile of his own. "Can you direct me to Mae Wilkey's place?"

"Mae?" The clerk's own smile brightened. "Why, she's in church at this hour, sir. It's across the street, three doors down."

"Thanks." Tom pulled up his collar to protect his neck from the icy chill in the air and exited the building. He frowned when his boot hit a warped board. He should have asked if there was a telegraph office nearby.

Tolling church bells met Tom's ears a half hour later. Thankful the sun was shining enough to keep most of the chill off, he sat on a bench outside of the General Store thinking back. It had been years since he'd attended a service. He didn't like the feeling the recollection caused. God had given him everything he had and he was thankful. He just didn't take the time to officially tell Him so as often as he should.

Glancing at the church, he saw that the doors were still shut. He got up to peer through the storefront window. The building was like a thousand others offering food, material, and sundries. His gaze focused on a table of men's shirts, and he grinned when he spotted a green one. Green was his favorite color. Visions of his earliest memories flashed through his mind. It was his fifth Christmas. He'd been given a shirt like the one he'd seen in the town mercantile.

Ma made the family's clothing, but the

exact material he wanted couldn't be ordered, so at great sacrifice his father purchased the store-made shirt using Ma's egg money. It still hung in his closet. Tom planned to give it to his son someday, if he ever found a woman he could truly love.

He glanced again toward the church and saw that the congregation was starting to file out. He watched folks appear, trying to spot a familiar face. Men, women, and children emerged. One lady had to be assisted down the six narrow steps that led up to the entry.

Pauline Wilson?

Seconds later an even older woman came through the doorway, alert, dressed in black, and carrying an umbrella. She skimmed down the stairs like a woman fifteen years younger. He studied her weathered features and decided she didn't have one Curtis feature. She certainly didn't favor his mother's side either. The Hollands were all stout people of German ancestry. For a second, memories of Grandma's kitchen and the smell of potato cakes sizzling in a hot iron skillet on the woodstove played havoc with his stomach.

A young woman and a teenage boy emerged. He tried to guess which one of the several men chatting at the foot of the stairs was her husband. The tall farmer with aristocratic features? Or possibly the man dressed in a red-and-green striped silk vest and dark suit? Tom mentally shook off the thought. He doubted any woman in her right mind would waste her time on that dandy. His gaze switched back to the doorway as an older couple started down the steps. No. Pauline didn't have anyone to care for her, especially not a doting husband. Three chattering boys came out of the building and nearly fell, they were laughing so hard. Shortly after, the pastor emerged, turning to lock the door. Pushing off the bench, Tom approached the tall, painfully lean man.

Straightening from his task, he started when he saw Tom and then put a hand over his heart. "I'm sorry, sir, but you gave me quite a fright!"

"No, please. I'm sorry to have startled you." Tom smiled warmly as he extended his hand. "Name's Tom Curtis, and I'm looking for Mae Wilkey. I don't know if she's a Miss or Mrs."

"Mae?" The gentleman's gaze roamed the now empty churchyard. "She was here a moment ago."

"Oh?" Tom turned to follow his gaze. Disappearing buggies met his efforts.

The man smiled. "I'm just filling in for the pastor this morning. He has a touch of dyspepsia." He straightened his vest. "Which reminds me, I must be getting on home. The missus will have dinner on the table, and she hates it when I'm late. Mae is probably already home. Jeremy has a big appetite, and he loves his Sunday fried chicken."

Jeremy. So it was "Mrs." A play by Thomas Morton came to mind: *Speed the Plough* or something like that. There was a character by the name of "Mrs. Grundy" — a lady with a prudish personality. He'd only read the play because his teacher had made him, but this Mae Wilkey sounded like her. He bet she looked like her too. Nose in the air. Straitlaced. Priggish.

"I'm sure she will welcome you inside so you can get out of the chill, and she'll have plenty on her table to share." The man pointed down the road. "She lives in that white house with the blue shutters."

Tom couldn't miss it. The buildings and houses were built so close you could spit on the neighborhood. Nodding, the pastor stepped back to let Tom precede him down the steps. Sunday fried chicken. Right about now, if he were home, he'd be sitting down to a plate piled high with his favorite meat at the boardinghouse.

Instead, he was in Dwadlo, North Dakota, looking for possible kin. The idea still didn't make a lick of sense.

Tom thanked the man and set off down the road. Smells of pot roast, fried chicken, and fresh coffee lingered in the mild air. Everything in Dwadlo was shut tighter than a tick burrowed in. The local café's "Closed" sign hung in the window in observance of the Lord's Day.

He counted the houses as he walked. He couldn't remember ever being in a smaller town, and the homes had been built within a couple hundred feet of the train depot. He thought with all the available land that folks would have spread out a bit.

Everything appeared to be tiny in comparison to Chicago dwellings. One house on the left had a large shed or some sort of outbuilding that sat near the back of the lot. The sound of rushing water met his ears, and he figured a river sat behind the house. Dogs and cats milled about the yard.

Tom focused on the house with the blue shutters. This must be the place, from what the pastor said. Resentment crowded him before he rejected the feeling. He should thank Mrs. Wilkey instead of begrudging her. If this Pauline Wilson was family who

70

needed him, he would want to know and be of help, but the letter had come out of nowhere, and he was having a hard time accepting the news. Exactly what could he possibly do? He couldn't move her into his boardinghouse.

Even if he left there and found a bigger place, Pauline would be alone almost every day in Chicago. It was a shame that someone in the area didn't start a home for aging people who were unable to care for themselves. In his travels he'd seen such establishments starting to spring up in Florida, Wisconsin, and Illinois.

Before he reached the house, a dog spotted him and bound out into the street, barking. Others followed. Backing away, Tom said, "Git!"

Three of the larger dogs took turns jumping up and planting dirty paws on the front of his shirt. Wet tongues lapped at him while small dogs tangled around his feet, yipping. Memories of being bitten when he was a boy flooded his mind and sudden fear gripped him. Stumbling, his satchel went flying, spilling its contents. He fell to the ground in a sea of fur, unable to fight off the animals. "Git! Git!"

Barks and yelps grew and the animals turned aggressive, latching onto the hem of his heavy coat. More dogs joined the fray. He was amazed they were only biting his clothing and not his flesh. Turning his back, he tried to push the animals off him. When that failed, he shouted louder. "Get off me!" The scuffle seemed to go on forever before he heard a sharp whistle.

The assault immediately stopped and the animals trotted off. Stunned, Tom lay on the ground, head spinning. His right hand felt the tears in his coat. He finally shifted his gaze to see the source of his rescue.

A young woman with the warmest brown eyes he had ever seen loomed above him — if a five-foot woman could loom above anything. She wore a long black cloak and huddled against the cutting wind. She spoke softly with concern on her pretty face.

"Are you hurt?"

He grunted. "Define hurt."

Kneeling beside him, she took the hem of her skirt and gently wiped his face. He much preferred the faint fragrance of jasmine lingering on the woman's skin than the animal smells lingering on the ground.

"My goodness. Those dogs are a pesky lot, aren't they?"

Pesky wasn't exactly how he would describe the all-out assault. "Are they rabid?" He searched the retreating animals for the frothing mouths or aggressive behavior of the dreaded disease. He knew that from childhood.

"Goodness no. They're healthy. Just boisterous."

Slowly sitting up, Tom held his head in both hands. "They came out of nowhere."

She assisted him to his feet. "Are there any lasting effects?"

He saw her focus on a long tear in his coat sleeve, and he checked for any open flesh wounds. "No, ma'am. My coat and shirt are torn, that's all." He bent to gather his personal belongings strewn over the yard, along with his extra clothes, which were now muddy as well.

"Those are easy to fix. If you have a moment, I'll mend the tears for you and then wash the mud off your things. I'll hang them in front of the stove, and they will dry in no time. Have you had your dinner?"

"I ate some jerky earlier." He dusted mud and snow off his knees.

"Jerky? For Sunday dinner?" Gripping his arm, she turned him toward the road. "You're coming with me."

Ordinarily Tom would protest, but his clothes did need mending, and if the aroma of frying chicken came from her house he wasn't going to argue — plus, she was pretty. Dogs howled in the background. "Does the dogcatcher live there?" he asked as they started to leave.

"No. That is the home of a lovely woman, and she can't turn any animal away. It started out innocently enough. Folks dump their strays here, and I'm afraid she's now let her compassion eat her out of house and home."

Rubbing the back of his neck, Tom followed the woman across the road and then up the path leading to a small front porch. He was so busy checking to see if the dogs were at his heels again that he followed her without being aware of his surroundings. When she opened the door, he spotted a youth standing in front of the cooking stove. Tom's gaze fixed on the table, where a heaping plate of fried chicken was surrounded by bowls of mashed potatoes, gravy, beets, and green beans. His empty stomach growled.

"Please make yourself at home. I'll get you something to wear while I mend that shirtsleeve — and your pants are all dirty. I'll wash those also."

"Thank you, ma'am." His eyes roamed the cozy kitchen. He breathed in the fragrant smells mingling in the room. He unbuttoned his coat, keeping an eye on the boy.

He didn't say a word, but a friendly smile welcomed him. The woman returned with a shirt and a pair of trousers.

"These will probably be too small. Our father was short in stature, but I'll have your clothing mended and washed in no time. I'm the town's postmistress, but I'm also pretty handy with a needle and thread." She pointed to the room she'd exited. "You can change in there."

He knew without trying on the garments that they wouldn't fit, but he took them from her and walked to the small room where a bed, chest of drawers, and women's clothing were strewn about. Closing the door, he stripped out of his muddy garments and put on the clean ones. When he emerged, he felt like a fool. The shirtsleeves were three inches too short, and the pant legs only came to the top of his boots. The woman discreetly studied his attire.

"Oh. Well, the repair will only take a minute. Sit down, please." She stepped to the sideboard and removed a cup.

Tom pulled out a chair and sat down. The boy remained quiet, lost in his cooking.

"Hope you like chicken."

"One of my favorites."

She moved quickly and efficiently around the kitchen. A moment later she set eating utensils in front of him and moved to the large coffeepot shoved to the back of the stove, addressing the boy. "The dogs tore this gentleman's coat sleeve and muddied his trousers and the extra clothing he was carrying. After dinner I'll mend and wash the garments and hang them to dry."

Nodding, he laid his turning fork aside and moved to sit down at the table.

Tom reached for the plate she offered and looked appreciatively at the delicious-looking food in front of him. This meal alone was worth the journey. Where was the husband?

"Jake usually joins us on Sunday, but he wasn't feeling well today."

Nodding, Tom opened his napkin.

She sat down and smiled. "It's a joy to feed a hungry man."

"Oh?" After spearing a couple of drumsticks he picked up the bowl of cream gravy. "Your husband has a hearty appetite?"

Shaking her head, she laughed. A clear, pleasant sound. "I don't have a husband." Her gaze tenderly focused on the young boy. "It's just me and Jeremy."

Nodding to him, Tom ladled beans on his plate. So far the lad still hadn't said a word. He just kept smiling at him. "You look to be a mighty fine cook, ma'am."

Color crept up her neck. "Actually, Jeremy does most of the cooking around here." Grinning at the boy, she admitted, "Sometimes he'll let me bake a chocolate cake, but not often."

Lifting his gaze, Tom focused on the young male, aware of the deep affection in her eyes. "Well, Jeremy, this is by far the best fried chicken I've ever had." The boy beamed, a blush infusing his youthful cheeks. Tom ate in silence as he tried to guess his age. Early teens? Mute perhaps? The woman's voice broke into his thoughts.

"I don't believe I've seen you in the General Store. Are you new to the area?"

"Arrived on the morning train." He disposed of the two legs quickly and reached for a chicken breast. "You?"

"Born and raised right here in Dwadlo. Jeremy is my brother."

Brother and sister. It made sense. "You said you're Dwadlo's postmistress?"

She smiled. "Afraid so. Not very exciting, is it?"

"No. It's a fine job. Could you pass the beets?"

She picked up a bowl and handed it to him. "What brings you to these parts in the dead of winter?"

"Pauline Wilson. Do you know her?"

Her cup slipped to the table. He reached to sop up the coffee when her hand grabbed his. "Are you Tom Curtis?"

When he tried to pull away, her grip tightened.

"Are you?" she demanded.

"Yes, ma'am. I'm Tom Curtis." His eyes narrowed as recognition dawned. If she recognized his name, then she must be the one who'd written the letter. "Are you Mae Wilkey?"

She nodded. "Yes. Thank goodness you've come."

Mentally shaking his head, he took a bite of potatoes. This was Mae Wilkey? She wasn't the woman he'd imagined. This woman spoke in soft tones, seemed eager to help, and if her brother's facial expressions meant anything, the young man loved his sister deeply.

Springing from her chair, she moved around the table and began heaping more chicken and beets on his plate. "I was about to despair of my letters ever reaching you."

He should have known by the way she was wielding food like a weapon that he was in for it. His hand blocked a third hot biscuit. "Please, ma'am. I've about had my fill."

Sinking back to her chair, she drew a long breath and expelled the words. "Thank you,

God, for answered prayer."

"So this . . . Pauline you wrote about. You said she's getting up in years?"

"She's in her nineties, and until a year ago she was doing quite well, but lately she's become very feeble. She falls often, she forgets to eat, and she roams the house at night and sleeps all day — not to mention that her mind isn't quite right anymore."

Tom had seen the likes and it wasn't pretty. "Ma'am, what makes you believe I'm Pauline's kin?"

"Yours was the only name and address I found in her desk. I've never heard her speak of family. She never married that I know of, and she mostly keeps to herself these days, but she's always been a good neighbor. I stop by every morning and evening to check on her, but she needs more." Her eyes pleaded with him. "She needs hot meals and more frequent baths. I feel certain she hasn't long on this earth, and having family to make personal decisions would mean the world to her."

"What kind of decisions?"

"Legal ones. Someone to care for her."

Shoving back from the table, he said, "Ma'am, I've racked my brain, but I can't remember a Pauline in the family — there may be, but I'm not recalling her." He shook his head. "However, if my name and address were in the drawer, it seems likely I had some connection to her."

"I wish I could help, but Pauline's mind —" Mae abruptly stopped speaking and shrugged.

Wiping his mouth on his napkin, he said, "If Pauline is kin, then you can rest assured I'll see to her care." How? He still didn't know. He supposed he could hire someone to stay with her and look after her needs, especially if she didn't have long on this earth.

"Are there any widows or single women in town who could assume her care? I would handsomely compensate them." Money wasn't an issue. He never had time to spend what he earned, so his savings had grown, and with the new promotion and benefits he'd be set for life.

Her features sobered. "I'm afraid there isn't. The town is very small, Mr. Curtis."

"I can see that. Unfortunately, Miss Wilkey, I put in sixty to seventy hours a week at work. I'm not in a position to care for a ninety-year-old woman. Few people live to be that old."

"Ninety-two, actually," she murmured, "and most of the time they don't. I don't understand why Pauline has lasted this long, and I'm sure this has come as quite a surprise to you."

"Quite," he said. He couldn't have been more surprised if a cannonball had landed on his desk rather than her letter.

"Would your wife —"

"I'm not married."

"I see." She pursued her lips. "This is a quandary."

"If I offered to compensate you well, could you do it?"

She shook her head. "I love Pauline, but with the post office and . . ." Her eyes discreetly indicated the young boy absorbed in his food. "Family responsibilities devour my time."

"What if I placed an ad in newspapers in surrounding areas?"

"You could, but would that be the best choice? Who knows what manner of person would answer? Some folks would do any-thing for money. Pauline won't be able to tell us if she is mistreated in any way." She met his eyes. "I couldn't sleep nights think-ing she might be neglected by a stranger."

Pushing away from the table, she said, "Why don't we pay her a visit? Perhaps when you meet her something will click. A family feature? Perhaps a turn of phrase?" She glanced at the boy. "Jeremy, I'm going to quickly mend Mr. Curtis' coat and shirt and wash the mud off his clothing. While the garments dry, Mr. Curtis and I will pay Pauline a short visit. Dinner was delicious." She leaned down to kiss his cheek.

Nodding, he continued to eat. She left to do her work and Tom finished his meal. When the boy offered a slice of piping hot apple pie swimming in hot cinnamon butter, he couldn't resist. If he'd ever been fuller, he couldn't recall the time. Mae would have to let out the waist on his pants if he stayed around these parts for very long.

While Jeremy cleared the table, Tom moved to the chair in front of the fire. The house, like the others he'd seen, was small, but not a speck of dust was visible. There was a large knitted red throw on the back of the chair he occupied. Next to it sat a rocking chair with a wicker basket filled with yarn. His gaze shifted to the knitting needles stuck in a ball of earth-colored thread. An end table separated the two chairs. A round braided rug was in front of the fireplace. Other than a small couch, the room couldn't hold more furniture.

The setting was relaxing. His room in the boardinghouse didn't have a homey feel. It contained a bed and a washstand. Mrs. Fletcher's downstairs sitting room had more warmth, but he never spent any time there. When he was in town he ate his meal and then excused himself to head for his room. His gaze shifted back to the two men's magazines sitting on the end table. Remains of her father, or was there a man in Mae Wilkey's life? Tom closed his eyes, enjoying the warmth and comfort of the quiet house after his long journey.

He was almost dozing by the time Mae return to the main room. Smiling at him, she reached for her cloak. "All finished. Jeremy, would you please hang the garments in front of the fire while Mr. Curtis and I visit?" She glanced at Tom. "Pauline lives across the street."

He stood and then paused as the words sank in. "Across the street?"

Taking his arm, she squeezed. "The dogs are just pets. I'm sure we can eventually talk her into relinquishing a few."

Dogs. Cats. Family connections he couldn't remember. Tom could always contend that he wasn't kin, but something inside him made him question that. He had no idea how his name and address landed in a crazy woman's desk drawer. He realized he could step away right now and return to his nice, sane boardinghouse that also served good fried chicken, claim his new job, and let Pauline become someone else's problem. However, his conscience would never rest until he had the answers he had come seeking.

"Ready?" Mae asked. "Here, since we don't have a coat to fit you, wrap this quilt around you. It will keep you warm until we get there."

He mustered an obliging smile as he took the makeshift wrap. He was as ready as a blindfolded man standing before a firing squad.

If he hadn't already looked like an imbecile wearing small cloths, he surely did now.

"Ready."

SEVEN

Tom couldn't help staring at the pack of mongrels prowling Pauline's yard. This time, with Mae at his side, the animals didn't trounce on him. Perhaps it was the clothing he was wearing or the quilt around his shoulders that stopped them in their tracks. He looked like a plain fool in a shirt and pair of pants three sizes too small. His gaze roamed the cats next and he shook his head. There wasn't a Curtis or Holland born who would live here.

"Pauline does seem to go overboard with animals." Mae worked her way up the three porch steps. "Git! When she started accepting every stray that wandered this way, things sort of got out of hand. Git down!" When she reached the top of the porch, she turned to urge him to the front. "Come on. Most don't bite."

"That's encouraging." He'd bite anything dressed in this shirt. He climbed the steps and paused as Mae knocked and then pounded on the door. Eventually it creaked open a notch and one faded blue eye peered out.

"Pauline, it's me, Mae!"

"Eh?" Pauline held her hand to her ear.

"It's Mae!"

"May is months away. It's January, I think."

"No." Mae wedged her foot between the door and the frame and stood firm. "Open the door, Pauline. It's your neighbor." She turned to whisper. "I'm sorry, Mr. Curtis. This doesn't appear to be one of her better days."

Nodding, Tom pulled the quilt tighter around his shoulders. He hoped no one in town saw him like this. A moment later the door flew open, and he dodged a couple of cats that sprang out. A bent woman stood in the doorway, her right jaw bulging with snuff.

"Oh, Pauline." Mae sighed. "You promised me you'd given up chewing."

"I did?"

She raised an empty can and spat into it.

Mae gently nudged the woman back from the door to allow entry. "You have company!"

Pauline stood back, eyes fixed on Mae.

"Honey, you're not company. You're family."

Mae turned and offered Tom a silent apology for the condition of the house. Today it appeared ransacked. Clothing was strewn over furniture and the floors. Pots and pans lined the baseboard in a train fashion. Feathers tied to strings hung over everything. Sighing again, Mae asked, "Have you been cooking today?"

"No."

"Then why are your pots and pans on the floor?"

Pauline turned to access the situation. "Are those pots and pans? I thought I was straightening my shoes in the closet."

Reaching for Tom's hand, Mae said, "I have a wonderful surprise for you."

"You do?" The old woman's eyes lit up.

"I might have found your kin! Tom Curtis, this is Pauline Wilson."

Grinning, Pauline clapped her hands with delight. "My kin! Why, that's just wonderful! Step closer, sonny. My eyesight ain't what it used to be."

Tom reached for the woman's hand. Her clasp had surprising strength. "Miss Pauline." His eyes scanned her features as he searched for any sign of recognition. She had his mother's nose — maybe — and the shape of her eyes favored the Holland side. Somewhat.

Her faded eyes traced him, and he could see she was having a hard time making the connection too.

"Goodness." She pumped his hand. "My own kin. I thought I had lost everyone. You've outgrown your clothes, son!"

"I believe you're right, Miss Pauline. Miss Mae's letter came as a real surprise." His eyes traced again her face, powerless to completely recognize one familiar feature. Most Curtises had brown eyes — and the Hollands had blue or hazel eyes. Pauline's faded eyes were blue, but not the deep hue his mother had.

"Well, honey." She drew him to the table, which was cluttered with dirty crockery and utensils. A cat was licking one dish clean. "Sit down and let me fix you something to eat."

Tom smiled. "That's not necessary. Miss Mae just fed me a huge meal."

"You been eating Jeremy's Sunday fried chicken?"

"Yes, ma'am. He's a fine cook." He sneezed.

"Oh, now. Call me Auntie."

He nodded. She apparently recognized something he didn't. "You are my aunt?"

88

"You said I was."

"No. I don't know if you're my aunt or cousin or anything. I'm sorry, but I can't make the connection." He sneezed a second time, and Mae handed him a dainty handkerchief. It held the scent of sweet jasmine, and he found it quite pleasing.

Pauline frowned. "You said you were kin."

He glanced at Mae. "She says I am." Another sneeze.

"He is your kin, Pauline. And he's here to help." Mae focused on him. "Are you coming down with a cold?"

"No, ma'am. I think it's the animals." He swiped at his itchy nose and glanced at Mae. How could the woman be so all-fired sure he was related to Pauline Wilson when he didn't know that himself?

Pale eyes brightened. "He's come to stay!"

His hand flew up in protest. "No, not permanently. I'm just here long enough to figure out our kinship and maybe get you settled somewhere." Even though she might not be kin, he could perhaps follow through with helping the poor old thing. After all, without a wife and family, he could afford it.

"I am settled."

Mae shot him a "move slowly" glance. The news that family had shown up had obviously unnerved Pauline. Wondering about it unnerved him too.

"I think we're tiring her." She helped the older woman to the couch, pitching a bundle of clothing aside in order to sit beside her. She reached for a blanket and folded it three times to fashion a middle cushion. "Why don't we all just sit here and visit? Maybe something will ring a bell for one or the other."

Tom joined them, and the three sat in silence, like blackbirds lined up on a board fence. Suddenly Pauline leaned out and peered around Mae to look at him.

"What did you say your name is?"

"Tom. Tom Curtis." He felt another sneeze coming on and put the sweet-smelling handkerchief to his nose.

She shook her head, pondering. "Ain't got no Curtis kin."

"What about Holland? That was my mother's maiden name."

Pauline shook her head. "Nope. Don't know anyone named Holland."

"Pauline," Mae cautioned. "Try to focus." She patted the older woman's hand. "I know it's difficult, but think. Does Tom show any physical evidence of family traits? Eye color? Hair?"

She raised her eyebrows. "Yes, they all had

hair and eyes."

Mae ignored that. "His mother's name was Holland." She glanced at Tom. "I believe that's what you said."

Tom knew Mae would give him another scolding look if he didn't stifle the laugh that tried to make its way out at the old woman's statement. He nodded. "Beatrice Holland."

"Beatrice!"

He met her faded gaze. "Do you know her?" Part of him wanted a firm no, but another part, one he identified as plain ol' curiosity, was eager to hear her response. The woman's almost skeletal frame settled back against the couch.

"No. Just always favored the name Beatrice."

"Maybe you like it because the name brings back fond memories of someone you once knew," Mae reasoned.

"Miss Pauline —"

She stopped him. "Call me Auntie."

For the time being he'd comply with her request. "Auntie." If the clothes didn't make him feel like a buffoon, saying the name sealed it. He felt about as foolish as judging a horse by its harness. "Do you have any idea why you had my name and address in your desk drawer?" The cat that sat before the fire suddenly got up and leaped into his lap, and then he promptly climbed Tom's shirt and curled around his neck.

Pauline drew back, seemingly affronted. "I don't have your name in my desk drawer."

Slipping to the edge of the couch, Mae explained, "Remember a while back when we straightened your desk? I took the liberty of writing down a name and address I found there. I wasn't being nosey. I was simply trying to locate your kin."

Pauline's eyes were now fixed on Tom, studying him from head to toe. The wood-stove pumped heat into the already swelter-ing room, and sweat beaded his forehead. Maybe she was in her right mind momen-tarily and was trying to make the connec-tion. Long moments stretched before she spoke.

"Sonny?"

"Yes . . . Auntie?"

"Who does your sewing?"

He glanced down at his clothing and hoped for the strength to get through this humiliation. "I . . . tore my shirt pocket, and Miss Mae kindly mended it for me."

Pauline's sharp gaze switched to Mae. "This is your idea of sewing?"

"Oh, no. That's Papa's shirt. And pants."

A frowned deepened Pauline's already creased forehead. Shaking her head, she tsked. "Honey, your papa's been gone a spell. I recall the day we laid him to rest. The sun was shining and the birds were singing. There was a dark thundercloud in the west, and the pastor had to cut the preaching short before the storm moved in. I was wearing a new pair of shoes — black — and a fine hat that was frilly but had a black ribbon tied around the rim. I was torn between getting my shoes muddy and my new hat wet and paying proper respect to your papa."

Tom glanced at Mae. The woman could recall all of that but couldn't remember her kin? And even if she wasn't his kin, he was beginning to feel an obligation.

Another sneeze made its way to the surface, then another and another. As he lifted his borrowed handkerchief to his nose he noticed again the scent of jasmine that lingered on delicate cloth and wondered why the pretty Miss Wilkey had never married.

EIGHT

The sun was slanting to the west when Mae and Tom let themselves out.

Mae walked in silence with Mr. Curtis, uncertainty bothering her. Had she made the proper connection between dear Pauline and this man? She'd caught both Tom and Pauline staring at each other for long periods during the afternoon, and she could practically see the wheels turning in Mr. Curtis' head. He struggled with the idea of lost kin as hardily as Pauline gleefully accepted her newfound family.

While they sat there, two hours passed before the older woman finally settled in her chair and dropped off to sleep mid-conversation. They quietly got up to leave and softly closed the door behind them. Mae glanced up at Tom Curtis. As he settled the quilt about him again, she noticed how the borrowed shirt pulled tight, amplifying his broad shoulders. She broke the awkward silence as they stepped off the porch and into the street. "Um . . . where do you plan to stay? I would offer accommodations, but I'm afraid I don't have the room." She'd slept on Jeremey's pallet until her younger brother came along. Father didn't have funds to build another room, so she'd made her pallet on the other side of the stove until Father died and she took his room.

"Haven't given it a thought."

She noticed how the set of his jaw tightened. Granted, the "meeting" had not gone entirely as hoped. It was clear that neither party could place the other. "Of course, you could stay with Pauline, but her home is cramped like mine, and —"

"Thank you for your concern, ma'am, but I'll find a room."

She studied on that and then admitted, "Dwadlo doesn't have a boardinghouse, Mr. Curtis. It did once, but the woman who ran it had to leave. Her sister needed her back East, and she couldn't find a buyer for the place, so it has sat empty since." She realized she was beginning to babble and stopped talking. But she kept thinking.

Obviously he couldn't sleep outdoors. It would be poor manners to unite a man with misplaced kin and then make him sleep outside in the dead of January. He seemed lost in thought, and she wondered if he was even listening to her.

"I won't rest well knowing I haven't provided you with home comforts." She paused and then snapped her fingers. "Of course. Dale can take you in for a spell." Mr. Curtis wouldn't be here long. It didn't take much to know that. He would be out of here the moment he found someone to care for his aunt.

Tom's steps paused, and he finally turned to look at her. "Dale who?"

"The man who owns the General Store. That's where Dwadlo's post office is too. Folks come in to purchase goods and get their mail at the same time. Dale lives in back of the store, and I'm sure he'd welcome the company."

"Miss Wilkey —"

"Please." She smiled. "Call me Mae."

"Mae, I'll only be here a day or two. Just long enough to figure out what to do with Pauline or get her settled somewhere. I can find a room."

"No, you can't." She sighed. "Like I said, there aren't any available. You'll have to settle for staying with Dale."

"Ma'am —"

She held up a forefinger. "Mae?" Noticing his handsome features in the dim light of evening, somehow she wished he would be staying longer. And she definitely didn't want him calling her ma'am.

"Mae, I think you're getting your hopes up. I can't take Pauline back with me. I live in a boardinghouse, and my job requires that I travel. I personally can't take care of her, but I can pay for her care here if she turns out to be my kinfolk. I'm going to have to check further into that possibility."

Pondering a moment, she shook her head. "There isn't anyone around here who can care for her, Mr. Curtis. Believe me, I've looked."

"Pardon me, Mae, but if you want me to call you by your given name, I think it's only fitting that you call me Tom."

"All right then, Tom. Dwadlo is a small community, and everyone has more mouths than they can feed now. I've asked as far away as Pine Grove and Branch Springs, and there isn't anyone. Trust me."

"All due respect, but why should I trust you? I just met you."

The man was absolutely right. Why should he trust a stranger? "True, but as you can see, we live a simple life here in Dwadlo. I wouldn't attempt to mislead you where Pauline's care is concerned, nor would I when trying to find you a place to reside while you're here. Dale is one of the most up-standing citizens in town. His living area is admittedly small — you'd probably have to sleep on a pallet on the floor — but I'm sure he wouldn't object."

"I'm a private man, and I wouldn't feel comfortable staying with . . . Dale. If there's a barn nearby I'll sleep there. And speaking of living arrangements, what would I do with all of the dogs and cats Pauline's acquired?"

"That is a worry," Mae admitted. "She's tried to give them away or give them back for a long time now, but she only accumulates more every year. I don't know what you'd do with them."

"It's one thing to assume Pauline's care and another to be responsible for those animals."

"I understand, but I'm certain God will work it all out."

"Do you understand? I have to wonder that if the tables were turned, and you were handed a 'could be' relative you knew nothing about, you'd have such a sunny outlook on the situation."

She understood what he was trying to say and wondered the same herself. She had no answer to that. "There's Pauline's shed . . ." Her voice trailed when she saw recognition hit his face.

His footsteps paused. "You should know something. I'm not an animal lover. I think pets are fine for most folks, but I was bitten by a mongrel once, and I can remember the long days we waited to see if the dog was rabid. Turned out it wasn't, but it made an impression on me. I steer clear of both dogs and cats. Also, they make me sneeze."

"What a pity. Pets are such a joy."

"Yes, ma'am. Pauline must be dying of happiness."

She barely noticed the remark because her head was spinning with possibilities. She must accommodate Tom Curtis. If he left without Pauline she wasn't sure what she could do. The elderly lady's plight worried Mae near to death, but she had to work. She had no other choice. Papa died a poor man, and she and her brother lived from week to week. Jeremy needed little, and she hadn't made a new dress in three years, but the good Lord provided. "Well, then," she began, "why don't I stay in Dale's quarters? I will be comfortable there for a few days."

"And where does Dale go?"

"My house. You, Dale, and Jeremy can stay at my place long enough for you to settle family matters." Maybe she overemphasized the word "family," but it was only fair that he accepted his responsibility. And with Jeremy there, perhaps he'd feel more comfortable.

"I don't mean to overstep my bounds, but is Jeremy . . ." He paused, wondering how to ask the sensitive question.

She understood. "Jeremy was injured at birth. He thinks like a nine-year-old in most areas. You saw how well he cooks. He's gifted with housekeeping and animals. Pauline pays him to feed and water her dogs and cats, and he dutifully fulfills his job."

"I'm sorry. I —"

Smiling, she said softly, "Don't be sorry. Jeremy is my greatest blessing in life." She paused. "Are you a God-fearing man, Tom?"

He focused on his boots. "I gather you're a religious woman?"

"I believe in the Bible's teachings. Do you?"

"Mae, if you don't mind I'd like to focus on a place to stay the night. It's been a long day, and I'd like to get some sleep."

When he didn't answer her question, it made her wonder if he was indeed a God-fearing man, but it wasn't her business one way or the other. "Of course. Let me tell Jeremy the plan and then we'll go ask Dale for his help." She was confident the store owner would be willing to fall in with the arrangement. Dale had known Mae and her brother all of their lives. He was like a second father, and there wasn't a kinder man on earth. "Oh. Dale sometimes smokes a pipe. Would that bother you?"

"I can live with it."

"I'll tell Jeremy to be careful to keep the animals away from the house."

Nodding, he walked on.

Be extra careful, she thought as she prepared to tell her brother the news. She'd do everything possible to make Tom Curtis comfortable for a few days. She would be fine in Dale's quarters. The arrangement would give her a chance to thoroughly clean his living space, and Jeremy could also help Dale with his daily baking.

Tom Curtis wouldn't leave without somehow arranging for Pauline's care.

Victory was so close she could taste it.

Within the hour Tom was settled at Mae's with a plate of hot biscuits and sausage patties in front of him. A steaming cobbler cooled on the counter. Fresh milk, which had been put outside to cool, sat on the table, and hot coffee perked on the stove. His boardinghouse didn't offer this much service.

Mae emerged from the bedroom with a

small valise. "I think that should do it. Jeremy, you take good care of our guests."

"I have to feed the animals."

"Of course. You can go now if you like."

Those were the first words Tom heard him speak. Reaching for a hot biscuit, Tom asked. "Should I wait for Dale before I eat?"

Smiling, Mae paused beside his chair. "Why do you ask? It appears you've made your decision." The back door closed behind Jeremy.

Tom winked at her. "Jeremy bakes a mean biscuit." He liked the way the color rose to her cheeks. How many years had it been since a man winked at her? He couldn't help but wonder again why Mae Wilkey wasn't married.

"If you like his biscuits, you'll love his corn bread." Picking up her bag, she glanced around the undersized kitchen. "Make yourself at home. You can't hurt anything."

She gave him another grin, and he noticed her features. She reminded him of a girl he'd known years ago. Bright and self-assured but not flashy. She wore her blond hair in a knot on the back of her head and her cheeks glowed with health. Her eyes were the color of dark toffee. The combination was nice, but Tom didn't have time for personal matters. He occasionally thought he should marry and settle down, but with the new promotion awaiting him, that seemed a distant prospect. He supposed now that Pauline had come into his life, and if she proved to be a long-lost aunt or cousin, he'd be in Dwadlo more often than he would like. The trips would be time-consuming. Another reason family life wouldn't work for him just now.

"Well, I'm off. Dale's mother lived with him until a few months ago. He's been lonely since her death. The company will be good for him." She smiled. "If you need anything, you know where to find me."

She left, and within minutes a rap sounded at the door. Mae told Tom earlier that when she explained the circumstances to Dale, he'd nodded, stripped off his apron, and gone to pack a small bag. Tom reached for the butter. "It's open!"

The doorknob turned, and a man stepped into the kitchen. The nondescript store owner appeared harmless enough and obliging as well. He was dressed in heavy-soled shoes, black pants, and a white shirt with the cuffs turned up. A pair of glasses perched on the bridge of his globular nose. He smelled of tobacco — a cherry blend.

Without a word, he walked to the bedroom and set his satchel on the bed. Frowning, Tom wondered where he was supposed to sleep. His eyes focused on the small couch that resembled a good-size rattrap. Mae surely didn't think his six-foot frame would fit on that torture box. Then he spotted two pallets by the stove and had a hunch of where he'd sleep. At least it would be warm.

Dale returned from the bedroom and sat down at the table. After a moment Tom asked, "Have you eaten?" The man shook his head and Tom motioned toward the food. "Help yourself."

Sitting upright, Dale stared at his plate but didn't make a move. Tom couldn't understand why he was just sitting there. "Better eat up. The biscuits are hot." The older man remained focused on his plate. After a moment Tom got it. Apparently Dale's mother had waited on him hand and foot.

Shoving away from the table, he reached for a plate off the sideboard and then filled it with two biscuits stuffed with fat sausage patties. He set the plate in front of store owner. "There you go. Enjoy." He returned to his supper. After a moment, he noticed Dale was still waiting.

"You need something else?" He watched Dale stare at his empty cup. "Oh — right.

Coffee." This was going to be a long two days. He stood, snagged the pot, and carried it to the table.

Dale shook his head.

"You don't want coffee? You need cream? Sugar?" The man concentrated on the milk pitcher. "Milk. Okay." Tom fetched a glass, poured milk into it, and set it down before turning back to his cold supper.

Dale lifted patient eyes and met his gaze. "What?"

Tom's head started to throb. He had to deal with a crazy old woman, he was up to his ears in dog and cat fur, and now he was expected to babysit a mute? He knew the man could talk. Mae would have mentioned if he couldn't speak. Didn't anyone but Mae talk in this town?

Dale's long-suffering eyes focused on his chest. Tom checked the table service. He had a fork, knife, and spoon. A tall glass of milk sat in front of him. Butter and something that looked like sorghum sat nearby.

Dale tapped his chest.

What? His shirt? Bib. He wanted a bib. Glancing around the room, Tom spotted a cloth on the kitchen counter. Getting up, he retrieved the item, tied it around the man's neck and pushed him closer to the table. He put a fork in his hand. "Now, eat."

When Dale still waited, Tom was tempted to eat his meal and be done with it. He moved to his chair and then noted Dale's bowed head. Prayer. Heaving a mental sigh, Tom bowed his head and said, "Much obliged for the food and cobbler. Amen."

Reaching for two warm biscuits, Tom was pleased to see that the man was finally digging in. The silence was broken occasionally with a clicking fork or the sound of a cup or glass meeting the table.

The older man cleaned his plate and then wiped his mouth on the bib. He sat up straighter. Tom caught the action from the corner of his eye. What now? "There's cobbler, if you want it."

He shook his head and waited.

Tom got up from the table, walked around to Dale, loosened the man's bib, and handed it to him, refusing to wipe his mouth.

Rising from the chair, Dale burped, put the cloth on the table, and then moseyed toward the bedroom.

Tom's gaze focused on the pallets, but his thoughts went to Mae Wilkey and Pauline Wilson. Unfortunately, he was stuck here for the time being.

And he already knew he was going to sleep on the floor.

NINE

"Where are all the barns around here?"

The post office cage occupied a small corner of the store beside the front window, and Tom watched Mae sort circulars while he kept her company. He picked up a magazine, leaned against the cage shelf, and began to read. He wanted a distraction from the crick in his neck that wouldn't let up from sleeping on a pallet.

"A few are outside Dwadlo, but as you can see, the town is mostly residential." Mae paused in her task and decided to address the unspoken subject between them head-on. "Have you definitely decided not to take Pauline back to Chicago with you?"

"As I told you before, I *can't* take her back with me."

"Oh, yes. Well. Last year I tried to find someone to stay with her, and I was willing to pay them what little I could, but there's isn't a soul around who has the time to care for an elderly woman. I couldn't see Pauline put in a poorhouse alongside the insane, the inebriated, and the homeless." She frowned thoughtfully. "I did hear of a nice place in Massachusetts — Boston's Home for Aged Women — but they charge a small fortune."

"I know of other homes that care for the elderly, but they're costly as well." With his new promotion, he'd be making better money, and along with his savings, without a doubt he could pay for the woman's care for the time she had left, but was she his responsibility? "Does Pauline have money? Any savings?"

"Does she look like she has savings?"

"No, but sometimes looks can be deceiving."

"She doesn't have money, Tom. You can trust my word on that. Dale lets her carry credit here — which he's almost never reimbursed for — or she wouldn't eat. She sells personal items from time to time, but that accounts for little."

"Let me make my circumstance clear. I'm not a rich man, Mae, but I do have some savings, and I probably make enough to pay for a fancy home for aging women. However, should I do that for someone I don't know?"

She shook her head. "You still claim you don't know her?"

He had tumbled the possibilities of Pauline being kin in his mind a hundred times, and still there was no recollection of the woman. "I *know* I don't know her."

"Then why stay?" As she turned away to resume her work, she glanced over her shoulder at him.

He met her questioning gaze. "That's what I've been asking myself all morning. I honestly believe I don't know her, but in the rare event I'm mistaken I'll do what I can to find her a home." Had he really just said that? He'd help her find a home, even though he knew in his heart she wasn't a member of his family? Was it Pauline's situation that was keeping him here, or could it be he liked Mae Wilkey more than he wanted to admit?

She slipped a flyer into a box. "That's very noble of you."

He heard the sarcasm in her voice, but before he could address it the front door opened and a woman stepped inside. Mae turned to greet the newcomer.

"Morning, Grace!"

The woman hurried toward the cage. "Hello, dear. I need postage for three letters, please." She rummaged in her crocheted bag.

"Yes, ma'am. That will be three cents."

"Oh, where is my coin purse?"

Grace searched and came up with a snuff box, from which she politely offered Mae a pinch. Mae shook her head. "No, thank you."

Stuffing the box back in her purse, Grace persisted with the search. Tom met Mae's amused gaze. She was so pretty when she smiled. Eventually the other woman struck gold, drawing his attention.

"Here you go." With trembling fingers she counted out three coins.

"Perfect." Mae slipped them into the cash box. "And how is the mister today?"

"He's loading feed on the wagon. I really must hurry." She cast an uneasy glance out the front window.

Mae stamped the letters, smiling. "Have a good day."

"Thank you, dear. The same to you."

The door closed behind her, and Mae continued sorting mail. Glancing up from his magazine, Tom asked, "What's her situation?"

"Grace?" Mae shook her head. "She's terrified of her own shadow. Her husband has to take her everywhere she goes and stay with her or she'll faint."

"Faint?"

"That's Grace's way of handling a nervous condition. She faints. Medford — that's her husband — has to do everything for her. Truthfully, she's shamefully sheltered. The couple has no children and have devoted themselves to each other. Grace buys all sorts of lotions and potions from traveling salesmen that promise to ease her condition, but none ever work."

A can dropped, and Tom looked up to see Dale restocking the shelves near the back of the store. His eyes focused for a moment on the quiet man, and then trying to keep his voice low, he asked, "Do you find Dale to be a pleasant person?"

"Pleasant enough."

"Does he talk?"

"Dale?" Mae burst into laughter. "Why would you ask such a thing?"

"I haven't heard him say a word. Apparently his mother was accustomed to looking after him. There must be a lot of that going around."

Mae frowned. "He talks, and he's extremely self-sufficient."

Tom turned to meet her gaze. "Dale? Self-sufficient?" Who had he just spent last evening with and waited on hand and foot at the supper table?

"Very. If you're having difficulty getting acquainted, please don't hold that against him. It's true that Dale's mother pampered him, but he's a wonderful man, even if he does have a shy nature and sometimes has a hard time expressing his thoughts to those he doesn't know. He'll warm to you. Just give it a little time." Leaning on her elbow, she grinned. "You are a good man, Mr. Curtis."

He shook his head. "Don't be giving me undeserved praise, Miss Wilkey. I haven't found Pauline a home yet."

"But you will." She sighed. "I slept well last night knowing that the situation was in good hands."

He hadn't closed an eye until the rooster crowed at dawn, but what she'd just said helped him make the decision. He didn't have any family members left, so why shouldn't he help an old lady who was also without family?

"About the dogs and cats." He'd steered clear of the subject until now, but there was no way on earth he could find homes for Pauline's animals.

"Yes . . . that is a problem." Mae studied the envelope in her hand. "I've told Jeremy to ask around, but no one wants or needs another animal. Frankly, I believe most have disposed of their unwanted cats and dogs in her yard because they knew Pauline would care for them."

"How can she feed them?"

"Well, the neighbors are good about that. They bring their table scraps and dump them in the large barrel sitting in the shed to keep the animals fed."

"Good of them, since most likely they're feeding their own animals."

"I understand your concern, and I'll help any way I can."

His concern. Now it was his concern. What could he do? He'd brought it on by saying he'd help. Laying down the magazine, he nodded. "Let me give it some thought, and I'll see what I can come up with. I don't have much time, though. I have to be back at work in a few days." He prepared to leave.

She exited the cage and walked with him to the front door. "I was hoping, if you stay long enough, that you would attend church with us Sunday morning."

"With whom?" He was planning on being long gone by Sunday.

"Pauline, Jeremy, Jake, and me. Afterward, we can have dinner together. Chicago is so far away. Surely lingering a few days here in Dwadlo wouldn't hurt." She glanced out the window at the house down the way with dogs roaming the yard. "Considering Pauline's condition — well, you never know when the Lord will call her home."

His gaze traced hers and also rested on the dogs. He wasn't used to this kind of upheaval in his life. Besides, he'd already made his assessment of Pauline's yard, and the last thing he wanted to do was have a midwinter picnic in it. Although, he couldn't say he wouldn't mind spending more time with Miss Wilkey. "I'm not sure I'll be around by then."

"But if you are?"

She turned, her warm gaze melting his protests. Oddly enough, something inside of him bought her invitation. "I'll see how things go." *Curtis, that's crazy. You have a well-earned promotion waiting for you in Chicago. Don't go getting involved with a woman, not at this point.*

He had to clear his mind. "Guess I need to get to work." As he was leaving, he called, "Have a nice day, Dale!"

Lifting a jar of tomatoes, Dale acknowledged his departure.

Closing the door behind him, Tom released a long breath. Shy? He'd have to describe the owner as downright strange.

A loud crash, and then the sound of glass breaking, came from inside the store. Tom

114

hoped Dale hadn't broken anything — like a bone. He didn't hear screams, so Mae must not be worried.

Shaking his head, he went in search of someone he didn't know to care for someone he didn't know.

Didn't make a lick of sense.

TEN

Later that evening Tom realized how hungry he was, so he stopped by the café. Dale and Jeremy would have eaten by now. Business was slow. The owner, Rosie, was cleaning up in the back room. A lone man brought his plate over to Tom's table.

"Can you pass me the salt?"

Obliging, Tom handed him the shaker. So far nobody he met had treated him like a stranger. Must be the small-town atmosphere. Surely there wasn't something about him that made folks pick up their plates and want to have supper with him.

The man took a bite before he even sat down. "Name's Jester."

The newcomer liberally salted his meat loaf. White grains fell on the red-and-white checked tablecloth. Tom sized up his dinner guest beneath lowered lids. The man was big — well over six foot, he'd bet, with a heavy red beard. He wouldn't miss two hundred and fifty pounds by a pound or two. "Mr. Hester."

"Jester. Just like it sounds. J-E-S-T-E-R."

"Jester," Tom corrected. How was he supposed to understand someone with a mouth full of food? Silence fell over the table while the two men ate. When Jester pushed back, Tom still had half his meal on his plate.

"Hear your Pauline's kin."

"That's what I'm told." It didn't take long for news to travel here.

"She's a good woman, but real strange. Know what I mean? I found her in back of the café a couple of days ago, planting a garden."

"In January?"

"Tell her that. This morning I caught her with her hoe and shovel, again behind the café, planting some sort of seeds in the snow, muttering something about growing a fine crop of bread."

"Losing your mind is a sad thing."

"Yes." Jester motioned Rosie over for a coffee refill. "Likely we'll all get there if we live long enough."

"I have a couple pieces of lemon meringue left." Rosie refilled both cups. "Dessert's on me tonight."

Tom refused with a shake of his head and a smile, but Jester accepted. "I'll eat anything that won't eat me first."

Chuckling, she left and the stranger returned to the conversation. "What do you think of Mae?"

"Mae Wilkey?"

"Dwadlo don't have but one Mae."

Shrugging, Tom picked up his cup. "She's pleasant enough." She'd be a whole lot more agreeable if she hadn't dumped a peck of responsibility on his plate. The gentleness of her touch when she wiped the mud from his face and the smell of jasmine came to mind. She was a kind soul. Why else would she be so concerned about Pauline?

"Yes, sir. She's a keeper. Never could figure out why she takes to Lil the way she does. Those two are best friends. Now, there's a woman who'll put a knot on your head for looking at her wrong."

A grin formed on Tom's lips. "You talk as if you've looked at her once or twice."

"Me? Never. She'd like to put a knot on my head, but she ain't met her goal yet."

Hearing that the woman was Mae's best friend fueled Tom's curiosity. "So who is Lil?"

"Oh, she's a loudmouthed female who lives just outside of town. Raises big ol' hogs. Always smells like one too. Like Pauline, she gathers any stray that comes her way. Stubborn as a Missouri mule. She and Mae met in school, and they been soul mates ever since."

"I gather Lil isn't spoken for?"

"Lil?" Jester threw back his head and laughed, a deep baritone rumble. "Don't know of a man who'd have her!" Lacing his coffee with heavy cream, he sat back, assessing his table companion. "Hear you're with the railroad."

Change of subject. Nodding, Tom swallowed the last of his coffee.

"Been there long?"

"Sixteen years."

"Me? The town's so small I run the livery and do the smithy work. Lost the missus a while back, so it's no problem. Now I eat all my meals at Rosie's." The owner returned and set the pie on the table. He glanced at Tom. "Sure you don't want a hunk of this?"

Tom waved the offer aside. That slab of lemon meringue pie, if eaten, would fell a moose.

"Guess you've met Jake." Jester took a bite of the dessert.

Fishing in his back pocket, Tom removed his wallet. "Don't believe I have."

"Jake Mallory? Claims he's going to marry Mae — if he ever gets around to asking."

Glancing at the bill, Tom shook his head.

"I only arrived yesterday." So Mae had a suitor. That didn't surprise him, but it didn't please him too much either. She was a fine-looking woman. Tiny, with a waist a man could span with both hands. Godly, pleasant personality, pretty dark eyes and blond hair — and she was a good sister to Jeremy. Until now he hadn't realized he'd noticed that many things about her.

Mouth full of pie, the man nodded. "You'll meet him. It'll take a spell to find somewhere to put Pauline, lessen you figure on stickin' around to take care of her yourself."

Tom supposed he needed to tell him that he'd been assigned an impossible task. "Do you know anyone who will take the dogs and cats?"

Jester glanced up, frowning. "No."

"Pauline?"

"No."

Tom had been given the same answer all day. He laid two quarters on the bill. "If you run across anyone, will you send them my way? I'm staying at Mae's."

The man choked and spit out the sip of coffee he'd just taken. Tom smiled at Jester's reaction and reached to whack him on the back. "Mae is staying in Dale's quarters at the store, and he, Jeremy, and I are at her place."

Fumbling in his back pocket, Jester produced a handkerchief and wiped his eyes. "Whew. You gave me a scare there for a minute. I know Mae has the patience of Job, waiting all these years for Jake to propose, but I thought she'd gone off her rocker."

Tom smiled and then headed for the front door. When he got there, he heard footsteps behind him. He turned to see that the man was following him. Jester apparently wasn't finished saying what he had to say.

"Put mine on my bill, Rosie! Thanks."

"Night, Fisk!"

The two men stepped onto the porch, pausing to lift their collars. Mae had done a fine job mending Tom's coat and shirt and cleaning his clothes. It was good to be wearing clothing that fit. The snow had stopped falling, but the cold wind rattled the bones. When Tom set off, he noticed Jester was still with him. "Thought you said your name's Jester."

"Did. Jester's my surname. Fisk is my given." The man glanced over. "Figure we're walking in the same direction."

Nodding, Tom trudged through snow drifts. "Have you lived here long?"

"Born and reared a couple of miles away."

"Then you've seen a lot of change."

"Some. The train's the biggest thing that

ever happened in Dwadlo." Jester's tone dropped to one of reverence. "I took the blacksmith job when the town formed. When I first moved here, I'd get up before the sun rose, pour my coffee, and then go sit on the train platform to wait until that big ol' steam engine would pull into the station, puffing smoke and wheels screaming against steel. Truth is, you can still find me there about any morning of the week." A wistful tone filled the man's voice. "I'd give an arm and a leg to drive one of those sleek, black iron horses."

"Maybe you'll get your chance one of these days."

Jester shook his head. "I'm a blacksmith, not an engineer. But if I were younger . . ." His words trailed off in a cold vapor.

Tom knew the longing. Railroading got in a man's blood. He knew the excitement he'd felt as a young boy living close to the rail yard. He'd hung out there from daylight to dawn. His mother thought he was in school until the teacher visited his home one day and reported on his actual activities. The engineers, conductors, and flagmen all teased him about being underfoot, but his love of the rail eventually paid off.

When he turned fourteen he'd snagged a job sweeping floors and slowly worked his way up the chain. He understood the tingling in the pit of a man's gut when he was around one of those steel monsters.

"Me?" Jester chuckled. "I'm pushing forty years old. Just about lived up my life, I 'spect."

Tom laughed softly. "I think you still have a few good years yet. Pauline doesn't think she's lived hers up yet, and she's ninety."

"Ninety-two, but she's lost her mind. She has one foot in the grave and another on a chunk of ice."

The men paused in front of the livery. Fisk stuck out a dry, rough hand. "Much obliged for letting me sit at your table tonight. Gets a might lonely in the evenings."

"How long ago did you say your wife passed?"

"Eight months next week."

"Sorry." After the shake Tom shoved his hands in his pockets. Sadness was evident in the big man's eyes, and suddenly he really did feel sorry for Fisk Jester.

Pulling his worn coat collar closer, the man smiled. "Wish the good Lord would have taken me with her."

"Appears He still has use of you." Tom wasn't an overtly religious man, but the assurance seemed in order.

Nodding, Fisk agreed. "That's what I tell

myself. Problem is, I can't imagine what He'd have in store for this old man."

Tom watched the man walk off and into the livery, darkness enveloping his tall frame. Turning into the night, Tom headed toward the Wilkey place, his mind skipping to a portion of the earlier conversation. Mae was spoken for — well, according to Jester, the man hadn't asked her yet, but he supposed it would be the same as being spoken for if everyone knew about the courting.

Her letter had indicated that work and family kept her busy. She had failed to mention that Pauline had become an anchor around her neck. Or maybe it was that her future husband — what name did Fisk mention? — wasn't willing to take on both a slow child and an old woman.

What if Mae Wilkey was using him to benefit herself? What if the note in Pauline's desk drawer didn't have anything at all to do with him?

But no. As much as that might now seem possible, common sense told him there had to be some reason for his name and address to be in that woman's possession. He had to try harder to discover what that was.

His footsteps grew heavy as he trudged toward Mae's cottage and his roommate, Dale. He hoped to goodness the store owner wasn't sitting at the table, bib tied around his neck, knife and fork in hand, waiting for supper.

Trying to put the thought aside, his steps slowed even further. What if he were? How far did the fellow intend to carry out this nonsense, and why did the man think Tom was his servant? Speaking of why, why did God suddenly decide to drop distant kin on him? Crazy kin, if she actually was kin, and a huge pack of cats and dogs. Shaking his head, he walked on.

Dale could sit at the table all night. He wasn't fixing supper at this late hour.

Eleven

Leaning against a stall, Tom watched Fisk forge a set of horseshoes. He'd spent the entire week searching for a home for Pauline, and when he wasn't doing that he'd passed his spare time hanging around the livery. "I don't get it, Fisk. I've asked everyone I've met about a place for Pauline. What do folks here do with their elderly?"

Fisk hammered the smoking red-hot steel, focused on his work. Today the milder weather brought a sweat to the man's brow. Ice melted along the boardwalks. Overhead, blue sky appeared innocent of bad weather.

"Don't know what to tell you, Tom. Most folks take care of their own. I'd take her in, but I'm afraid the town would frown on the situation." He glanced up. "That's a joke, in case you failed to catch it. Don't know what I'd do with her."

He flashed a grin that made him look a decade younger than his almost forty years.

Tom had taken a liking to the man. He was good company, and other than himself, he'd never met a man who had more railroading in his blood. "Kind of like me."

"Guess I could put her to work shoeing horses."

Dwadlo citizens wouldn't find fault with the living arrangement, but Pauline might. Tom couldn't help but laugh at the thought of frail Pauline Wilson trying to shoe a horse, but he didn't doubt she'd give it a go. Tom knew, from what Mae told him, that when she was in her right mind she was cantankerous and self-reliant.

Shoving away from the stall, Tom admitted, "I have to visit a couple over in Pine Grove. Heard they might be interested in boarding Pauline for the right price."

"Thought you were going to be out of here in a few days."

"I've thought various things since I arrived." The thought uppermost in his mind was that he wasn't going to find a suitable place for a ninety-two-year-old woman. "I have a promotion waiting when I get back to Chicago."

"That right?" Fisk glanced up. "What do you do for the railroad?"

"Upper management."

The blacksmith whistled. "Your family

must be real proud of you."

"Don't have family." Tom settled the hat he'd bought from Dale and then buttoned his heavy jacket.

"You mean other than your aunt."

Shrugging, Tom smiled. "If you say so. You going to the café tonight?"

"Always do. You plan to be there?"

"Suppose so." Tom had eaten most of his meals there because he didn't have the stomach to help a grown man eat when he was capable of doing it himself. Last night Jeremy missed Mae so much that he had packed up and left the men to join her at Dale's place, though he promised to provide Dale with lunch and dinner every day. Tom told him not to worry about him; he'd fend for himself.

Now it was just Dale and him.

Tom road out to Pine Grove at first light the next morning, and he wasn't happy with the outcome of his visit. The couple, though young enough, was only out to make a buck. They had no real interest in Pauline but appeared very interested in how much and how often they would get paid.

Was he any better than them? He'd tentatively made a decision as to what he was going to do, and staying in Dwadlo to care for a woman he was certain wasn't his kin wasn't part of his plan.

He was willing to support her financially, but that was as far as he'd go. He knew Mae could use the money, so he'd give it to her and let it help her in all aspects. Even though she didn't think she could do it all, she was strong and he had faith in her. She could care for Pauline because it was unlikely the woman would live much longer, but he just needed to ask Fisk if he was making the right decision.

When he pushed open the heavy livery door later that morning and saw the strong, red-haired man forking hay to the waiting animals, he grinned.

Fisk paused and reached for a jug of water. After taking a swig, he lowered the bottle. "Well, how'd it go?"

"Not well."

"So what's next?"

"I'm leaving tomorrow."

Fisk took another long swig and then wiped his mouth on his heavy shirtsleeve. "Just like that?"

"Just like that." Seeing as how he'd gotten into the mess that quick, it seemed only fair to walk away under the same circumstances. Almost the same.

"You're going to just up and leave Pauline

on her own?"

"Mae can take care of her."

"But she shouldn't have to," Fisk argued. "She's your auntie."

That term was starting to sting. Auntie. He'd tried all week to find one thing about the woman that he recognized, but he couldn't. And she'd done the same. Last night they had sat in her house — each on an end of the couch because the middle cushion was missing — and tried one more time to connect. Nothing. Not an inkling of recognition on either side. This had turned into a game of futility with no clear winner. "What would you do in my place?"

"Me?" Fisk set the pitchfork aside. "Can't say. I've never been in your boots, but I think it would be a might hard to walk away from the situation."

Hard? More likely impossible. Tom knew he would look like a selfish soul who had let an old woman die alone, but he'd done his best. No one could expect him to stay around here until Pauline passed, could they? That might be years away. Or it could be tomorrow. Other than her mind failing and a few fainting spells, she seemed to be doing all right.

"Well." Fisk shook his head. "I don't think you got the stomach to do it."

"Watch me."

Oh, he had the stomach. He had plenty of gumption, and no young woman with big brown eyes was going to stop him from leaving.

Tom settled his hat more firmly. "Tomorrow's Sunday. I'm going to catch the outbound train in the morning. Mae will understand."

"Think so?" The sound of steel meeting steel pierced the air. Fisk had finished feeding the stock and had gone back to his fire. " 'Pears you don't know women." Fisk laid the hammer down. "Mae won't appreciate it, Tom. She has her own problems, plus she's got no man to take care of her."

"She has Jake, doesn't she?"

Laughing Fisk replied, "Not till there's a ring on her finger. And even after that I doubt he'd be much help."

"What's that supposed to mean?"

"Don't mean to talk a man down, but Mallory's lazy, that's all."

Tom had yet to lay eyes on the marriage-dodger, though he hadn't gone out of his way to seek him out. He knew how difficult things were for Mae, but he had his own problems. After he was settled into his new position he'd come back again for a visit, but for now he'd done all he could.

Fisk used a pair of tongs to pick up the shoe he'd been pounding and dunked it in a barrel of water. Steam plumed. "Don't know what he's waiting for. Any man with good sense would grab her and run like a thief. She's a keeper. But if he hasn't proposed to her yet, I don't think it's likely he ever will."

Something deep inside Tom hoped Jake never proposed. Mae was a hard worker, but she could certainly use a husband's help. However, if what Fisk said was right, she'd never get what she deserved from Jake. She was a beautiful woman wasting her youth on someone who obviously didn't appreciate her.

Shifting to one foot, he studied the situation. His basic instinct was right. He should leave and be done with the matter. The situation would work itself out without his help. It had in the past, and it would after he was long gone.

Though images of Mae's earnest eyes flashed before him, causing him to question his decision, he knew he couldn't let her suck him into quicksand. Pauline, Mae — they were strangers to him, and though he hadn't asked for this promotion, it was offered to him and he deserved it. He'd told Letterman that he hadn't given a thought as to who would replace Earl Horner, but that was pride talking. For years Tom had prayed to advance, to be singled out for his dedication and long hours. When he'd first started he'd been the company's lackey, doing anything they asked and going anywhere they sent him without complaint.

At sixteen he'd made choices to buy land and byways that a man with twice his experience made, and he hadn't failed the railroad yet. He figured he'd earned the promotion and planned to work his backside off to prove they had made a wise choice. But he couldn't do it here in this tiny poke town with an old woman he knew wasn't his aunt and a young woman who had pretty eyes. Just how dumb did they think he was? He nodded to Fisk. "I think I'll mosey on over to Rosie's and get a cold drink."

"Have you tried the root beer at the General Store?"

Tom turned. "The what beer?"

"Root beer."

He shook his head. "I'm not a drinking man."

"Good thing 'cause Dwadlo don't have a saloon, 'cept an old farmer's place outside of town, but Dale got in a few cases of this stuff they're callin' root beer. Seems it's been around a long time but hasn't reached

Dwadlo till recently. It's mighty tasty. Even got an edge up on sarsaparilla."

"I have heard of it. Tastes like sarsaparilla."

"Close enough." Fisk reached for an earthenware bottle and held it up. "I've had me four bottles since yesterday."

"Then I guess I ought to have a taste." Nodding, Tom walked away, his earlier question echoing in his ear. Exactly how dumb did Mae Wilkey think he was?

Mae turned when the front door opened and saw that Tom was trying to step inside the store. Dogs swarmed him, barking and snagging onto the hem of his pants.

"Git!"

Growls, barks, and a few mild oaths filled the nearly empty store. The ruckus grew louder until he managed to wedge between the screen and the growling animals. The sight of him made her giddy. It wasn't that he was so handsome — well, he was handsome in a rugged sort of way. And his clothes were nothing special, though they were always clean and neatly pressed. And it wasn't even the way he smelled, though the soap he used was most pleasant. Jake was attractive, dressed at the height of men's fashion, and always had a whiff of tobacco and rum about him — a man's scent he favored but she didn't — but Jake did not affect her the way Tom had been doing since he arrived.

She reflected that, as he did make her head swim a little, it was probably a good thing she hadn't seen much of him since Monday. The talk about town was that he'd asked everyone in the area about taking Pauline in but received nothing but negative responses.

He was suave and professional this morning. She felt color rise to her cheeks when he sauntered over to the ice barrel filled with bottles of root beer. No doubt about it, he was an intriguing man. Jake was more polished, but the contrast was nice. She felt good on Jake's arm, secure. *Would this man's arm offer the same assurance and comfort?* She fought back the unexpected thought, cleared her throat, and said, "Good morning, Tom!"

He fished around in the cold water for a bottle and then withdrew one. "Morning, Mae."

"Opener's right there on the counter." She saw him reach for it and then fix on Jake, who stood beside the mail cage. Mae quickly moved around the counter. "Have you two met?"

"I don't believe so." Jake extended a well-groomed hand. "Jake Mallory."

Tom returned the handshake. "Tom Curtis."

"Mr. Curtis. Pauline's nephew?"

Tom took a drink and then lowered the bottle. "So I'm told."

Jake clasped Tom's shoulder. "You're doing a fine thing, Curtis. Pauline's a marvelous woman. You'll enjoy her company." His tone was warm but his eyes were distant. He turned to Mae. "I'll see you later?"

Nodding, she walked him to the door, where they exchanged a few private words. When the screen closed behind him, a smiling Mae returned. "Enjoying the root beer?"

"Yes, ma'am. It's real tasty."

She stepped behind the wire cage again and began sorting letters.

He finished the drink and set the empty bottle on the counter. "Have you got a minute, Mae?"

She glanced up. "Certainly."

He motioned toward the bench. "Maybe you need to sit down for this."

His tone suggested trouble, something Mae wasn't prepared to face. Was he going to tell her he was leaving? Would he just dump the whole situation back in her lap? Her pulse thrummed in her throat as she seated herself.

Sitting down beside her, he came right to the point. "I can't find anywhere to place Pauline. I've looked, and I've offered a handsome wage, but nobody has room for an aging woman. Most already have parents they're trying to care for or too many children. Or they plain don't want her."

Nodding, Mae bit her lower lip. "Perhaps if you tried —"

The frustration of the past week showed itself in the way he sprang from the bench and started to pace. "I've tried everywhere, Mae! Nobody wants an extra mouth to feed, and what do you think I'm supposed to do with all those dogs and cats?"

"We know that is a problem, but . . ." She'd tried everything she knew to find some of the animals good homes, but her efforts had proved dismal. Usually after she'd ask, Pauline would somehow acquire another one overnight, so she'd given up.

"Problem?" He shifted stances. "Problem? Do you know those dogs have ripped her couch cushions to shreds?"

"Oh, that." She sighed. "That's at least her fourth set of cushions this year. I'll make new ones."

"Look." He sighed and sank back to the bench. "I'm sorry. Really I am, but I have a job waiting for me. I can't stick around any longer."

She bit back tears. He had every right to leave. She wasn't sure if his going caused the tears or she had grown accustomed to seeing him around. Dwadlo simply didn't attract new families. It had been years since anyone happened through town and lingered. Not since the railroad station was built. Tom brought a reminder that a whole world existed outside Dwadlo, one she'd never considered. Clearing her throat, she said, "I'm sorry that you must leave, Tom."

"I'm sorry to go, and even sorrier that I have to leave Pauline here, but I'm at the end of my rope."

"Well, may I respectfully mention that it was a rather short rope?"

"I wasn't aware I had a particular length to this matter. I'm leaving on the morning train."

Mae's eyes shot up when what he said sank in. "Leave Pauline? Here?"

"I can't take her with me."

"Doesn't the train carry more than one passenger?" She bit back a further sarcastic remark, aware that she was overstepping her bounds, but the crushing notion that he could just up and go, making Pauline her responsibility again, took her breath away.

Though Jake had never said, she often wondered if her insistence to care for the aging woman was the thing that prevented him from proposing.

That, and the dogs and cats. Jake would never accept them into his comfortable, sophisticated life. That he had ever come back from that fine Philadelphia law school to practice in Dwadlo still amazed her.

Tom rubbed the back of his neck. "I understand your concerns, but I can't take care of her myself. How am I supposed to look after a woman Pauline's age in a one-room boardinghouse?"

"I suppose you would need to move —"

"Move! I can't move, Mae. Besides, my job requires travel — a lot of it. Are you suggesting that I drag Pauline along on business trips?"

"I'm not suggesting how you should live your life, Tom, but I am suggesting that she's your kin and therefore your responsibility!"

"Oh. So that's how the wind blows."

Crossing her arms, she met his flashing eyes. "That's *exactly* how the wind blows."

Twelve

When Tom wouldn't budge on his decision, Mae turned her head and stared out the front window. She saw Jake's top hat blow off and watched him hopping down Main Street trying to recapture it. She sighed.

"The wind 'blows' many ways, Tom. And I have done my part in caring for your aunt. She is a dear person, but I have plans too."

"Oh, yes. Your impending engagement. I've heard about that." His eyes also traveled to the comical sight taking place outside the window.

Her gaze slowly shifted back to meet his. "Who told you about Jake?"

"The relationship isn't exactly a secret. Almost everyone in town has made it a point this week to tell me you're expecting this man to propose. How long have you been waiting? Six years?"

As soon as the words left his mouth he wished he could take them back. Now he'd stepped in it. He had no call to make the statement sound so . . . insulting. She slowly rose to her full five feet and met his stare head-on.

"For your information, Jake was in law school and then started his practice. Furthermore, Mr. Curtis, my *private* life is none of your concern."

He stood and met her eye to eye. "Well, listen to you, Miss Wilkey. You had no problem getting involved in my *private* life when you roped me into something I knew nothing about!"

"Roped you?" A flush crept up her neck. "Roped you! If . . . oh, if you were half the man Jake is, there would be no need to *rope you* into taking care of your own kin!"

He broke eye contact. "You're just testy because you can't rope Jake into proposing."

Sizzling now, she tightened her stance. "How dare you!"

"How dare you ask me to make the trip cross-county to assume the care of a woman I've never laid eyes on?"

"Shame. Shame!" She shook her finger at him. "Denying your own flesh."

"I don't think she is my flesh. I haven't heard a thing this week that convinces me otherwise."

"Ohhhh." Pushing past him, she returned to the cage, trying to swallow her anger by silently reciting last night's Bible reading: "The Lord is faithful, who shall establish you, and keep you from evil."

In her heart she knew Tom wasn't evil, but how could one man infuriate her so much? Reaching for a stack of flyers, she shoved one into a slot. On top of his obstinacy, the train was late again this morning, which meant she'd be late getting the mail sorted and into the boxes.

Tom appeared at the cage. "I'm leaving —"

"Have a nice trip."

She ignored his deep sigh.

"Look, Mae . . ."

Keeping an eye on her work, she pretended to not have heard the plea in his voice. How could he just waltz off and leave Pauline's care to strangers? True, the town was his aunt's extended family, and she wasn't a stranger but a close neighbor, but a decent, God-fearing man would never allow others to look after his kin.

Mae fought to ignore the prick of conscience that suddenly nagged her. *Why are you so angry? What if Pauline isn't his family? Haven't you also tried and failed to find someone to assume her care? If you, an area resident since birth, couldn't find help, then how do you expect this man to work a miracle in a few short days?* She closed her eyes and took a calming breath.

"If there were a solution to this dilemma, I'd have found it," he said.

She noted the tiredness in his tone.

"But there comes a time when you have to admit you have done all you can. I have a job, Mae, and I need to be back at my desk. It's purely business."

She let him explain away. Whatever he said couldn't account for this crushing sense of disappointment. Had he tried hard enough? The answer came quickly. She'd seen him out early and late searching for a solution.

And, truthfully, Dale couldn't be easy to live with. He was a good man with quaint ways, but he had lived with his mother, Saline, for fifty years. She was a woman who had spoiled him shamelessly, and he had to be stepping on Tom's nerves. She should have thought of a different sleeping arrangement. Even Jeremy couldn't adjust to the change. Maybe it wasn't too late. She turned to face him.

"Is it Dale?"

"Pardon?"

She turned away from him again and shoved another flyer in a box, her ear tuned for the train whistle. "Is Dale the reason why you're giving up so soon?"

"I'm leaving because I have a job that's going unattended." He frowned. "Wait. You know Dale is . . . eccentric?"

"Of course I know. I've worked with him all of my life. His mother . . . um . . . shall we say spoiled him a bit?"

"Well, yes. Let's say that."

Inwardly groaning, Mae realized she hadn't drawn an easy breath the last few days. She had wondered if Tom might leave even sooner because of Dale's eccentricities, but her prayers had held. Until now.

Outside an explosion rattled the windowpanes. The floor shook beneath their feet and the whole building quivered. Stunned, Mae paused to peer out the front window. "What was that?" She noted Tom's puzzled expression.

"Sounded like dynamite. Anyone blasting in the area?"

"Not to my knowledge." Coming out from behind the cage, her heart pounded.

"Are you sure?"

She racked her mind to recall any work like that going on nearby, but she was sure there was none. "Positive."

He walked toward her and placed his hands on her shoulders. "Well, something out of the ordinary's happened. You stay here."

The warmth of his touch and the strength in his hands should have comforted her, but the concern in his eyes made her even more uneasy. She met his intense gaze and simply nodded. No words would form.

Tom dropped his hands and started toward the door. "I'm going to investigate."

Before he reached the door, however, it burst open and a boy ran inside. The look of terror on the child's face told them what they already knew, that something was terribly wrong.

"Train wreck!"

"What?" Tom paused in front of the boy.

"The train . . . it done jumped track up the road a piece. A few people are hurt, but most appear to just have bruises and scratches. Doc Swede says bring all the camphor bottles, balsam, and lint you got!"

Mae quickly stripped off her apron and watched Tom follow the boy outside, the door slamming behind them. Train derailment. Her chest heaved from the heavy thumps inside it. A train wreck.

Dwadlo had never experienced the likes.

Mae grabbed a basket and filled it with the requested items while watching out the window. Buckboards and wagons began to assemble outside the store. The situation quickly became confusing when all available manpower in the area started to arrive to help.

Fisk rode up and held the reins to a saddled mare. The blacksmith grinned. "Got you all fixed up." He tossed the reins to Tom.

Mae, basket in hand, closed the door and was on Tom's heels. "I'm going too." She was surprised when he didn't protest. Swinging into the saddle, he reached down and pulled her up behind him. His strength was that of a hardworking man, and this time she was comforted by it.

The town's residents swiftly rode south with a pack of howling dogs on their heels. Gusty winds blew snow particles in Mae's eyes, and she held Tom's trim waist tightly. Her mind whirled. The closest doctor, other than Doc Swede, lived in Branch Springs, which was seven miles away. *No serious injuries. Thank You, Father. Doc Swede isn't equipped for such matters.*

It took them almost no time to reach the disaster. Smoke billowed, and a black engine hissing steam was on its side. Three overturned wooden cars and two passenger cars looked as though they had been tossed about like rag dolls. Tom drew closer, and Mae saw dazed passengers with bloody bandages tied around arms, foreheads, and legs milling about the wreckage. Bits and pieces of mail and other documents littered the ground.

Tom was off the horse just before it stopped, handing Mae the reins. She pulled the animal to a halt and also slid off, immediately setting to work. Her heart swelled when she saw Tom's devotion to those injured in the catastrophe. She glanced around. Where was Jake? Why wasn't he here helping?

Wagons loaded with water barrels pulled up, and many able-bodied men, women, and children scattered to help dazed victims. Terrified people roamed the area. Mae was thankful the sun was beginning to knock the bitter cold off the morning air, but the light did nothing to warm the chill in her heart at the sight in front of her.

Hours later the sun moved lower in the sky, though it was only midafternoon. It wouldn't be long before the darkness brought the bitter cold again. Mae collapsed by the fire beside Tom, and he absently offered his cup of coffee. Since arriving on the scene, wagons had moved the stranded passengers to Dwaldo's train station, where they were met by anxious families. Lowering the cup, her eyes searched the teeming area. "Have you seen Jake?"

"He was here for a short time earlier, but I saw his buggy leave a couple of hours ago."

Nodding, she took another sip of the coffee and handed the cup back. Funny. She had never drunk from Jake's cup or glass. Their kisses had been short, very staid events. The thought had never crossed her mind until this moment, but Jake had never offered her anything in a kind gesture. Not even a sip of tea. She glanced at Tom, and noted that his face was lined with fatigue and worry. "Are you all right?"

"Fine, considering I'm looking at an enormous financial loss."

She glanced at the derailment, trying to make sense of his statement. "Loss? How could this affect you?"

"Company loss. I work for this line." His eyes scanned the still smoking carnage.

"Oh, no." He might have mentioned the name of his railroad earlier, but she couldn't recall it.

"Yes, Chicago and North Western." His eyes fixed on the overturned locomotive. "The loss is great — not to mention the interruption of service."

Mae fit the pieces together and gasped. "Oh my goodness! Dwadlo is now cut off from the outside world!" There would be no mail, no grocery orders, no fine fabrics shipped from the East. Her eyes returned to the wreckage. "For how long?"

"Until we can lay a temporary track." His gaze measured the impassable rail.

"That's all?" She wilted with relief. "Laying a little bit of track shouldn't take that long." She recalled when the line to Dwadlo was built. It had taken months to lay track from here to Wisconsin, but this was a simple repair job.

His mirthless chuckle didn't match her optimism. "Well, not normally, but it's winter, Mae. We have to contend with snow, rain, mud, and getting the right material and manpower to put down the track."

"Then . . . it will take some time." Relief flooded through her like melting snow. If the train didn't run, he couldn't leave. Suddenly guilt plagued every part of her as she acknowledged to herself that she enjoyed his company. Her thoughts went to Jake. She never felt this sense of . . . what? Appreciation? Love? There was something new and different about being with Tom. When had that missing link broken her connection with Jake? She shook the thought away.

"How long do you estimate?"

"I don't know. Maybe less than a week if we can get the supplies sent right away."

She deliberately sobered. "That's too bad, but a week isn't the end of the world. We can make do that long." She was hoping it would be longer than a mere week, but at least it would mean a few more days of Tom's company.

"You have other ways out of town."

"That all go nowhere except to Pine Grove and Branch Springs, who get their supplies from us. The closest large town is Elkton, and it will take a while for supplies to reach us from there."

Sitting in silence, they took turns drinking from the same cup. Events were happening so fast she couldn't keep up. Finding Pauline's kin, Tom coming to Dwadlo, Tom saying he was leaving, the train derailment — and now Tom staying. She studied him from the corner of her eye. Perhaps he'd decide to stay in Dwadlo. She caught her thoughts again, mentally apologizing to Jake for letting them wander so far. What had gotten into her? Tom was a new face, that was all. An interesting, exciting new face. Any woman would feel a faint stirring when he was near. "The store serves as our telegraph office."

"I have to contact the railroad immediately. It looks like I won't be leaving as soon as I'd hoped."

What was that crazy leap her heart just took? She shivered against the chill and held her hands toward the dwindling fire.

"We'd better get back to town so we can warm up."

"Yes. And we can probably get your wire out before day's end."

He stood, and she instantly missed his warmth beside her.

"Dwadlo is a lucky place." He doused the fire with snow and then held out a hand to help her up.

She thanked him with a smile. Picking up her empty basket, she placed the cup inside it. "How can you say we're lucky after what's just happened?"

"Because if this derailment had been in town instead of out here, Dwadlo would have been destroyed."

"What a dreadful thought!" That was one more thing to praise God for. He must have had His hand on their small community. "I'm sure it will all work out, Tom. The Lord will see to it."

"No doubt."

His note of irony didn't escape her, but life had a way of changing one's plans. She smiled again and then caught herself. It was a wicked smile. Chastising herself once more, she closed her eyes and rotated her head to work the kinks out of her neck. All the bending while attending the injured had left her stiff and sore.

With Tom's help, she joined him on the horse's back. "Shall we keep the same living arrangements? Or if Dale is too much, Jeremy and I can find another place to stay —"

"It's okay. He never says a word. I can manage now that Jeremy brings his meals."

Dale had two different sides, but now wasn't the time to inform Tom of that. If the present arrangement suited him she wasn't going to argue. She imagined he'd find out soon enough about Dale's varying personality. For now, Pauline's immediate future was safe and Tom wouldn't be leaving.

That smile appeared again. Leastways, not this week.

Thirteen

It was late afternoon before Tom had a chance to send a wire to Clive Letterman about the derailment, but a reply came back quickly. The simple message read:

YOU'VE BEEN PROMOTED AGAIN STOP YOU'RE NOW WRECKING MASTER STOP GLAD TO HEAR THERE ARE NO MAJOR INJURIES STOP EQUIPMENT AND SUPPLIES ON THE WAY STOP STAY TILL IT'S DONE STOP.

Grinning, Tom wadded up the missive and pitched it into the wastebasket.

Mae glanced up at him. "What did your boss say? You look happy."

"He has a strange sense of humor." C&NW could afford to have one at this point. There didn't appear to be a single serious injury. The derailment was costly, but it would have been far more devastating had there been casualties. The disgruntled but thankful passengers had been relocated to their destination, and it looked as though the incident was over.

"Such as? Today's event was anything but humorous."

"No, it was nothing about what happened. He's just ribbing me. He's sending supplies, and he says I'll be staying on to oversee the rail repair."

He was staying until it was done. Butterflies flitted in her stomach, and though Mae fought the urge to smile, it did little good. He glanced at her and she quickly sobered. She couldn't let him see how pleased she was with the news.

"Are you okay?"

Straightening, she shrugged. "Fine. Thank you." *Lord, forgive me for having these thoughts.* She was going to be sure to read extra Bible passages tonight before she went to sleep.

Tom grabbed a root beer from the barrel. "Clive's a good man. He's relieved there were no serious injuries."

The front door opened and Pauline walked in. "What's all the ruckus? Did somebody blow up the bank again?"

Mae helped the woman off with her coat. It was almost dark, and the poor thing had no business being outside at this hour. "Now, Pauline, you know perfectly well our bank has never been blown up."

The old woman scratched her head. "It hasn't? That's a relief. I could have sworn I was involved in something like that once before. That's why I stayed inside all day. I didn't want them to lock me up again."

Tom snickered. "I think with that pack of dogs around your place, you're pretty safe."

He hadn't spoken loudly, but Mae heard him perfectly well and shot him a glance, glad Pauline was nearly deaf. "The train derailed. That's what you heard."

"Train? Well, I swear. Was anyone killed?"

"No one had more than a scratch, praise God." Mae fell into step behind her as Pauline wandered the store. The woman was as honest as the day was long, but she didn't worry about price or money when she shopped. She put it on her "account." Mae couldn't recall the last time her account had been paid up.

"Ain't gonna stop church services tomorrow, is it?"

Mae doubted that the service would be canceled, and she had a hunch the pastor would emphasize the need for faith and strength to overcome present obstacles beyond the town's control.

Pauline set a porcelain wash pan on the counter and then went back to browsing. Mae stared at it. Why would she need that? The elderly lady moved to the thread section, sorting carefully through the colorful spools. Muttering under her breath, Mae went to help. "Is there something you need, Pauline?"

"Hmm . . . no." She picked up a spool of black and examined it. "I've always favored this color." She moved on to the dry goods section. "What's all the fuss in town? Has something happened?"

Mae turned in time to see Tom shaking his head. "Something quite substantial." Mae continued to trail behind Pauline. It embarrassed her to search the woman before she left the store.

"How much did they get?"

This was one of her friend's really bad days, and Mae felt sorry for the woman.

"There were no bank robbers, Pauline. The train derailed this morning. Thankfully, no one was seriously hurt, but the track is torn up. It's going to take a while to fix it." Mae gently removed a bottle of hot sauce from the woman's hands and smiled.

"Well, I don't mean to be hateful, but I don't have a good thing to say about the railroad. They shouldn't have brought that black monstrosity through here. Been nothing but a nuisance. It upsets my dogs every time it pulls into the station." Pauline turned to focus on Tom. "Sorry, sonny, but that's the pure truth. You got something to do with the railroad, don't you?"

"A little, ma'am. Not enough to worry you."

"It's certainly brought Dwadlo a fair amount of prosperity," Mae pointed out as she gently took a package of hairpins from Pauline's grasp. Dwadlo was the end of the line, but the station brought needed supplies to outlying areas. Otherwise, the town would be nothing but a tiny spot in the road.

"They treated me badly." Pauline sniffed.

Tom cracked a peanut. "I'm sorry. Was it my line? Chicago and North Western?"

"Can't recall." She waved a dismissive hand. "How do I know? I only know that I don't know any railroad person except you, sonny, but I'm obliged to like my kin." She paused. "Or does the Good Book say to love your neighbor more than your kin? Sometimes that's a might easier to do."

Mae patted her shoulder and moved her to the counter. "Let's see, now. We have —"

"I'm not through yet."

Mae pointed her to larger products, such as canned tomatoes and beans. She turned her head when she saw a tin of baking soda go in Pauline's purse.

"Unfortunately, Mr. Curtis isn't going to leave town as soon as he wanted. The railroad has assigned him to help lay the new track."

"That right?"

Mae checked her necklace timepiece. "Mr. Curtis, since there's been a delay in your departure, would you join us in church tomorrow morning?"

"You'd better warn him to wear britches that won't catch fire," Pauline muttered.

The things Pauline could come up with. Their pastor did get a little thunderous, but that was the spirit of God — or so he claimed. Mae never saw the need to shout and become red-faced when she spoke of God's love and grace, but she wasn't called to the pulpit. She smiled. "Will you join us, Tom?" She checked her timepiece again. It was growing late, and she was plain worn-out.

After taking another sip of his root beer, Tom set the bottle down. "I haven't been to church in years."

"Then it's high time you went. Isn't that right, Pauline?"

She nodded. "Overdue, sonny. I'll dress up real nice for my kin." She picked up a woman's housecoat. It was a very fancy bit of finery that had come all the way from New York, but the robe's cost scared off even the most affluent in town. Today it caught Pauline's attention. She swooped up the silly extravagance. "How much is this?"

"Oh, Pauline, it's quite outrageous, and you can't wear it to church."

"How much?"

"Nineteen dollars."

"Whoooee."

"Yes, very expensive." Mae gently took it out of her hands and put it back on display, but Pauline retrieved the robe and stuffed it in her purse. "Put it on my bill."

Mae mentally groaned. Her bill was past the point of ludicrous, and Dale certainly couldn't afford this luxury. She would let Pauline take it home, and then she'd bring it back to the store Monday morning.

Pushing away from the counter, Tom reached into his pocket and pulled out a money clip. Peeling off two bills, he handed them to Mae.

She started to refuse the offer, but Pauline had so few pretty things, and after all he was her kin. "Thank you," she murmured. "That's most generous of you."

"Consider it a gift from the railroad. Speaking of which, do you have any strong young men in town who need work?"

Mae wondered if he was evading the church question and decided she'd let it rest for now. "Why?"

"Their help would come in handy in laying the new track."

She put the bills in the money box. "Is that what you do for the railroad? Oversee rail repair?"

"Not ordinarily. I'm in management now, but I've laid a few thousand miles of track over the years. I've worked about every job the railroad offers."

"Really."

Lifting his bottle of root beer to his lips, he grinned and winked before he took a long drink.

She watched the muscles in his throat move as he swallowed and felt a blush creep up her neck. She wasn't accustomed to his playful side. "I'm sure the men in town will welcome the work, and I'm also certain the railroad will pay a handsome wage as you are in a bit of a bind."

He lowered the bottle, studying her. "Why, you little conniver."

She held up a hand and smiled. "Purely business, Mr. Curtis."

She squealed when he leaned over and held the dripping cold root beer bottle over the top of her head. Lunging for the container, she playfully wrestled for the weapon. His long arm easily kept the bottle from her reach. Feminine squeals and male laughter was filling the room when the front door opened and Jake stepped inside.

Mae caught the newcomer's entrance from the corner of her eye and immediately snapped to attention. Straightening her bodice, she said, "Hello, Jake."

Looming in the doorway, the lawyer's eyes appraised the situation. "What do we have here?"

What indeed? How could she have acted like a hooligan, losing complete control of her decorum? What would her father have said had he been alive to witness his daughter tussling with a man — and in public, no less?

She summoned a shaky smile. "Well . . . you know about the derailment. Tom and I were . . . um . . . discussing the incident."

Stepping inside the store, Jake closed the door. "Indeed."

She tried to stay calm while his eyes assessed her hair, which now hung loose down her back in curls. She must have lost the pins in the friendly scuffle.

"And by the looks of you, you were also a victim?"

Tom set the bottle on the counter. "There's no need for sarcasm, Mallory. I'm sure this does look a little . . . inappropriate. I apologize for my behavior. I dripped water over her head and she reacted."

Jake's gaze focused on Mae and he lifted one brow. "Pardon me?"

Pauline giggled. "Have you tried the root beer yet, Jake? It's real fine."

Mae closed her eyes with relief when the old woman peered around a shelf. With Pauline present Jake couldn't possibly find the situation upsetting — merely curious. Yet she still felt the heat rising to her cheeks, and when Tom turned to face her she wondered if he could see it.

"Please accept my deepest apologies, Miss Wilkey. I am under a bit of a strain today and forgot my manners." He gave a courteous but pretentious bow.

Patting her flyaway hair, she nodded briefly. "Apology accepted, Mr. Curtis. It has been a most trying day for all concerned. I do hope to see you at services in the morning."

"Well, what is life without hope?" He flashed her another smile.

Mae held her breath when he tipped his hat briefly to Jake, gave her another wink, and then left the store. Why did she feel guilty when she'd done nothing wrong?

When the door closed behind him, Tom's grin faded. *You're stuck here now, Curtis. You'd best be saving your winks for available women.*

The lazy smile returned when he stepped off the weathered porch. Still, it had felt good to see the look on that stuffed shirt's face. Mae was a wonderful woman, full of life, and he enjoyed her company. She deserved someone better than Jake Mallory. Tom had to fight to harness his thoughts. Mae was close to being spoken for, and that was that. Bad-mouthing another man never gave him pleasure, but what could she possibly see in someone who considered himself to be the biggest toad in the puddle?

A wagon pulled up to the hitching post. A woman dressed in men's clothing set the brake and got out. Though he'd never met her, Tom realized she must be Lil, the woman Fisk had told him about. Before she could climb down from the wagon, an older man wearing suspenders and hip boots walked up. Tom had spotted him around the store this week. "Curtis!"

"Sir?"

The farmer's eyes sized him up, and then he turned to spit a stream of tobacco. Wip-

163

ing his mouth on his sleeve, he accused, "Name's George Stewart. I'm a might riled, son. You killed my bull."

"Pardon?"

"You work for the railroad?"

"Yes, sir."

"That train killed my bull. One of my best. So if you work for 'em, then you owe me fifty dollars."

"Fifty?" Tom shook his head. "I regret that your bull was killed in the accident, Mr. Stewart, but the railroad pays seven dollars a head."

"Seven dollars!"

"I might get them up to ten, but not a cent more."

"That there was prize stock, Curtis."

He noticed the woman had climbed down from the wagon and approached. He stayed focused on the farmer. "I understand, sir, but that's the offer. Seven — possibly ten dollars." Grumbling under his breath, the farmer glanced at the rough-edged woman.

Shrugging, she said. "What are you going to do with a dead bull, George?"

The man's eyes narrowed. "You'd settle for ten dollars for one of your prize sows, Lil?"

"If she were dead and I didn't need the meat, I would."

Scowling, George apparently worried the offer over in his mind. "Okay, Curtis. Ten dollars and you move the carcass."

"When am I supposed to have time to do that —"

The woman stepped in front of him and offered a handshake. "I'm Lil Jenkins. If I can have the meat from that bull to do with what I want, I'll clear it away for you."

"By yourself?"

"No. I got a friend who will pitch in."

"Deal." Tom had bigger headaches than a dead bull.

"Consider it done."

FOURTEEN

Nighttime shadows had deepened by the time Mae hung the new sign in the store window before retiring for the day.

HELP WANTED
Men with strong backs and hearty souls needed to repair railroad track. $1 per day. Apply inside.

She was pleased Pauline had finally agreed to go home, though it had taken almost an hour to convince her to do so, and Jake had left without much of a fuss about what had happened between her and Tom. He had never been playful with her the way Tom was that evening, and it saddened her. But the day's events saddened her too.

Mae couldn't think of the last time Dwadlo experienced an accident. She intended to extinguish the lights and go straight to bed when she heard footsteps approaching. She turned to see the hog farmer through the window.

"I need your help, Mae," Lil said as soon as she had opened the door and stepped inside.

The postmistress stared at her friend's clothing. "Goodness, Lil, what happened to you? Where did all that blood come from? Are you hurt —"

"No, I'm fine, but I have a mess on my hands. I have to move a dead bull."

Mae was sure she'd heard it all now. The vivacious, spunky Lil was known to tackle anything, but moving a dead bull at this late hour? And though she hadn't asked, Mae was certain she was part of her friend's crazy plan. "How do you propose that we — meaning you and me, I'm guessing — move a dead bull?"

"Haven't had time to give that solid thought, but we gotta move it quick. We can still salvage the meat before it freezes." She latched on to Mae's arm and urged her out of the store and down the steps.

"Now, just a minute —"

"No time to jaw, Mae. We got to dress that bull."

"How did it die?"

"Train got it. The poor thing got knocked so far back from where the train stopped that no one noticed it till a short while ago."

"Do you have your butchering tools and a lantern?"

"No. I wasn't planning on butchering anything when I came to town today."

"Wait here. I'll get some things." Whirling, Mae went back into the store and returned a few minutes later with a large saw, two of the sharpest knives she could find, a meat cleaver, and a lantern. Lil immediately began thinking aloud about ways to move a two-thousand-pound animal.

"We need Esau."

"Lil, listen to you. When he comes around folks get nervous, you know that. Besides, are you planning to drag the bull to your place?" Mae put the tools in the back of the wagon and climbed aboard.

"We can't drag it to my place. There'd be nothing left. That's why we'll have to butcher it where it is."

"You know more about this kind of stuff than I do. Where is it?"

"Not far from the accident site. It must have wandered onto the track and caused the wreck. George Stewart was hot under his collar because the accident killed one of his stock. He wanted fifty dollars, but Curtis held firm. He gave him ten, but we have to clean up the mess."

"Tom said *I* have to clean up the mess? How dare he make that commitment for me!"

"Easy, girl. I offered to clean it up. And it was my idea to ask you to help me. No use letting good meat go to waste."

"I guess not, but couldn't one of the men in town take care of the matter?" Exhaustion was overtaking her. Mae didn't know if she had it in her to dress a bull tonight. The accident had stripped her of energy. Her bones ached, and she longed for a hot bath to sooth them.

"No one was available." Lil climbed up onto the driver's seat of the wagon. "Typical, ain't it? Can't find a man when you need one." She looked at Mae. "Guess that's why we ain't married!"

"Maybe." Climbing up the side of the wagon and onto the seat, her so-called beau ran through her mind. But Jake would ask for her hand someday, she was sure of it. Lil slapped the reins across the horses' hindquarters and the wagon lurched forward.

When they rode past Pauline's house, Mae noticed the lamplight in the window. Undoubtedly her elderly friend was sound asleep in her chair.

They arrived at the broken track and Lil

followed it. They came upon the carcass a ways beyond the accident site. The felled animal was huge — more bull than Mae wanted to tackle, but she had no choice. She was here now, and she would make the best of it. She thanked the Lord for the moon or the task before them would have been even more daunting.

Lil quickly built a fire and then grabbed the tools while Mae positioned the lantern for good light. Lil made the first cut and then began skinning the animal before Mae stepped in to help. Within thirty minutes she had stripped out of her gloves and discarded them. Her fingers quickly lost feeling, but she couldn't work with her hands covered.

"There's some nice roasts here," Lil said.

"Very nice, but I'm not hungry. I'm tired and cold." Mae heard a noise in the distance. It was dark and quite late. Who — or what — was out there? "Lil, did you hear that?"

"Yep. No telling who it is." In the distance dogs approached. Jeremy kept Pauline's dogs penned at night, so they shouldn't be hers. The ruckus grew louder, and Mae paused as she watched a small figure, with a familiar pack of dogs on her heels, enter the ring of light. Pauline. Dressed in long johns that were covered with her new robe.

"Oh, Pauline." She dropped her knife and went to offer the elderly woman her coat. She would catch her death. "What are you doing here? I thought you'd be sound asleep."

"Saw you and Lil go past the house and knew something was up. We got another train wreck?"

"No." Poor Pauline. When had the train ever run at this hour? "You need to go on back home. Here. Put on my coat. It's too cold outside for you."

"I can't do that. If I leave with your coat, you won't have anything to wear. Besides, I'm not cold. I'll just sit by this cozy fire."

Lil was never one to coddle. "Pauline, put on that coat and git home."

"I don't want to go home. Maybe I'll go tell Fisk what you're doing out here in the middle of the night."

Lil snorted. "Go ahead. He won't care."

Nodding, Pauline sat down on the railroad track in front of the fire. "You're right."

"Then why bring it up?"

"Will you two stop it? Let's just get this job done and go home." Mae bit her lip to keep her teeth from chattering as she went back to work on a hind quarter. "Pauline, can you at least keep the dogs away from

171

the meat, please?"

"Okay." The old woman whooshed her hand through the air. "Git away from the meat."

The gesture and command did little good, and the animals nosed along the ground, tracing the fresh scent of blood. Pauline huddled on the rail. "Want me to help?"

Both Mae and Lil simultaneously turned, answering, "No!"

Mae softened the response. "You just watch."

"Git away from the meat! Sonny would do this if you asked him to."

" 'Sonny' is the reason I'm out here at this unmerciful hour," Mae groused. She intended to give Tom a piece of her mind tomorrow morning. Lil might be grateful for his generosity, but right now Mae would give twenty dollars to be asleep in her warm bed. The cold moon climbed higher.

She watched as Lil took three big slop feeders from the back of her wagon to hold the meat. Mae figured they could wrap up the bounty and distribute it tomorrow, but she didn't know where. The store didn't have capacity for this amount of fresh meat. Maybe Lil intended to keep it.

"Are you taking the meat home?"

"When would I eat all of it?"

"You wanted it."

"I didn't want to see it go to waste. There's bound to be folks who could use it."

The dogs milled about as Mae wielded her knife. "Jeremy would like to have one of these big roasts." Shooing the pesky animals aside, she glanced at Pauline, who was now trying to move a couple of steaks to the feeders. "Sit down, Pauline. You're getting your lovely new robe messy." Blood splattered the front of the garment. Mae grew faint when she thought of how much Tom had spent on the frivolous piece of clothing.

"Git away from the meat! Go!" Wiping her sticky fingers down the front of her robe Pauline smiled. "It's a purty thing, isn't it? Sonny bought it for me. He was always a thoughtful child."

Lil glanced up. "You remember him?"

Reseating herself on the rail, Pauline smiled as she spread her fingers toward the fire. "No, but a man's bound to be good if he'd pay nineteen dollars for this piece of junk."

Lil turned to Mae. "Make her go home."

"I can't make her do anything, Lil."

"She's gonna die of exposure, and these dogs are slowing us down. They are even getting away with some of the meat!"

"She'll get cold enough that she'll leave."

"Where's Esau?" Pauline asked.

"In his shelter." Lil dropped a steak in a makeshift pan.

"What shelter?"

Lil continued to slice meat. "The one I built for him, old woman."

"Lil," Mae rebuked.

"Well, she gets on my nerves."

"Be kind."

"Why?" Pauline asked.

Mae sighed. "Why what?"

"Why is he in the shelter?"

"He belongs there. It's cold out, and he has to take care of his skin."

"Humph. Why does it get dark so much?"

Lifting her head, Mae frowned. "What?"

"When did they change the time? I eat breakfast and it's dark. Then I eat dinner and it's dark again. That's all I do. Eat in the dark."

"You get up too early," Lil said.

"I get up when I wake up."

"That's earlier than most folks."

"Why, I suppose it's not. When the good Lord opens my eyes, I get up."

"You don't have to get up the moment your eyes open." Mae sliced a piece of loin. "I've noticed your lamp burning at all hours."

"Then you must be up."

"No. I happen to wake up and look out the window." Mae straightened. This situation was beginning to try her fortitude. Fortunately, they were nearly finished. "If you don't mind, Lil, I'll take Pauline and the dogs home before she freezes to the rail."

"Mind? I'd give you a —"

Mae cut off the not-so-patient response. "Thanks. Do you want me to come back?"

Lil continued her work. "No need. I'll be done soon."

Pauline peered up at Mae, toothless. "I suppose it's time to eat again?"

She glanced at the night's clear winter sky. "By the moon's location, I'd say it's close to midnight."

Pauline whistled. "It's past my bedtime — or it's time to get up. I'm not sure which."

Saying goodbye to her friend, Mae wrapped her arm around the woman's thin shoulders, sheltering her as much as she could from the cold wind that had sprung up. She turned and whistled for the dogs to follow. Pauline's lovely new housecoat was ruined. Mae would try to get the blood-stains out of the fabric, but she doubted she'd have much success. Tom Curtis was a generous man, but he needed to choose his purchases for his aunt more wisely. "It's past my bedtime too."

By the time she got Pauline home, cleaned up, and tucked in warmly, it was well after two a.m. before Mae crawled between the sheets in Dale's bed behind the store. Stirring, Jeremy lifted his head from his pallet and called into the bedroom. "Mae, you tired?"

"Mae's really tired." Stretching out, she wiggled her cold feet under the blanket. Her soft bed and warm covers felt like a small part of heaven. The wind howled around the eaves, but she was safe and secure. She could only pray that Lil was home and in her own bed as well.

"I left a plate of food for you in the warming oven."

"Thank you, darling, but I'm too tired to eat." She was too tired to move.

"I talked to Mr. Curtis tonight when I took Dale's supper to him."

"Oh?"

"He told me he'd put me to work."

"That's nice. Did Mr. Curtis assign you a job?"

"Yes, ma'am." Jeremy yawned and laid his head back on his pillow. "I wanted to do a man's work, but he said I would be the best at carrying water and keeping the dogs away, and he didn't want anyone else to do it except me."

"That's very nice. Not every man is good with animals like you are." Poor darling. *God, please allow him one day to do a man's work. I'm not asking for a miracle. Just a life of purpose that fulfills his needs. Jeremy will never be like other men, but he is gifted in so many ways.*

"I work very hard," his sleepy voice drifted to her. "I'm gonna fry fourteen chickens for the workers' dinner on Monday."

She closed her eyes. "Oh, Jeremy." That meant he'd wring fourteen chickens' necks, heat boiling water, pluck feathers, dress and cut up all those birds, and then fry the meat in order to help. If that wasn't a man's work, she didn't know what would be. "I'm sure the workers will deeply appreciate your efforts."

When she looked in the living room, she saw that the boy was already fast asleep. She'd wanted to tell him that Pauline was trying to build a large pen to contain the animals and soon that job might be easier, but there would be time tomorrow.

Pauline building a pen? She smothered a chuckle. That should be interesting.

FIFTEEN

Sunday morning dawned with a hint of snow in the air, yet as the sun peeked over the distant hills Tom was pleased that seventeen men turned out before church to sign up to repair track. Dale stood on the General Store's front steps and silently registered each name in a log book.

This morning the store owner wore a suit, white shirt, and tie. Tom had heard him get up earlier than usual, and then he'd left the house before the first pot of coffee boiled. Taking a second glance, Tom noticed that nearly every man in the crowd looked to be in their Sunday-go-to-meeting clothes.

"Where's Mae?"

Shrugging, Dale handed him the roster.

Fisk stepped up to Tom. "She sent word she was running late this morning, but she'll be at church."

"Thanks." Tom skimmed the names on the list. Then he looked up to survey his crew. Young men and old stood quietly before him, and in a moment he decided they would do. "It should only take a few days to lay a temporary track. We'll come off the original one below the accident site and bypass the wreckage. Later the railroad will send a crew to restore the original line. Fisk, are you sure you can spare the time?"

The blacksmith nodded. "Won't have much to do without that train coming through."

A farmer stepped up. "We'll all work as long as needed, Mr. Curtis. Without that train, Dwadlo's locked down tight as a corset."

"The task will be backbreaking," Tom warned. "We'll work through rain, snow, and whatever else comes our way." The warning didn't faze them. Everyone's head bobbed, and the men's faces reflected determined understanding.

"Looks like you're all dressed for Sunday services. The supplies won't arrive until sometime tomorrow anyway. Go on to church. I know it's the Lord's Day and I respect that. We'll start clearing wreckage first thing in the morning. I want to thank all of you for coming, and I look forward to working with you at first light."

The crowd began to disperse when he saw

a woman approaching him. "Something I can do for you, ma'am?"

"Yes, I believe you can. I'm Mrs. Crowley, the town's seamstress. May I speak to you privately?"

He nodded. "Yes, ma'am."

"There's a girl in Pine Grove getting married in two weeks. She's expecting a rather large herring order to arrive for her reception."

"Herring? As in fish?"

She nodded. "Will the train be running by then?"

Closing the log book, he met her gaze. "If the supplies get here on time, and the weather holds so we can work, then yes. She'll have her fish."

"Herring," the lady whispered. "She's very sensitive about the word."

"Fine. Herring." As the woman turned and walked away, Tom headed back to Mae's place to wash up, shave, and put on some clean clothes. There wasn't much he could do until after the morning services. He needed to thank God that, though the accident had caused a few injuries, costly repairs for the railroad, and a bit of a headache for him, lives had been spared.

When he walked into the kitchen, he found Dale seated at the breakfast table, fork and knife in hand.

"We're having oatmeal this morning." Tom had stopped asking for preferences and now merely made statements. He took the resulting grunt as a positive sign and tied Dale's bib around his neck. Dale dropped his fork and picked up a spoon.

The men ate in silence with only an occasional noise from Dale to indicate when he needed more coffee, cream, or milk for his porridge.

When Tom was through, he carried his bowl to the sink and then walked back and stripped off Dale's bib. And he wondered why no one wanted to assume Pauline's care. The woman could at least wait on herself.

"I'm going to church this morning." He dumped Dale's bowl in the wash pan.

Dale lifted a hand to acknowledge the statement.

He supposed by Dale's clothing that's where he was headed as well, but he didn't volunteer his destination. "I'll see you later."

Dale nodded, dabbing the corners of his mouth with a napkin.

Meals had turned out to be less of a problem than he'd expected. Because Jeremy took care of providing Dale with lunch and supper, Tom didn't have to cook anything but breakfast, which was a good thing. He didn't know how to make anything but oatmeal.

Slipping on a heavy jacket, he nodded a goodbye to his housemate and left. Tom's mother had been the churchgoer in his family, but she'd tried to instill God's Word in him. He didn't get to church often, but he and God had long talks on his travels, talks that strengthened his faith. One day he planned to settle down, take a wife, and sit in a long pew with her and his kids. And if God blessed the union, they would have three boys and a couple of girls sitting with them.

The crisp, early morning air made him feel alive as he walked the short distance to the country-style building. Already buggies and buckboards lined the churchyard. The wintery landscape made a pretty sight with its drifts of earlier snow still white and piled deep. Most of the snow had melted off in flat-lying areas. He paused at the bottom of the steps. Time had passed quickly. A week ago he'd sat on a bench outside the General Store and waited for services to let out, thinking he'd be long gone before now. But here he was, heading into church and looking forward to sitting with Mae Wilkey, who definitely was no Mrs. Grundy.

Inside he counted nine rows of simple wooden pews. The benches were old but well cared for. He spotted Mae, Jeremy, and Jake already seated on the front row. Because Jake was on one side of Mae and Jeremy on the other, sitting next to her would be impossible. Tom took a seat in the row behind them.

Mae turned to welcome him with a smile. "It's so nice that you could join us today. Would you like to sit with us?"

He nodded a greeting but remained where he was. She looked pretty in an emerald green dress and matching hat. As beautiful as she was, she also looked tired with dark circles under her eyes. The accident had taken more of a toll on her than he first thought, and he decided he was going to make sure she rested this afternoon.

He turned toward the door and watched as the pews started to fill. Fisk came in and took a seat beside him. Tom spotted the farmer whose dead bull he'd bought sitting three rows back.

The next time the front door opened, in waltzed Pauline wearing a housecoat. He took a double take. Was that the one he bought her? It was — the exact housecoat he'd bought her yesterday. Blood and dirt were smeared all over the front. He had a hard time making out the original color.

Fisk snorted. "Holy smokes. She's finally done it. She's killed someone!"

Sashaying down the row of pews, Pauline paused beside the one Tom was sitting in. He couldn't believe the way she looked standing in the aisle, as if she'd just survived a massacre in her nightclothes. She lingered for a moment, smiling, and he wasn't sure if she was happy or just plain loco.

"Do you mind if your ol' auntie sits with you this morning?"

What could he say? He couldn't very well tell her go home and clean up. What had she done? "No, ma'am." He and Fisk switched places, both scooting down a little to allow her access to the pew. Pauline sat down beside him. Mae's horrified look caught his attention.

She mouthed, "Take her out of the room!"

"Take her out?" Tom mouthed back. How would it look if he up and jerked the elderly woman out of the pew and carried her outside? He'd have the whole town in an uproar.

Pauline preened, as if she were dressed in her Sunday best. He, and he assumed everyone else in the church, was mystified. He hoped the preacher wouldn't pass out when he set eyes on Pauline.

The pianist struck the first chord, and the congregation rose to sing the opening hymn. Pauline's voice could be heard above the others as she joined in the singing. Tom's mind whirled. Where had all that blood come from? It looked as if she had killed something or someone, and he did not want to think about what or who. He'd seen cleaner butchers after a hard day's work.

When the congregation sat down, Dale walked up to the pulpit. When the store owner faced the congregation and opened his Bible, Tom was the one who nearly passed out. He narrowed his eyes and fixed them on the man he'd yet to hear a peep out of. Was he the preacher? His answer came fast and loud.

"The LOORDDA is good!"

"The Lord is good," the members repeated.

"The LOORDDA is faithful."

"The Lord is faithful."

Tom fixed on the Goliath voice coming from the man who hadn't spoken a word to him in a week. He was the pastor? Why hadn't Mae mentioned the fact?

Dale merged straight into the sermon, a blistering lecture that soon had Tom on the edge of his seat.

"The fires of hellla will consume you!"

185

The little man who never talked now had plenty to say. Sweat pooled on his forehead and ran down his cheeks. The stove in the back of the room pumped out heat. "Turn away from your evil ways!

"The Loordda is good! He will not fail youuu!" Dale turned in a half circle. "Matthew seven, verses thirteen and fourteen, exhorts us to 'enter ye in at the strait gate: for wide is the gate, and broad is the way, that leadeth to destruction, and many there be which go in thereat: because strait is the gate, and narrow is the way, which leadeth unto life, and few there be that find it.' "

The farmer Tom purchased the bull from settled deeper into his pew, head nodding. Stomping his foot, Dale bent closer to the floor. "Turn from your evil ways! Now — today — before the Loordda sends His wrath upon you!" Tom glanced over to see sweat rolling down Fisk's temples. Mae lightly touched a handkerchief to her pale cheeks. He wasn't sure if the woodstove was making it hot in the small building or if the heat was due to the pure energy Dale was pouring into his sermon. All he knew was that he was starting to feel a little warm under the collar too.

"Turn!"

Tom started, his eyes fixed on the man

he'd tied a bib on that very morning.

"Turn from your ways least Sataaan gets a holt on you!"

Two hours of a pulpit-pounding, sweat-inducing message followed. When the service concluded, Tom stepped out of the church he'd entered thinking he knew about the Lord and had come to give his thanks to Him. Now he was nursing a gut-gripping uncertainly that he was doomed to burn in an eternal pit of fire before the next hour was over. Heaven was real. Hell was real. Tom had just never heard the facts enforced so emphatically.

Had he read the same Bible Dale spoke from for the last two hours? Was that even the same Dale who sat at his breakfast table? He'd never see the man in the same light again.

The pastor stood at the bottom of the stairs, shaking hands with each and every parishioner. When Tom filed by, Dale grunted, grabbed his hand, and gave him a firm shake.

Tom nodded and walked away, completely at a loss for words. How could he describe Dale's dual personality? The man had certainly fooled him. He would never have imagined the little guy was capable of such conflicting traits.

Pauline emerged right behind him, and as soon as she let go of Dale's hand she slipped her bony arm through his. The wind caught the bloody robe and ruffled the soiled fabric. "Now, Tom . . . that is your name, right?"

"Yes, ma'am." He studied her for a moment, and he knew he had to ask. "How did you get your new robe so dirty?"

"Dressing a bull."

She had dressed a bull. She must have been out with Lil last night. Why hadn't that been his first guess?

"You're coming home with me for dinner."

"Ma'am, I have a lot to do —"

"Hush. Kin eat together on Sundays. I won't take no for an answer." She warmly smiled up at him. "I've fixed a nice big meat loaf."

Her face and hands were clean, but glancing down at her bloody, dirty attire and recalling how much of a disaster her house was, he knew he wouldn't be able to eat a bite.

Sixteen

After Sunday dinner, Mae stood next to Tom at the entrance to Pauline's shed and watched Jeremy scoop slop from the feed barrel. Dogs and cats scrambled to get their share of food.

This was the second Sunday Jake had excused himself from dinner. Jake didn't work on Sundays. Mae was starting to think he was pouting.

Crossing his arms, Tom leaned against the doorway. "Mae, why didn't you tell me Dale was the town pastor?"

"Um . . . you didn't ask." She picked up two water buckets and carried them over to the rain barrel.

He turned and fell into step with her. "I have one more question."

"And that would be?" She set the buckets down and turned toward him. Flashes of distant lightning lit the black line of clouds moving in from the west. The storm was probably hours away, but it looked as though they were in for several more inches of snow.

"How does a man preach like that when he hasn't said a word to me this whole week?"

"Well, he's quiet when he's not in the pulpit. I hope he hasn't stepped on a nerve."

Quiet? He was a smoking pistol. And maybe Dale did step on a nerve or two, but Tom wasn't going to tell Mae that. He didn't want her to think he was weak. Lifting his hat, he recalled the blistering warnings. Every word the man had said was true. He'd brought home the thought that a person either lived his belief or he needed to ask himself if his faith was lip service only.

Thunder interrupted Tom's musings, and he glanced at the darkening sky. Thunder snow didn't happen often, but when it did the snowfall was guaranteed to be heavier than normal. He had been hoping bad weather would hold off until after the supplies arrived. The cleanup would take several days under good conditions, and the situation would be difficult without nature causing problems and delays. If the supplies arrived on time, there was a chance the temporary track could be laid by the end of the week. That would be cutting his self-imposed deadline close, but he had a decent crew, and he knew the men would work hard to get the train back up and running on schedule.

He broke through the ice of the rain barrel so Mae could dip water, his eyes skimming over her head to the lay of Pauline's land. Mostly flat. Good drainage. The river was a decent distance away, so flooding would be minimal when the snow began to melt.

His gaze shifted to the other end of the street to the train station, the lowest point in town. Pauline's place would have made an ideal location. The station sat on uneven, swampy ground, and he'd bet that during the spring thaw, or when it rained, the platform was even more of a sinkhole than normal. Mae's voice broke into his thoughts.

"Did you enjoy the service?"

His mind returned to Dale. The man was something behind the pulpit. "Can't say that I did."

She turned, surprised. "Why not? We're very proud of our pastor."

"He knows his Bible, that's for sure. I just don't like to take a verbal horsewhipping when the time comes I decide to worship God in His own house."

"Oh, that. Yes, he can get loud. He's been

'called,' you know."

Loud? Tom's ears were still ringing. He wasn't deaf; at least, not prior to the sermon. He didn't want to talk about his morning in church, so he changed the subject. "I'm guessing that you and your lady friend —"

"Lil."

"Yes. Lil — and Pauline, from her own admission and the looks of her robe — dressed that bull last night."

Setting the full water buckets at her feet, Mae paused to rest against the barrel. "I didn't get home until the wee hours of the morning."

"You were out that late butchering that thing?" He shook his head. "Why didn't you come get me? I didn't know Lil would ask for your help."

"When Lil came looking for me last night and wanted me to help her dress that bull, I actually planned to give you a piece of my mind this morning. I was plenty put out at the time, but later I realized you had been quite generous to give the meat to Lil to do with what she wanted, so I had no cause to complain. Besides, your hands are full."

She shoved a lock of hair away from her flushed face. His gaze focused on her, and he had no desire to look at anything else until he realized she sensed his overly long inspection. He cleared his throat. "I appreciate the thought, but if any more dead livestock turn up, let me handle the disposal. However, I'm glad Lil got the meat."

A bit of red tinged the tips of her ears, and he wondered if she felt improper chatting with him. If so, he didn't share the concern. The third finger of her left hand didn't wear a ring, yet she seemed embarrassed about something.

"I . . . I've been meaning to apologize to you for my harsh words," she said quietly.

"When was that?" He couldn't recall her speaking an unkind word. Quite the opposite. She appeared to go out of her way not to step on his toes while still treating everyone else in her sweet, caring way.

"Yesterday, when you said you were leaving. I was completely out of line to question your decision, and I want you to know I'll do everything to ease your inconvenience while the rail is being repaired. Often these things turn out to be blessings instead of misfortunes. Perhaps the good Lord is allowing us more time to find someone to help Pauline."

Her remark took him by surprise. Accustomed to dealing with hard-nosed clients, he wasn't comfortable with her concession. Sympathetic. Considerate. Mae Wilkey was a charming puzzle. Her compassion numbed his suspicions that he was being taken for a ride by her, which in the light of the past week, and the town's complete acceptance of his presence, appeared even more cockeyed.

"Thank you, Mae. I appreciate your understanding my position in this matter." And that was the plain truth; a smitten schoolboy's honesty. "But I want you to know that, however this turns out, I'll see to Pauline's care. You have my word." He'd just as soon kept his plans to himself, but he'd known from the moment he'd laid eyes on the elderly woman that she was no longer alone in the world. It wasn't because of any great need to help. He wouldn't get another good night's sleep knowing that if nothing else he could offer financial assistance.

"Thank you."

There was sadness in her voice, and he couldn't quite put his finger on why. Was she content with her situation? After six years, he'd think an independent woman like Mae would take the hint that the man she hoped to marry was running from commitment. She didn't appear to be prone to bury her head in the sand when a problem presented itself, except maybe where Jake was concerned. "What do you ladies plan to do with the beef?"

Frowning, Mae fished in her coat pocket and took out a handkerchief to lightly wipe her nose. "We're not sure. It was one of the biggest bulls I've ever seen. We have meat running out of our ears. Hank Latimer has a bit of room in his ice house, but it won't hold it all. Lil said she knows some folks in the hills who can use some, and everyone in town can have a share. If another dead animal pops up, I don't know what we'll do with it."

He studied the approaching storm front. "Sundays appear to be pretty slow in Dwadlo." He nodded toward the empty church. "Does Dale hold evening services?"

"No," she admitted, flashing an impish grin. "I don't think folks could absorb that much guilt in one day."

"Looks like bad weather's going to be here before dark."

She turned toward the ominous-looking clouds. "Sure does."

"Do you favor parties?"

"Parties?" Her eyes lit up. "I haven't been to a party since the Fourth of July. Dwadlo always celebrates the Independence Day with watermelon, fried chicken —"

He interrupted her. "What if Fisk and I got a good fire going over at the livery and roasted that extra beef? Pretty women shouldn't spend all of Sunday working."

Jeremy's voice rose above the barking animals. "A party!"

Tom grinned and caught Mae's eye. "You said you liked parties."

"But a party on the Sabbath?" Doubt replaced her earlier enthusiasm. "And what about the accident . . . it would seem sacrilegious to hold a party after such a disaster."

"Nobody was seriously hurt. And even if we had planned to work today, the weather would stop us from doing much. Besides, I think the people of this town could use a good outing to lift their spirits. If party is too strong of a word, we'll call it a church supper." He saw the glow return to her cheeks.

"A church supper. Why, it's the perfect solution, Tom. The extra meat shouldn't go to waste."

Studying the sky again, he said, "I figure we have enough time to stoke that fire and cook the meat before the storm moves in." He called over his shoulder. "Jeremy?"

The teen appeared in the shed doorway. "Yes, sir?"

"I need a man to do a man's job."

A wide grin spread across the boy's features. "Yes, sir!"

"Go tell everyone in the town that there's going to be a meal at the church this afternoon. Tell them to be there around four and to bring anything but beef." He winked at Mae. "We have beef coming out our ears." Jeremy darted around him and ran down the road, followed by a dozen yapping dogs.

Tom trailed Mae into the shed, where she poured fresh water into three containers. "What's with all the wire and posts?"

"Pauline is trying to build a fence to contain the animals. They've outgrown the shed."

"She's building it?"

Empting the last bucket, Mae sighed. "She thinks she is, but she'll need help. I tried to talk her out of the idea when she burst into the store last week and asked for wire, posts, and nails."

"She can't build a pen large enough to hold all of her animals without help, and for the next little while every available man will be laying track."

"I told her she couldn't, and you know what she said? 'Hollyhock. I've built many a chicken coop on my own.' Then she shot for the nail barrel, filled a large sack, and headed for the door. She said she'd have Jeremy carry the posts and wire for her. The last thing I heard her yell as she left was 'Put it on my bill!' " Mae shook her head. "Your aunt certainly has a strong will."

The word "aunt" still got under his skin. Shifting, he crossed his arms. "I'll send a couple of men to build the pen as soon as I can spare them."

"Thank you. As I've said before, you're a good man, Tom Curtis."

She straightened and their eyes met. He wanted to ignore the sudden lurch in his stomach, but he was a man and she was a very attractive woman. Still focused on each other, he said, "Will you talk to her and make sure she understands that she can't wear women's —"

"Lingerie in church?" she finished with a nod. "I'm so sorry about its condition. She followed Lil and me last night. She wanted to help, but she ruined her lovely new robe. I was horrified when I saw her wear it to services. I'll speak to her immediately about her inappropriate dress in public."

"It was a little . . . embarrassing." He frowned. "Didn't it make you uncomfortable?"

"Somewhat. I never dreamt that she would mistake the garment for suitable Sunday attire."

His tone turned teasing. "I thought you

might be too busy looking at your intended to notice what she was wearing."

A lovely red color instantly covered her cheeks, but her eyes remained fixed on his. "Don't be silly. Of course I noticed. That's why I asked you to take her out of the church." She glanced away, changing the subject. "I also noticed that you went home to Sunday dinner with her."

"You noticed that?"

She shrugged. "You didn't seem overly eager." She bit back a grin.

"Did it show that much?"

She nodded. "I know Pauline makes meat loaf on Sunday, and I believe I've heard you mention that you don't . . . um . . . care for meat loaf."

"Was that what I ate?" He shook his head. "She said it was meat loaf, but whatever I had didn't resemble anything I've ever eaten before."

"Pauline gets creative when she cooks."

He didn't want to think of the implications that could imply. Thunder rolled in the distance. "I'd better get started on that beef."

"I'll bring some dessert and corn bread. What's your favorite kind of pie?"

"Peach."

She paused. "Mine too. Jake doesn't like

peach. It gives him dyspepsia."

Jake gave him heartburn, but Tom couldn't pinpoint why. The man was friendly enough. Perhaps a little too possessive of Mae, but then Tom supposed Jake had good reason to protect his interests. His eyes lightly skimmed her trim figure. He'd do the same.

"Peach it is. I have a couple of jars in my pantry."

Nodding, he tipped his hat. "Sounds good."

Sounded too good, he decided when he reached down to unlatch a couple of mutts from his ankles. He tripped over a short spaniel who wouldn't give up.

Dwadlo's postmistress was starting to look way too good to him in light of the fact that she belonged to another man. His gaze focused on her as she crossed the field leading to her house. Way too good.

Seventeen

By four o'clock buggies lined the church-yard, tops up under the threatening sky. Men, women, and children streamed into the church carrying covered dishes. The room was soon filled with mouthwatering aromas.

Just before leaving her temporary quarters at the store, Mae took a passing peek in the mirror. She'd changed into her best dark blue wool dress and had tied a lemon-colored ribbon in her hair. Funny how she didn't take the time anymore to do the same for Jake, but their courtship was so informal now that she didn't bother.

He, on the other hand, always dressed for prestige and privilege. His tailored suits fit impeccably. His shirts were the newest fashion with stiff collar points, vests just so, and his trousers were exactly a fourth of an inch from the top of his polished square-toed shoes. Recently, he'd discarded the bow tie he customarily wore for a narrow bit of material with a knot at the top he referred to as a "four-in-hand." Mae knew, though, that he wasn't dressing for her. He dressed for business. She often felt under-dressed and dowdy when she was beside him. Did she make him feel less of an important man with her sensible dress and understated preference for fashion?

"Oh, Mae, your hair's pretty. I like your bow."

"Thank you, sweetheart." She glanced up at her tall little brother. "You look mighty handsome yourself." A blush rose to his cheeks as she walked over to give him a hug. He was so special. "Let's get the food we're taking and head for the part— supper."

By the time they reached the church, Mae's festive mood was infectious. Laughter mingled with the scent of fresh-brewed cof-fee. She and Jeremy walked over to the food table and set their pies, corn bread, and pickled beets next to the other dishes. Eas-ing the peach pie to the back, she lightly drew a napkin over it, praying it would go unnoticed until Tom spotted it. And Jake. She'd baked Jake's favorite, custard. She'd even taken extra care to add additional eggs and the vanilla she'd purchased from a traveling salesman, who vowed there wasn't a better bottle of flavoring to be found.

News of the gathering had obviously reached Lil. She showed up a few minutes later bearing an overflowing plate of fried pork rinds. Men's eyes lit up like small children's at Christmas. The Fourth of July had come to Dwadlo early this year.

A man scooped potato salad on his plate. "Shore sorry about that bull, Stewart."

The farmer lifted a burgeoning plate and grinned. "Sorry I had to lose him, but I'm ten dollars richer and gained a whale of a supper outta him."

Tom listened as talk turned to how they were going to move the locomotive, passenger, and wooden cars. He'd learned Dawdlo had one old ox that was on its last leg. It would take a full morning to round up enough animals to move the heavy loads.

Fisk approached, chewing on a piece of T-bone. "Lil has an elephant."

Tom turned to face him. "She has a what?"

"An elephant." Fisk licked the bone dry. "Circus train came through a couple of years ago. The old bull elephant they had took real sick, and they had to either dispose of him or leave him behind here in Dwadlo. They had about decided to shoot him, but

Lil stepped in and claimed him before Pauline could."

Tom couldn't believe his ears. An elephant! Pulling at his collar, sweat broke across his forehead in the warm room. An elephant. God was good — Pauline wasn't the one who had acquired the thing. "Where does she keep it?"

"She built it a mighty fine shelter. Heated and all. She nursed him back to health, and he took a liking to her. He's harmless."

"Elephants are wild animals, Fisk. They can turn on you."

"Shoot, Tom. Lil rides that ol' thing for fun when she takes a notion. Esau can do the job."

"Esau?"

"The elephant. He can move your locomotive."

"I don't know." Tom had never been around an elephant, and he wasn't sure this was the right time to get to know one. Using oxen, horses, and mules had to be safer than having some gigantic pachyderm wandering around. What if the animal went out of control?

"Well, you can talk to her about it. She's over there jawing with a bunch of the other women."

Fisk moseyed on, licking his fingers. Tom

couldn't help wondering why the blacksmith apparently didn't fear the elephant. Could it be possible that the answer to his prayers had been delivered by a circus? He just hoped the whole project didn't end up turning into a three-ring show.

The old church was quite lively as festivities got into full swing. Harry Miller tuned his guitar and Miller Sands warmed up on his banjo. Tom was just wondering how much longer it would be until the storm hit when the sound of thunder rolled in the distance. He looked up to see Pauline approaching him. At least she'd discarded the bloody housecoat and replaced it with a clean dress. The tiny woman appeared to be in control of her faculties tonight. She extended her arm.

"Shall we take a turn around the floor, sonny?"

It was hard to believe the woman was so spry at her age. Smiling, Tom took her into his arms and swung her gently onto the dance floor. Her slight, thin frame still had a lot of life in it. Her steps matched his, faded eyes alight with pleasure.

"Oh, how I love to dance! Didn't think I'd ever get the chance again."

The lively atmosphere put a bold bounce in her step. Tom led her carefully around the other couples, his gaze searching for Mae. He'd seen her come in earlier carrying steaming dishes. Jake's suit caught his eye, and he found a bright-eyed, flushed Mae in the lawyer's arms. Something akin to jealousy stabbed him in the pit of his stomach. He focused instead on Pauline. "You dance well."

Nodding, she chuckled, "I haven't lost it, have I?"

"No, ma'am." He turned her away from Jake and Mae. "You haven't lost it."

"You know, son." She sobered, her gaze suddenly focusing on Tom's face. "I still don't think I know you from a hole in the wall, but if you are my kin, I'm right proud of it."

He smiled at her and realized he may as well accept her as his aunt, even though he knew she wasn't. It would be kind of nice to pretend he still had family. After all, he'd already decided he would make himself responsible for her financial security. "Me too. I wasn't aware I still had kin, so I guess I should thank you. You're a fine woman, Auntie." God had perfect timing. He hadn't thought he missed family until this very minute. A flush overshadowed the heavy rouge on her weathered cheeks.

"Oh, my. You take my breath away. A man

hasn't said anything like that to me in . . . come to think of it, I don't recall the last time."

"I can't believe that. You're a lovely woman, Pauline. I bet you have had your fair share of admirers."

"Well, yes. I'm sure I have."

She sighed and twirled like the fanciest-reared lady and settled back gently in his arms. Even now he could see that she was once a pretty woman. In her day she'd probably had many a suitor.

"I was a looker, sonny boy."

"I just bet you were." Pauline was in sound mind tonight, and he figured she wouldn't want trite responses. "Time can only steal your body. It can't touch your soul, and you're a good soul." Her toothless grin warmed him, and he was suddenly glad he'd come to Dwadlo.

"Are you married, Tom?"

"Never had the time, Aunt Pauline."

"I understand. You seem like a bright boy. You'll settle down one of these days." Her eyes fixed on Mae. "Now, there's a good woman, but, dad gum it, she's taken."

"Yes, ma'am, I know." The music changed, slowing to a waltz. Still moving about the floor with Pauline as his partner, Tom studied Jake. The lawyer looked just like

207

every other dandy Tom had ever seen. He was a man who liked to flaunt his social position, and Tom was well aware he could offer Mae a good life as Mrs. Jake Mallory. The stuffed shirt would probably build her the fanciest house in town, and their kids would be well-educated. And, unless he missed his guess, the attorney would try to send Jeremy off to one of the fancier institutions in the East, but he'd never achieve his goal. Tom hadn't been in town long, but certainly long enough to know that Mae would fight Mallory tooth and nail to keep her brother with her.

"Do you find Jake handsome?" he asked Pauline. He couldn't judge such matters, and women's taste in men often stumped him.

Pauline turned her head to study the man. "Yes, he's quite attractive. Always been good to me." She pressed closer and whispered in Tom's ear. "I don't think he likes my animals, but then who does 'sides me?" Throwing back her head, she cackled.

Grinning, Tom stifled an involuntary sneeze at the mere thought of dog and cat hair, and he moved to the sounds of the guitar and banjo, letting her laughter wash away his cares.

The past couple of days had been rough,

but thanks to a dead bull, the evening would restore the town's mood. They would realize that the inconvenience of the accident was small. The rail would be repaired, the town wouldn't go under, and life would go on.

If Jake wasn't an imbecile, he would eventually get around to asking for Mae's hand. After a week in Dwadlo, Tom almost didn't want to go home, but he would return to Chicago to bury himself in his new position. Work long hours. Grow old alone. He laughed to himself when he thought about this morning's service. Maybe he would purchase a robe, butcher a bull in it, roll in the dirt, and then wear it to church. That would shake up Chicago.

He nodded to Dale, who waltzed past gingerly holding Widow Freidman in his arms. A chuckle slipped out. Growing old. A sense of humor would help. His gaze turned to Mae and Jake again, and he watched her face flush with exertion. What would it be like to hold the woman God had waiting for him? To spend the rest of his life with his wife in his arms? Smile at her. Allow his love to seep through his gaze and saturate her like thick molasses until she openly longed for him the way he desired her.

He hadn't exactly been looking these past years, but he would have noticed if the right woman had crossed his path. To date he'd yet to find someone he longed to talk to, to hold. Someone he felt he couldn't bear to be separated from . . . until Mae. The memory of passing years that had flown by too quickly closed around him. His aching muscles told him he wasn't getting any younger. And to make matters worse, the only woman he wanted to court belonged to another man.

The music stopped and his stomach growled. What he really wanted was some of that peach pie Mae had made. "Auntie, could I interest you in something to eat?"

"Eat? Is it time to eat again? Well, land sakes, it is dark outside, so let's head for the food."

He'd watched when Mae pushed the peach pie to the back, but covering it had done little good. Most of the slices were gone, but he managed to grab the last piece before Fisk got to it.

"Sorry, my friend, but that's my piece of pie. Peach is my favorite."

"I like any kind, so you can have it."

Tom took his first bite, and it was the best he'd ever tasted. He was savoring the sweet taste when a huge clap of thunder shook

210

the church and folks spooked. The storm was too close. A man opened the door, and folks rushed to have a look outside. Tom set his pie down and listened while husbands called to their wives to pack up their food and get ready to leave. The music died away, and the scramble to clean up and get families home turned fast and furious.

Squeezing his arm, Pauline pulled him down to whisper in his ear again. "I see the way you look at Mae, sonny. It'll happen one of these days. As sure as the good Lord grows green grass, it'll happen for you too."

The only answer he gave her was a smile. He ushered his newly acquired aunt to the back of the room to retrieve her untouched dish. He needed to see her safely home before the storm broke.

Enthusiasm swept the crowd the next morning when Tom and his crew started for the work site. Fortunately, Dwadlo had escaped the worst of the weather. He was thankful the storm had dumped only a couple of inches of icy pellets. He figured folks to the north got the worse of it. Maybe the Lord did indeed have His hand on this tiny community.

Getting ready to leave the center of town, Tom spotted Jake standing on the sidelines, watching the parade of activity, and he had no idea if the man had come to work or just to keep an eye on the situation. He tossed the lawyer a friendly invitation. "Might as well join us, Mallory. Pay's good." When Jake's only response was a nod, Tom turned to follow the workers.

What does Mae see in the man?

When Tom noticed some dogs cheerfully moving toward the accident site, tails wagging, he mentally groaned. He broke away from the rest of the men and cut through an empty lot to bypass the animals. Halfway down the snow-covered path, he sensed eyes on his back. He paused and turned to look. Nothing but snow met his gaze. Proceeding on, he watched his left side, and sure enough he spotted a small shadow trailing his. He turned quick enough this time to see the shadow disappear into the brush.

Scanning the thick growth, Tom didn't detect anything stirring except for a crow cawing in an overhead tree branch.

He walked on. The shadow reappeared, and now he heard footsteps in the snow behind him, but this time he refused to stop. Whistling, Tom parted the thicket and maneuvered through the winter landscape as though this was the exact route he wanted to take. When he came to a low overhanging branch, he grabbed it and pulled it down as he ducked beneath it. Releasing it a moment later, he grinned when he heard the expected "ow!" Now he had an idea of who was following him. He decided to make a game of it.

He wove in and out of the brush, trying to get the culprit to make a mistake, but the intruder proved persistent, keeping a safe distance.

The shadow fell behind far enough that Tom used the opportunity to double back and pick up the pace, and suddenly he found himself right behind the guilty party. He couldn't help but grin at Jeremy's wide-eyed, startled look when he realized Tom was following him.

Mae's brother stood in the snow holding two towel-wrapped packages, his wind-chapped cheeks flushed pink. "I didn't mean no harm, Mr. Curtis."

"Why are you following me?" The boy appeared to search for words, and Tom remembered the young'un's condition. He softened his tone. "Jeremy, did Mae send you to tell me something?"

He shook his head, and Tom focused on the two packages in the boy's hands. "Did she send my dinner?"

A negative head shake again.

He gently took the boy by the shoulders. "What is it, Jeremy? Is it Pauline? Does she need me?"

"I want to work, like a man. I was going to fry some chickens, but cooking's not much of a man's job, and neither is keeping track of the dogs. I do that all the time anyway. I want to do *real* work."

"Real work?" The boy wanted to lay track. "Jeremy, I think caring for the animals is a man's work, but I need strong, grown men to tote and carry heavy material. We'll be handling rails and ties. I'm afraid you'd hurt yourself."

The child's chin sank and it broke Tom's heart, but he couldn't take the chance of the boy injuring himself. Patting his shoulder, Tom gently turned him and said, "Go on back to town." He'd like to oblige Jeremy, but he had enough worries waiting ahead.

He resumed the short trek to the wreckage. The sounds of men's shouts, metal clanging against metal, and wreckage being cleared broke the early morning silence. He could say one thing for the folks of Dwadlo — they weren't afraid of hard work. He turned to check his shadow, and his heart sank when he spotted the hem of Jeremy's yellow coat disappearing into the thicket.

Mae was doing a fine job of raising him, but there were times in a boy's life when he needed a man's companionship. He sighed. "Come here, Jeremy."

The boy emerged, trailed by two dogs, and all three of them had their tails tucked between their legs.

He motioned him closer and the boy complied. "Son." He placed his hands on the boy's thin shoulders again. "You've done a good job caring for the animals. I'm going to promote you."

Jeremy smiled. "Okay."

"The high winds make it hard to keep the lanterns lit. I need someone I can trust to make sure each light is burning and the pots are filled to the brim with oil before they leave the site."

Jeremy's face fell, and Tom realized the boy was bright enough to know when he'd been offered yet another token job. His expressive eyes conveyed a man's need, and Tom knew he would only settle for something a man could do.

"But," he cautioned, "this means you'll be in charge of the kerosene. No one comes near that barrel unless *you* authorize it. Supplies will be scarce until the track repair is finished. Think you're up to it?"

A grin broke across the boy's features.

"Yes, sir!"

"The job only pays an extra nickel a day."

"I'd do it for nothing."

Negotiation wasn't Jeremy's strong suit. "Can you handle the job and take care of your duties at home? Mae doesn't need any additional work, especially now, and you can't forget that you still work for Pauline, helping her with the animals."

"I can do everything," the boy assured him.

Tom focused on the dogs. "There are rules to working for the railroad, and one rule is you have to keep all animals off the job site. They get underfoot otherwise and in the men's way."

Nodding, Jeremy accepted the duty. "They won't bother you."

"Thanks, son." Jeremy's shoulders were now back, and he walked like a proud man with a purpose. Tom was glad he could help, even if it wasn't much. At least the boy would benefit from the experience. The two men walked on, shadows in sync.

Tom had to grin when he realized that Jeremy had now hoisted a pick over his shoulder. The boy must have brought the tool in hopes of getting the job.

Fisk moved about the site, pitching great chunks of metal onto a growing pile of twisted and useless parts. His massive arms plowed through the wreckage like a fox in a henhouse. When Tom and Jeremy approached, he glanced up with a wide grin.

"Already making a little progress, boss."

Tom acknowledged the work with a grin at his new appellation, but he looked up and down the site and knew they had a long way to go. "Jeremy."

"Yes, sir?"

"It's time to start. Go over to the supply wagon and fill water buckets from the barrels. Everything you need should be there. Don't forget to take a ladle with you so the men have something to drink from."

"Yes, sir. Right away."

"Oh, and do you know how to build a fire?"

"I do, Mr. Curtis."

"There's dry wood in one of those wagons. Would you build three fires for me and space them a few yards apart?"

"I can do that. And after I get the fires built I can brew some coffee."

Tom was proud of the young man's enthusiasm. "Good idea. Now, Fisk, that's what I call a man willing to work hard to earn his pay."

Maybe the boy was going to be more help than he'd thought.

Eighteen

Tom grabbed a pick and started to work. The new job felt awkward. He should be inside an office somewhere, where it was warm and he didn't have to use his back to make a dollar. Yet it felt good to work side by side men he admired.

All of the new hires stayed busy, and every so often he'd see Jeremy struggle by with buckets of water or keeping the fires ablaze. The boy knew how to work hard.

The sun was now overhead, raising the temperature to a bearable level, and even some of the snow had started melting. Tom glanced up when he saw a female rider approach. For a split second his heart experienced an odd quirk, but when he saw that the rider was Lil, his pulse slowed. She rode into camp wearing a man's hat, coveralls, and scuffed red leather boots.

Several men called out to her when she dismounted, and she waved them a greeting. Tom paused and watched her exchange a few short words with Fisk before turning and striding in his direction.

"Curtis." She reached out to pump his hand like a man would greet another man. She had a grip like a vise.

"Nice to see you again, Lil. What can I do for you?"

"I'm here to work."

"Thanks, but the women are in charge of the meals. I'm sure they'd welcome an extra hand in town."

"I can't cook. I eat out of cans and jars." Her eyes swept the wreckage.

Tom skimmed her rough exterior. She was sturdy as all get-out, but a woman's place was in the kitchen. "Now, Lil —"

Her hands fisted, and she rested them on her hips as though she expected trouble. "Don't go giving me this 'woman' talk, mister. I may be a woman, but I can outwork any man here." She pulled on a heavy pair of gloves. "I'll join Fisk in what he's doing if that's okay."

Leaning back against a locomotive wheel, Tom released a long breath. Well. By the determined expression on her face, he supposed it would have to be.

It was going to be a long week.

■ ■ ■ ■

By midafternoon dark clouds blocked the sun and heavy sleet was falling, stinging faces. Winter wasn't Tom's favorite time of year even in Chicago. No matter how much a man was bundled up, the chill went straight to the bone. Everyone in Dwadlo said they hadn't seen the likes since most could remember.

The frigid January temperatures made it hard enough for the crew to work when it wasn't sleeting or snowing, so Tom decided to call it a day. "Okay, boys, lets wrap it up and get out of the cold. I'm sure we'll see enough of it over the next few days. No need for anyone catching their death."

It didn't take long for tools to be gathered, the supply wagon loaded, and the men to make their way home.

Tom had hoped Tuesday would be a better day, but it proved just the opposite. Construction stalled when the railroad sent lighter rail gauge than needed, and it wasn't temporary track. At least Fisk had been right about moving the locomotive. An elephant should be able to do the job. Who would have thought an elephant lived in North Dakota, out in the middle of nowhere, cared for by a woman? Tom had to laugh. When he got back to the yard in Chicago and told the story, he doubted anyone would believe him.

What the railroad couldn't ship by rail was being sent by wagon. The problem was the weather, which had yet to cooperate with his plans. He hated all the delays. A sense of restlessness started to nag him. This was going to take longer than he'd anticipated.

Late Tuesday afternoon, when he was sure nothing else could be done, he saddled the mare he'd borrowed from the livery and asked Fisk for directions to Lil's house. It was time to inquire about using the elephant to speed up productivity.

Despite his growing frustration with the situation, Tom had to smile when he thought of Lil. He couldn't help a grudging respect for her. She worked like a beaver. Though he didn't know much about her, he knew she raised hogs, dressed like a man, and cussed like a pirate — and she and Mae were close friends. He couldn't think of a more unlikely pairing.

Fisk had been quick to tell him where the woman lived, and he made it clear that he didn't want to make the trek with him, so Tom went alone. Lil's house sat in a hog wallow some distance outside of Dwadlo.

The tin roof of the shanty sagged beneath the heavy snow atop it. The dogs that had followed him from town immediately got into it with Lil's pack when they darted out of a large barn, taller and wider than most.

He neared the porch and she appeared, shotgun leveled at her hip right at him.

Getting off his horse he called, "Lil, it's Tom Curtis." Then he tried to shake a growling mongrel loose from his pant leg.

Lowering the weapon, she smiled at him. "Why, git yoreself on in here, Tom Curtis!"

Out the corner of his eye he caught sight of Jeremy riding in on a donkey. He silently watched the young man slide from the animal's back, reach for the ropes looped around its neck, and use one to tie the donkey to a rail. Then he waded into the pack of barking dogs, culled Pauline's strays, and tied them to Lil's fence railing.

Tom shook his head. He had to admit, the nickel a day he paid that boy was well spent. Striding toward the shanty, he stepped up onto the porch.

"What brings you out this way this afternoon?"

"Well, um, Fisk mentioned you have an elephant." The implied inquiry felt as silly as the words sounded. This would go down as a first for him and the railroad, hiring an elephant, but he was left without a choice.

She nodded. "Yeah, I got one."

"You actually have one?"

"Just said so, didn't I?"

"You didn't mention the fact yesterday."

"Figure you'd come to me if you needed Esau."

She peered up at him and he smiled. She had a smudge of red jam on the corner of her mouth. She might actually be an attractive woman if she ever cleaned up and dressed like one. "Fisk told me his name. Can't rightly say I've ever heard that before, except from the Bible."

"I took one look at that big ol' hairy skin and knew that was my Esau." She paused. "He was a hairy, hairy man."

When his mama had read the Bible to him, Tom had never thought of naming an elephant or anything else for that matter, after one of Isaac's sons.

Her eyes turned to the slate-colored sky. "You planning to work this evenin'?"

His gaze followed hers. The clouds showed signs of breaking up. "I don't think so. The day's gone. But, weather permitting, tomorrow we can continue to clear the wreckage. I was wondering if I could . . . use your elephant."

"Use him how?"

"To move the locomotive and the cars."

"Well, he could shore do it," she said. "I've made a pulling harness for him — ain't the best, but it helps when I'm uprootin' trees."

Tom relaxed a little. He was relieved to have at least one problem off his hands. Just two to go: Get the right rail, and find Pauline a home. But there was one question that kept nagging at him. "Is it safe to work with him?"

"Safe? Aww, Esau's a big ol' kitty. He wouldn't hurt a fly."

Flies didn't concern him. The removal of the overturned steam engine and wooden boxcars did. He needed brute strength. He hoped the animal was up to the challenge. "Can you have him at the job site early in the morning?"

She nodded. "I'll ride him there. I have to take special care of his skin in the cold, but he can handle it for a day. I'll have to have him back home and inside before dark."

"Much obliged." He tipped his hat and turned to step off the porch. The dogs lunged on their ropes and a few broke loose. Chickens squawked. Feathers flew. He paused when he heard Lil clear her throat, loudly, so he turned and met her stoic expression.

"He gets a dollar a day — same as me."

Nodding, Tom set his jaw. "Dollar a day." He'd never paid an animal one red cent before, but he figured there was always a first time for everything.

By morning word had spread that Esau had been hired to move the locomotive and cars. When Mae, Jake, and Pauline arrived at the work site just after sunrise, the area was teeming with curious observers. Over the previous two days most of the snow surrounding the engine and cars had been cleared away, but if today was sunny, the entire area would become a mud pit. Mae had put her boots on, but Pauline insisted she didn't have any and shoes would be just fine.

Mae recognized most of the people in the gathering crowd, including many who came all the way from Branch Springs to help. On Jake's insistence, she'd closed the store and post office for a couple of hours to accompany him to the site. If truth be known, she came more to see Tom than to be with Jake, and that thought bothered her.

Thoughtfully, Jake had included a reluctant Pauline. He had yet to volunteer a hand in the repair of the track, but Mae knew that manual labor was not his strong suit. Pauline had grumbled all the way to the site because she still nursed a grudge against the railroad interfering with the town's serenity, and it didn't seem likely she'd ever let go of her resentment. But as exciting and entertaining moments were few and far between in Dwadlo, she willingly climbed into the buggy.

Mae spotted Jeremy in the distance as soon as they arrived. She saw quite a few dogs tied to various objects. He was putting logs on the fire next to the water barrels to keep them from freezing. He loved his "man" work and took it seriously. He also seemed to love working with Tom. Mae was sure she'd heard his name at least a hundred times in the last two days during conversations with her little brother. She was happy to see him bond with another man, but she was afraid that Tom's departure would devastate Jeremy, and she didn't want to see that happen.

More families arrived, with men and women carrying small children and babies bundled in warm clothing. Once word had circulated about the elephant working here today, a huge crowd was certain to show up. The whole scene had taken on a circus-like atmosphere.

When Tom appeared, she noticed a frown on his handsome face. Tired lines had formed around his eyes. Was he getting enough sleep? The accident consumed his days. She stood up in the buggy and waved. He lifted a gloved hand in greeting.

"Sit down, Mae." Jake shook his head. "The man doesn't need more distraction."

Mae sat down, fuming inside. How dare he reprimand her like a child! If they weren't in public she'd give him a piece of her mind. Jake had been acting a bit strange lately, and she had no idea why. Maybe he just missed her brother's cooking. Since they had moved into Dale's place, Jeremy hadn't cooked dinner for him.

She opened her mouth to talk to Jake about his behavior, but before she could speak the crowd let out a loud roar. When she looked up her anger was forgotten. Her excitement swelled as Lil and Esau came into view.

Dwadlo would never forget this day!

Nineteen

Mothers moved small children closer to their sides, allowing plenty of room for the massive animal. Lil sat like a proud parent showing off her newborn. Mae's eyes focused on the enormous coat and smiled as she thought of the elephant's name. Esau certainly was hairy.

She looked over at Tom. His eyes were fixed on the gigantic force moving toward him, and she noted his uncertainty. Life had thrown him a curve, and he must spend his nights wondering how on earth he had found himself in this situation. Sadness gripped her. When the rail was complete, he would leave. Right now, watching him take charge of the difficult situation, she knew that for her Dwadlo would never be the same. She gave herself a mental shake. *Mae, that is a most shameful thought for a woman about to become betrothed to another man!* She glanced at Jake, seated in the buggy next to her, observing the activity with keen interest.

The massive Goliath lumbered closer to the overturned locomotive. Lil called, "Stay back, folks! Let Mr. Curtis connect the riggin'!"

Mae's heart nearly stopped when the animal came closer to Tom. Her hand absently came up to cover her mouth. *Protect him, Father . . .*

Pauline clasped her hands. "Sonny boy could be crushed like an ant!"

The animal's sheer bulk dwarfed Tom. Mae couldn't stop the gasp that escaped while she watched the unfolding scene. She caught back an appalling thought. If Esau were to overstep his bounds, she feared Pauline could be right.

Jake abruptly turned toward Mae. "Did you say something?"

"No . . . I just . . . uh . . . the elephant scared me." She wasn't afraid of Esau. She'd been around him before. Had Jake sensed her fear for Tom?

"Curtis is a smart and cautious man. He knows what he's doing. He'll be fine."

Please God . . . let it be so.

Jake stared at the scene in front of him. "You seem overly impressed by the man's work, Mae. It hardly takes a genius to work with a dumb animal. See how your railroad man is getting dirty messing with that filthy animal. Most repulsive."

Tom looked fine to her. He worked fearlessly with Lil to get Esau into his harness. At one point he'd slipped and gone down, but he'd only hit the snow-covered ground. It wasn't as though he'd rolled in the mud and looked like one of Lil's muck-coated sows. However, according to Jake, that was exactly how he looked. If she didn't know better, she'd think the lawyer was jealous. But that was ridiculous.

"What I see is that you don't plan to help." Mortified by her imprudence, Mae couldn't believe she'd voiced her displeasure with him, yet she felt no compulsion to take it back. Jake turned toward her, and from the look in his eyes and the expression on his face, she could tell he wanted to scold her for being insolent.

"Oh, look!" She pointed at Tom and listened to the crowd's appreciation when he finished connecting the harness-like apparatus to the elephant. "He did it!"

Jake glared at her again, but she joined the crowd's cheers and clapped her hands. For the first time in a very long while she felt liberated, and she was mindless of Jake's insecurity.

"They're ready to move the engine!"

"Lil!" Tom shouted above the growing racket.

"Yes, sir?"

"See if you can quiet the crowd." He didn't know how the news had spread so fast. He'd hoped to move the engine and cars without an audience. This certainly wasn't a spectator event, and he didn't want to excite the elephant.

Placing her fingers at the corners of her mouth, Lil whistled. The piercing sound caught the crowd's attention. "Shuddup!"

Conversations ceased.

Nodding at Tom, Lil said. "Go on."

He checked the rigging twice and then motioned for her to back the animal to the engine. "Slowly!" he warned.

Giving another whistle, Lil spoke to the elephant. "Back."

Esau lifted one large foot and took a step backward.

Tom shivered, thankful Esau listened to his master. The morning was freezing, and he wondered if the temperature would ever get out of the teens. His hands and feet were already numb, and he doubted he'd even feel it if the elephant stepped on his foot. He wasn't comfortable in such close quarters. Esau's tail whipped his cheek, and he quickly averted his head, dodging the weapon on the return swish. He felt like a fly next to the gray beast. "Does he have to do that?"

Lil nodded. "That's normal behavior. Relax."

He was as relaxed as anyone standing inches away from tons of flesh. He bent to straighten a rope, and when he looked up the animal hiked its tail.

Oh good grief! Fear struck him speechless, but the anxious moment passed without incident. The onlookers chattered freely, pointing and laughing. He hadn't planned to provide the morning's entertainment.

Lil yelled again. "Quiet!" She used the harness to climb up on Esau's back.

Tom secured a sturdy chain to the locomotive and then to the harness. "Okay! Move him a couple of steps!" He bent to pick up the slack in the chain, and when he turned all his breath was squeezed out of him. The elephant had moved backward instead of forward. Swallowing down hysteria, he tried to breathe as a solid wall of flesh flattened his nose. *Forward!* his mind screamed.

Lil leaned down to peer over the animal's side. "Did you say somethin'?"

"Forward! Move him forward!" Only the sharp command sounded more like "mood hen fodward!"

"Esau. Forward." The weight of the animal came off of him, and Tom gasped to fill his lungs. When he turned, Mae was suddenly there, hovering over him.

"Are you hurt?"

"Go back to your buggy!" Heat filled his cheeks and he consciously dusted his pants. "I can handle this."

She stepped back and gave him a look that said she had no intention of returning to the buggy. The skirt of her dress below her heavy coat caught his eye. This was no place for a woman.

"Careful," she called up to Lil. "It's tight quarters back here!"

"Shore thing. Ease up, Esau."

Tom stepped out of the way and motioned for the animal to step back. The elephant took two steps toward him and stopped. He readjusted the harness, checked the connection to the engine, and then motioned for Lil to move the animal forward. Mae came to stand beside him.

"Does your intended know you're out here in the cold with me?"

Nodding, Mae pointed. "He's sitting right over there watching us."

"He doesn't mind?"

"I didn't say he didn't mind. I said he was watching."

"You should go back to the buggy, Mae. I don't want you to get hurt." He said the words he knew he should say, but the truth was that he liked her there, with him.

Mae smiled. "I've been around Esau a lot. Lil and I are friends, or did you forget?"

"Okay, then. Just stay out of the way. I don't want you getting hurt."

"Why, Mr. Curtis, I'm flattered."

At that moment the sun peeked through the clouds and Mae was bathed in light, looking like an angel. Her hair was shiny, her complexion fair and flawless. She was indeed one fine woman.

Within an hour the overturned locomotive was upright and off to the side, safely removed from the damaged section of track. By early afternoon Esau, with the help of the crew, had cleared the rest of the damaged cars and now stood to the side, contentedly munching on hay. Bystanders still walked around the elephant, amazed by his size and power. Fisk, on the other hand, was fascinated with the engine. He was like a child, climbing around the locomotive, slipping onto the engineer's seat, and touching every knob and handle. He was doing everything kids do when they pretend to drive a steam engine.

Eventually, though, the crowd started to disperse, and Tom studied the work site. He hated to end the workday so early, but without the needed supplies, there was nothing more they could do. He glanced down at his mud-caked clothing and thought he resembled one of Lil's sows. Mae's soft voice interrupted his thoughts.

"You look a mess."

His gaze lazily scanned her own grubby attire. He smiled. "I'm afraid you don't look so good yourself, Miss Wilkey. You've ruined your pretty dress."

Sighing dramatically, she grinned. "I know. Jake said I have to walk home."

Tom turned to watch the man's back disappearing down the road. "Seems Jake isn't very accommodating. Is he always this thoughtful?"

"His buggy is new, and the upholstery is quite expensive. He is . . . well, you see, Jake . . ."

"Don't make excuses for him. He has enough of his own." Tom saw her eyes begin to tear up. "You didn't do anything wrong, Mae. In fact, you're the most giving, most helpful person I know." She looked at him and blinked hard, trying not to cry in front of him. "And, if you don't mind my saying so, you're the prettiest woman I've ever seen."

She fell into step with him but remained silent. He was afraid he'd embarrassed her. He probably shouldn't have made those cracks about Jake, but the more he saw of the man, the less he liked him. He should probably apologize, even if he'd meant every word he'd said. Reaching down, he took her hand and stopped walking. She looked up at him, and as he searched her beautiful brown eyes, he realized he had an almost overpowering urge to kiss her.

"What's wrong?" she asked when he didn't say anything.

"Nothing. Everything seems right."

"Well, you stopped walking. I just wondered why."

"I wanted to apologize . . . in case what I just said insulted you in any way."

Mae shook her head, her gaze on him unwavering. "You didn't insult me, Tom. And for your comments about Jake, well, I suppose everyone in town feels the same way about him."

"Why do you stay with him?"

"Because . . ." Mae looked at the ground for a moment and then back up to his face. "I guess he's like a habit, and no one else has given me a reason to leave him."

"I'd love nothing better than to give you that reason and kiss you right here, right now. But out of respect for you, and Jake, I won't."

Sadness crept over her features, and she looked confused. "I'd love nothing better myself, but I . . . have commitments elsewhere, and I know you want to get back to your life."

"My job," he corrected.

"You're working right now, aren't you?"

He hadn't thought about it, but he was working. Clive was joking about another promotion. His was still waiting for when he got back to the office. Tom thought about that. He hadn't run a crew in years, but he was enjoying the physical labor. Every bone ached, but he'd slept like a log the past couple of nights. He'd grown soft sitting behind a desk every day. "You're right. I am working."

"Then something else must be drawing you back." She pulled her hand from his.

"Mae." Tom took it back and wished he could take her in his arms, but he knew if he acted on how he felt, she'd be more hurt when he left, and he had to leave one day soon. He sighed, squeezed her hand, and said, "Let me escort you back to town. We'll talk only about neutral subjects, okay?"

She smiled as they started walking again. "I hear the weather might be better tomorrow."

"I hope you're right. It's difficult to work when you're freezing to death."

Mae giggled. "I know. I was out there with you!"

"Right." They both laughed and stared at each other like schoolchildren. "Say, when is Jeremy going to fry up some more chicken? Or make one of his apple pies?"

"I'll speak to him tonight, but you know his 'man' job keeps him very busy."

"So I've heard. I don't know how the boy does it. He cooks, cleans, and keeps up his responsibilities with Pauline's animals and the work at the site."

"I appreciate the compliment, and I'll be sure to pass it along to him."

"He's a good boy, Mae."

"Thank you, but then I'm partial."

"You raised him."

"Father passed when Jeremy was nine. Since then it's been just me and my little brother."

"Your mother?"

"She passed giving birth to Jeremy. So you could say I turned big sister and mother overnight." Mae nodded. "Our world here in Dwadlo is small."

"Have you ever wanted to leave? See the sights?"

"What sights?"

He thought of the places he'd seen and the experiences he'd had. "The Grand Canyon, with the Colorado River winding through steep canyons; Mount Hayden; the unbelievable marvels found in Yellowstone National Park. There's a whole big world out there, Miss Wilkey." He smiled. "Maybe you'll see some of it one day." One day maybe he'd like to show her this other world.

"No," she said. "I'm sure I won't. I was born here, and I'll die here, but that's fine with me. I love my life."

His gaze drew hers. "You deserve more. Contentment is good, but never rule out excitement." He spotted a winter bush with bright red berries growing along the road-way. He let go of her hand, stepped over to the plant, and picked a stem. "A flower for milady." He bowed slightly when he presented it.

Breathing deeply of the fall-like scent, Mae smiled. "Thank you, milord."

"Ah, a tiny gift of delicate berries, whose beauty cannot compare to yours." He noticed a slight blush appear on her cheeks.

"I didn't know anyone could be so poetic about a stem of winterberry holly."

"There are many things you don't know about me." His expression sobered. Pauline's house came into sight, and he spotted the woman wrestling with a tangle of wire. Dogs barked.

"Oh, dear. She must be working on her fence."

"Now? In this weather? It'll be dark soon. Is she crazy?" Tom already knew the answer to that. He looked at Mae, and they both burst out in laughter.

"Pauline is determined to build that pen to hold the dogs, so you know what that means."

"She can't build a pen by herself." Tom rubbed his brow. He walked closer to the older woman. "Pauline! Mind if we help?" She glanced up and gave him a toothless grin.

"Thought you had work to do, sonny. But I reckon if you want to help, it'd be okay."

Tom knew it wouldn't take the fragile woman long to tire out, and then he could get the fence up uninterrupted. He glanced at Mae. "How are you with a hammer and nails?"

"The best."

Pauline picked up a hammer.

Tom said, "It's pretty cold out here."

"I haven't been warm all day. Besides, it can't be colder than the other night when I dressed that bull."

"You win. Let's get to work, Miss Wilkey."

He was right about one thing. She was prettier than any winterberry growing wild along the roadside.

Any roadside.

TWENTY

Mae noticed that Pauline tired of fence building about ten minutes after she and Tom arrived to help. The woman's efforts were barely visible when he took the hammer out of her hand and nudged her toward the house. "Why don't you fix us a big pot of coffee —"

"Water," Mae corrected hastily. "Please draw a big pitcher of water."

"Water. Yes, I'll do that. I hope I have enough sugar." She wandered off repeating the task under her breath. "Water, Pauline. Get a pitcher of water."

Tom frowned. "Why not coffee?"

Mae shook her head and reached for a roll of tangled wire. "Why confuse her more?"

"You're right. Does she put sugar in water?"

"She won't this afternoon. She's out of sugar."

Jeremy appeared with the pack of dogs

trailing him. Mae heard the ruckus before she spotted the source. When the boy approached, he called, "Hey, Mae, can I take the dogs to the river?"

"If you promise to be careful."

Tom reached for a post. "You think it's safe to let him near the water?"

"Jeremy is cautious. He understands about the frozen crust and how easily he could fall through." Turning to her brother, she said, "Go on, but be back before dark."

Once her attention was on the task at hand again, she couldn't help but think that Tom's presence made the work seem almost fun. Unrolling the wire, she carefully straightened the kinks while Tom handled the pick. His swift strong swings broke up the frozen ground where they would set a fence post. Admittedly, she was a tomboy at heart. Household chores bored her, but when Mae could work outdoors she savored the task. Lifting her face to the sky, she said aloud, "Thank You, God, for this perfect day!"

Tom glanced up in the middle of a swing. "Did you say something?"

"Just talking to God." She unwound more wire. "Don't you do that?"

"Not in the middle of building a fence."

He swung the pick and she shamelessly

focused on the play of strength in front of her. Jake was a handsome man, but he wasn't athletic. Hours spent in a stuffy office left little time for firm muscles like Tom's. She wondered how he came by them. Didn't he work in an office too?

"How do you keep so fit when you work inside?" She caught her words and offered a shy grin. "I suppose I shouldn't ask such things."

"Ask anything you'd like." Pausing, he leaned on the pick and grinned. "I'll take your remark as a compliment."

"It was meant to be."

"I don't spend all that much time in the office. I travel a lot, which means riding horses to inspect land, jumping gullies, and fighting off stray dogs. My work keeps me in shape."

Now he was teasing her, and for once she was thankful for her wind-chapped cheeks. At least he couldn't see her blushing. She bent closer to her work. "I'm afraid Pauline's forgotten the water. I'll go get some."

Nodding, he brought the pick over his head and swung. Snow and frozen ground flew.

Mae checked on Pauline, who was sound asleep in her chair. A full pitcher of water sat beside her on the floor. Smiling, Mae tucked a warm throw around her friend's tiny frame, picked up the container, and went back outside, softly closing the door behind her.

Rounding the corner a moment later, she noticed that Tom had unbuttoned his coat. The work must be making him sweat even with the low temperature. She pulled off her gloves, dipped her fingertips lightly in the water, and flicked them at him as she walked past.

Straightening, he stared at her. She pretended complete innocence as she set the water jug down. Glancing at the sky, he frowned and returned to work. He knew good and well it wasn't raining. The sun was shining, and there wasn't a cloud in the sky.

She tipped the pitcher ever so slightly, and then moseyed over to the roll of wire, flicking him with more water on the opposite side. This time he didn't lift his head.

Moments passed, and she eased back to get more water. When she straightened she met a broad expanse of chest. His eyes locked with hers.

Bursting out laughing, she ducked when he reached down and grabbed a handful of snow. Her stomach lurched with anticipation when he walked toward her with a white fluffy weapon in hand.

"Don't even think of it."

She put her gloves back on and, frisky beyond her imagination, she swooped and gathered a handful herself. The snow felt cold as she packed it together.

"Don't do it, Mae."

Casually rolling the ball in both hands, she smiled. Would she throw it? She hadn't had a snowball fight since she was a girl. Her grin widened. She wasn't a girl anymore, but she felt like one at that moment. Something definitely must be in the air — something she'd never experienced.

"Hey, Jake." Tom lowered his hand and glanced over her shoulder.

Whirling around, she realized he'd suckered her. When she turned back a big ball of snow hit her chest.

"Why . . . you!" She let her own missile fly and a snowball fight erupted. Shots sailed back and forth. Breathless, she closed her eyes and sank into the middle of a snowbank and started flinging whatever came to hand, laughing so hard she couldn't catch her breath. He was a merciless opponent! When she opened her eyes he loomed over her menacingly with a large mound of snow in his hand.

"Give up?" he asked.

"Never!" she vowed with laughter. Jake flashed through her mind. She couldn't imagine the finely dressed attorney rolling around in the snow with her — or any woman. Grabbing her sides, she doubled over, and tried to gain control of her hysteria. Trying to keep her still, Tom lifted her chin with one hand and calmly rubbed snow in her face with the other. She squealed, dissolving in mirth.

Suddenly he straightened. Turning, he looked behind him and then said, "Afternoon, Jake."

"Oh, no you don't. Not this time." She scooped up a fistful of the white stuff, stood up, and let fly.

Tom ducked and Jake caught the assault full force. Her hand flew to her mouth. Where had he come from? With a gasp, the man stiffened and absorbed the shock. Snow slid down his cheeks.

"Oh . . . dear . . . Jake." The incredulous look on his face almost made her laugh. Mae reached in her coat pocket and took out her handkerchief. "I'm so sorry."

Jake's eyes were burning embers of fury as he glared at her. "Mae!"

She opened her mouth to say something more when she heard the sound of Jeremy's frightened sobs. Fear struck her speechless.

Turning, she focused her attention on him instead of her angry beau.

Tom stepped over and put his arm around the crying boy. "What's wrong, Jeremy?"

"Twelve and Fourteen fell through the ice, and I can't get them!"

"Twelve and fourteen?" Tom glanced at Mae.

She met his questioning gaze. "He named the dogs by number in the order they were acquired."

Jeremy wiggled out from beneath Tom's sheltering arm and grabbed his hand. "You have to come, Tom Curtis. We gotta help them."

Mae watched Tom and her little brother race toward the river. She looked at Jake. "I'll explain later, I promise!" She started to run after them.

"Mae! Come back here. You're acting like a hooligan. Curtis can take care of those dogs!"

She stopped to turn and glare at him. "Yes, but Jeremy's my brother!" She left Jake muttering to himself as she headed to the water, picking up her pace.

Tom's long strides had quickly covered the ground, Jeremy jogging by his side. She finally caught up with them and saw tears rolling down her brother's cheeks. Mae rarely had seen the boy cry.

"Mae, hold up here," Tom said. "I'm going out there — Jeremy!"

"Jeremy!" she shouted. "Stay here with me!" But he had run ahead. She and Tom both hurried to catch up with him.

"Jeremy!" Tom called again.

"Yes, sir!" The boy had stopped at the river's edge.

"Let's tie all your ropes together!"

"Yes, sssir . . ."

The quiver in the boy's voice broke Mae's heart. She was terrified, but she had to trust Tom. He would not put Jeremy in danger. Surprised at the length of the rope after they quickly tied the individual lines together, she watched Tom tie one end to a tree and the other to his waist.

"The ropes will keep me safe. If I lose my footing, don't panic. You can pull me out easily enough. Don't do anything unless I tell you to."

"Yes, sir." Fresh tears rolled from the corners of the boy's eyes.

"It's going to be okay, Jeremy. Twelve and Fourteen are born swimmers. They'll stay afloat till I can get them."

Jeremy stared up at him. "But it's so cold."

"God gave them heavy coats, and they

haven't been in the water very long. Trust me."

Mae's heart pounded as Tom laid down on the ice and started to slither over it, using his elbows to pull himself forward. She held her breath when he was only a foot away from the struggling dogs, fearing his weight would cause him to fall through the already weak ice.

He reached into the water, snatched one of the struggling animals, and set him on the ice beside him. The poor dog was shaking so badly he could hardly walk.

Jeremy broke into a smile. "Fourteen!"

Tom turned onto his back and held up the other dog. "And Twelve," he added with a smile. Mae heard a loud crack and knew the ice was giving way. "Tom!"

"Pull me in!"

Mae and Jeremy grabbed the rope. Together they gave one big tug, and Tom slid toward shore, safe from the thin ice. He handed the dog to Jeremy and got to his feet.

Jeremy hugged the wet, freezing animal and then bent down to Fourteen, who had made his way to them. "Thank you, Tom. You're the bravest man I've ever known!"

"You're welcome, son."

Mae fought back tears. Tom was safe and

so were the dogs. God had heard a small boy's prayers. *Thank You, Lord, for hearing mine too.*

She approached Tom and welcomed the gentle touch of his gloved hand as he wiped the tears from her cheek. "Tom —"

"I'm all right and everybody's safe. Let's get back and get us all warmed up."

Mae fell into step with her two favorite men. Since when had Tom become one of her favorites? It wasn't right that she had these thoughts, but they seemed so natural. Was she falling in love with him? *Lord, please guide me and help me make sense of my confused heart.*

"Tom Curtis?" Jeremy asked

"Yeah?"

"Do you believe in God?"

"Yes, I do, Jeremy. It would be hard not to believe in Him, don't you think? He helped us find your dogs, kept them safe and sound, and so far He's protected us."

"What made you believe? Mae says she thinks I'm still too young to fully understand how to believe in God, but I do. I know He's there."

Mae's heart filled with pride at her brother's admission of faith. Even with all of his problems, he was smarter than most. She fell behind and continued to listen as they made their way into town. Jeremy needed a man's presence in his life, and right now Tom was filling that role beautifully.

Tom was amazed at the young man's question. He put his arm around Jeremy's shoulder, noticing that Mae now walked behind them. "Well, I got to thinking about how blessed my life has been. I had good parents, a good home, always had a good job, and things were getting better all the time. One night I was lying on the ground looking up at the stars — I guess I was about twenty-five or so — and I got to counting up all those good things in my life and they kind of overwhelmed me.

"My mother had taken me to church when I was small, but nothing much stuck. Then, as I grew older I didn't go to services a great deal, but she continued to read the Bible to me." He glanced down at the boy. "That night, looking up at that beautiful sky, I was so full of gratitude, and I realized I could only have one Person to thank for the way things had turned out for me." He paused, reliving that moment.

"So what happened?"

"I got on my knees and made God's acquaintance."

"You said you went to church when you were a small boy."

252

"I did, but I personally met God that night under the stars."

"You met God face-to-face? You saw Him?"

Tears welled in Tom's eyes and he stopped, turning toward the boy. "No, son, I didn't actually see Him face-to-face, but that was the night I realized that God lives . . ." He gently tapped Jeremy's chest. "In here. Right inside each and every one of us."

The boy's eyes grew wide. "How did He get in there?"

Tom continued on, suddenly realizing that now, through the innocence of this child, was the true moment he met God. He cleared the lump in his throat and answered the question. "He was in there when you were born, Jeremy, and if you ask Him, He'll be there with you all of your life."

TWENTY-ONE

"Land sakes," Lil said, scooping up a handful of peanuts and cracking a shell.

Mae caught the action from the corner of her eye. "I'm putting those on your bill, Lil."

"Go right ahead." Grinning, she tossed a nut in the air, caught it with her teeth, and then spat it out on the floor.

"That's appalling."

"Proper-shmopper. When did you turn all ladylike?"

"Spitting on the floor isn't a fancy idea." Mae carefully recorded two cents on the hog farmer's account. Lil circled the cage and stepped inside. Mae tried to shoo her away, to little avail. "You're not supposed to be in here. Why aren't you working out at the accident site?"

"Tom said he would need me more when the supplies arrive, so I thought I would come see you. What do you do in here when no mail is coming in?" Lil sat down on the small chair and propped her feet on the tiny desk. Her muddy size ten boots dripped something on the floor Mae would rather not put a name to.

Mae pointed to the puddle. "You're going to clean that up."

Lil shrugged and popped another nut in her mouth. "Oh, don't get your bustle in an uproar. Dale's laying track, isn't he?"

"Thankfully, he is."

"So where's the cute railroad man? You know, the one who's got you all dewy-eyed?"

"Lil! That's a terrible thing to say. You know Jake and I are —"

"Nothing! That's what you and Jake are to each other. He don't look at you with that sparkle in his eye any more than you look at him that way. Who are the two of you kidding? A blind man could see y'all aren't in love. He's just your bad habit."

"Lil, don't you be saying those things. I love Jake and we're going to get married. You know we are, so stop talking about us like that."

"Okay. Because you're my friend and always will be, I'll shut up." Lil lowered her feet and leaned forward in the chair. "Now, tell me where Tom is. You know, the man you're not interested in."

Mae knew Lil well, so she chose not to respond further to her teasing. If she said anything more, Lil would keep on about it all day, and she wasn't in the mood. "Early this morning the supply train was waiting for Tom just before the accident site, where the track is still intact. He was the first man out there, and he had to come back to tell Dale so he could hurry the men along."

Mae wouldn't dare tell Lil that she had been able to chat with Tom over her first cup of coffee — with the sun just peeking over the horizon — and that for her the day had begun beautifully. She closed the box lid. "Now that the site is clear of the wreckage, the crew has started the repairs. It shouldn't be but a few days before the train is running to the depot again."

In a way the thought pleased her. On the one hand, it meant that Tom could go back to his work in Chicago, but on the other hand a nagging sense of emptiness filled her when she thought about his leaving. But that would be for the best because Jake had started to make accusations. He'd found her and Tom together too many times in what he called "questionable situations."

Lil cracked another peanut. "Heard you and the boss got in a snowball fight yesterday."

Her friend's statement brought back last night's argument with Jake. He had openly accused her of being attracted to the railroad man. She presented her best argument, but even she realized her words rang hollow.

She needed to change the subject. "Did you hear about the dogs falling through the ice?"

"Yeah." Lil tossed a shell in the direction of a wicker basket. "Twelve and Fourteen? I heard Curtis saved the day." Reaching for a tin box, she searched in it until she found a red button and stuck it in her overall pocket.

"Please. Help yourself to anything you need," Mae said dryly, deliberately picking up the credit book and dutifully recording an additional four cents on her friend's account.

Closing the book, she eased around Lil and the puddle on the floor and stepped out of the cage. Mrs. Pryor had brought in five dozen eggs earlier, and she had yet to put them on the counter. "Jeremy was beside himself when the dogs fell through the ice, but Tom solved the problem. He was quite helpful."

"I'm sure he was. Unlike Jake."

"Tom was there at the time, Lil. Jake wasn't. Well, he was, but he didn't do anything."

"Doesn't surprise me. He's never there. He hates those dogs."

"Yes, but he loves my brother, and he would have helped."

"Not if it meant getting dirty."

Lil knew Jake too well, and unfortunately so did Mae.

For some reason she felt as though she'd known Tom Curtis all of her life too. Her mind skipped to the coming evening when Jake would be over. Last night he'd insisted on seeing her, even though they hadn't been able to have their regularly scheduled dinners together since she had started staying in Dale's quarters. She assumed she'd be in for another stern lecture on "proper etiquette."

She understood that discovering one's intended playing in the snow with another man would be disconcerting for someone with Jake's conservative nature. She had already explained and apologized for her insensitive actions and didn't want to go through it again, but Jake had given her that look, the one that said he didn't believe a word she said. A headache bloomed at the base of her neck. The telegraph machine beat a rat-a-tat-tat and she moved to accept the message.

"Who's gittin' a telegram?" Lil asked.

Mae motioned for her friend to keep quiet. She wrote as the erratic beats came in, copying the message twice. When the machine fell silent, she turned toward Lil. "It's for Tom — from the railroad."

Lil shelled another nut. "I knew it couldn't be for anyone from around here." She brushed empty shells off her lap. "When was the last time anyone in Dwadlo got a telegram?"

"Hmm . . ." Mae returned to the counter. "I don't know. Probably a couple of years ago when Mr. Anderson's mother passed."

"Oh, yeah. That came all the way from Philly, didn't it?"

Nodding, Mae put the last of the eggs on display, her mind on the recent wire. The railroad wanted the track finished by Wednesday of next week — just seven days from now. Tom would be leaving shortly after that. His earlier words flashed through her mind: *There's a whole big world out there.* Until she'd met him, she hadn't thought much about what she might be missing, but it didn't matter anyway. Her life was here, and it always would be.

Lil stood and stepped out of the cage and said, "Want to eat supper at the café tonight?"

"I'd love to, but since I've been at Dale's,

I haven't had dinner with Jake, and he's coming here tonight."

"I forgot. This is Thursday."

"Yes. His regular night." Sighing, she remembered that Dale was low on baking soda. Jeremy would make biscuits, even though Jake favored white bread. She often wondered if Jeremy liked to play with the lawyer's mind by purposely irritating him.

"Well." Lil stretched. "Guess I'll mosey on out to the work site and pester Fisk a while."

Shaking her head, Mae smiled. "You two do love to annoy each other."

"Yep. It's the only fun I get anymore."

The front door opened, and Mae turned to see Joanne Small's mother walk into the store.

"Hello, ma'am. What brings you out this morning?" Mae knew the reason, but she had to be polite to the woman. She'd been in twice since the accident to check on the herring shipment.

"Is the track repaired?" The full-bodied woman paused before the counter.

"No, ma'am, but they're working on it. I believe it will be in plenty of time for Joanne's wedding."

"Are you certain?"

Mae understood the woman's concern. "I

can't promise, Mrs. Small, but the work is coming along nicely. Supplies have arrived, and it should only take a few days to lay temporary track."

"A few days? That's all the time I have." The woman glanced around the store and then back at Mae. "I haven't slept a wink since the train derailed." She drew a handkerchief to her mouth. "Oh, for the days when weddings were a simple occasion. When a man and a woman took vows before their family and just a few friends. Joanne's guest list grows every day."

Mae reached out and patted Mrs. Small's hand. "I know you're concerned, but the herring will arrive on time. Go home and try to rest." She gave her a brave smile. "I'll send Jeremy to let you know the minute the track is finished."

"Thank you, dear. I know I'm a bit of a pest, but this wedding has me all aflutter."

"I understand. It will work out. You'll see."

"Thank you, dear," she said again. Mrs. Small walked toward the door and then turned. "You will send Jeremy the moment the train is running?"

"The very moment. I promise." Mae sighed when the woman pulled the door closed. "Poor thing. She's making herself sick with worry."

"What if the fish don't get here?" Lil pitched another shell and missed the can.

"Pick that up. If the herring doesn't arrive, Joanne's big day will still go on. It wouldn't be the end of the world to have the wedding without it." Mae walked over to where Lil stood.

"I've never heard of a wedding with herring. Have you?" Lil dropped more peanut shells on the floor.

"You know Joanne. She likes things fancy. Are you going?"

"Where?"

"To the wedding."

"I don't like them shindigs. Besides, I use herring as bait. I don't eat it."

"It's considered a delicacy."

"It's bait. Just because Joanne's papa has enough money to burn a wet mule don't mean that I'm gonna take a bath in rose water, put on a dress, and force bait down my throat."

"Don't blow your corset. I was only asking." Mae changed the subject. "You must have been proud of Esau."

Lil's face beamed like a proud mama's. "He's a dandy. I bet Pauline was coming out of her skin watchin' my elephant work and knowing I'd outbid her on the animal."

"I didn't notice." She'd been too focused

on Tom — according to Jake. "The last thing Pauline needs is an elephant." An elephant to worry about in addition to the stray dogs and cats would surely have sent Tom over the edge. "What would Pauline do with an elephant when she can't care for the animals she has?"

"Why, she could put him in the new pen you and Tom are buildin'."

Mae groaned at Lil's statement. She should be used to the way word spread in Dwadlo. Turning a cynical eye on her, she said, "Weren't you on your way to annoy Fisk?"

"Well . . . yeah, that's where I'm headed." Tipping her battered hat, Lil grinned. "When you get a free evening, let's eat supper at the café — once you get your man problems figured out. Fisk eats there every night. I wanna see the look on his face when I walk in."

"You're hopeless. Fisk is a good man, and he's still obviously grieving for his wife."

"Maybe if he'd open his stubborn eyes, he'd notice there are other women around who might treat him as good."

Mae turned. "Why, Lil Jenkins. You actually like the man."

"I do not." She shoved her hands in her pockets. "And don't you be spreadin' that around."

Grinning, Mae shook her head. "And all this time you've had me convinced you thought the blacksmith was cow droppings."

"I never said that."

"You've implied it a hundred times —"

"Can we change the subject? I'm getting sick to my stomach."

"Because you've eaten too many nuts."

"Because my best friend is a nut. Can you go to supper or not?"

Mae raised her eyebrows. "Not tonight. Jake, remember?"

"Oh, right. Mr. Wonderful."

Twenty-Two

The scent of baking biscuits filled the store as Mae hung the "Closed" sign. She'd seen Jake's buggy pass a while ago, but last-minute customers had detained her. He would be displeased that she wasn't there to greet him when he arrived at Dale's quarters.

"Hello!" she called cheerily when she brushed past Jeremy and headed for the small living area. Jake was pacing back and forth in front of the fireplace. No doubt his mind was on something other than the beef stew simmering on the stove.

"Good evening, Jake. Sorry I'm late." She leaned toward him to give him a peck on the cheek, but he moved his head away from her before she touched him. He stopped pacing and stared at her.

"It's ten after." He showed her his pocket watch and tapped the face. "I said six o'clock, Mae. That does not mean ten after six. It means six o'clock."

Mae silently growled inside, but she didn't dare show Jake she hated being treated like an errant child. "Mrs. Wetlock ran low on salt, so she came in right at closing. Then another telegram came in for Tom. I had to write it down and would have had to deliver it, but thankfully Mrs. Wetlock offered to take it to him on her way home. So I could have been even later."

He paused to focus on her, glaring. "Is that right?"

She wilted beneath his harsh scrutiny. The mere mention of Tom's name caused a ruddy tint to creep up his neck. His eyes hardened, and she recognized the impatient glint all too well. She was puzzled. Being late was no reason for him to get this angry.

"Can't Mr. Curtis fetch his own wires? Why should someone have to deliver them?"

"He wasn't aware he had a message, and because it was from the railroad, I thought he'd need to read it right away." She gently placed her hand on his arm. "Let's eat. Something smells glorious."

Ordinarily a good meal distracted him, but not tonight. He pulled his arm away from her touch. "I don't believe you understand how it looks when you spend time alone with another man."

"I wasn't alone with him. I sent the message with someone else."

"You were alone with him yesterday. I caught you."

She clenched her teeth and suppressed her objections to his ridiculous statement. "I'm sorry, Jake. It won't happen again." He stared at her for what seemed like an eternity, and then he paced a couple more times. He stopped in front of her again, and she wasn't sure what to expect.

"First, I accept your apology. Second, I have business I'd like to get out of the way before we consume our evening meal."

"Oh? Well, if you don't mind, I need to sit down first." Mae stepped over to the couch and sank onto the cushion, nudging off her boots. She'd been on her feet for hours. Unfastening a few hair pins, she allowed her hair to cascade down her back. "All right." She couldn't recall any pending business that affected both her and Jake, but then so many things were on her mind these days.

He eyed her sudden personal disorder with apparent disdain, absently straightening his shirt points. Normally she'd have taken the time to put a bit of rouge on her cheeks and a little powder, but her disheveled appearance was one more penalty for being late. She was just plain weary tonight.

Jake cleared his throat. "Shall we get down to business?"

"Let's."

"It has come to my attention recently that a certain woman in town is acting most improper for a woman betrothed to a man."

She scratched her scalp vigorously. It felt so good. "Mmm — who's that?" Couldn't be Lil. She always acted improperly, and she wasn't betrothed to anyone. Mae chuckled, recalling their earlier conversation. "Jake, do you know that Lil has her eye on Fisk? All this time she's pretended to argue with him to get his attention. Can you imagine? That girl is —"

"Mae!"

She glanced up and immediately sobered at the disturbed look on his face. "What?"

"I am talking to you."

"Yes." Her hand dropped. Why was he acting so contrary? He seemed more serious tonight than usual. She had a lot of comments about his present behavior, none of which he would appreciate. She sighed. "Go on."

"It has come to my attention that you have been spending entirely too much time with that railroad man."

"Tom?"

"Is there another railroad man in town of whom I am not aware?"

He was using his lawyer's voice on her now. She straightened. "Of course not, Jake. You can't be serious." She'd never known him to show an ounce of jealousy, but then she'd never given him a reason to warrant his concern. She'd been completely faithful, even though officially she wasn't engaged to him.

"People are starting to talk."

"Who? I can't imagine anyone in Dwadlo who would find fault with my behavior."

"You're telling me that allowing a man to drip water on your head is appropriate conduct?" Jake shook his head. "How about the snowball fight? Do you think that was appropriate? If you do, then I have to say I question your judgment, Mae Wilkey."

She was too tired to argue, and she had to admit she'd made some mistakes, especially in Jake's eyes. "I suppose you're right." He was still making an ugly face at her, and she knew he wanted her apology spelled out and acknowledged. "You are right, Jake. My behavior was improper, and I regret it. I used poor judgment, and that will never happen again. I'm sorry."

"Indeed. Then you would agree that folks have a reason to talk?" He stood in front of her. "It grieves me to have to speak to you about this, Mae. You must understand that as my intended wife I cannot have you running around like a common strumpet."

Her jaw dropped. How could he think that after knowing her almost all of her life? "Strumpet? Jake, that's most unkind."

"How else would I define your recent behavior? Cavorting around with a man who appears to have no morals —"

"Tom has morals. Why would you say such things?"

"Because a decent man doesn't try to move in on another man's territory."

Mae stood up and took a few steps toward the kitchen area. Jake's accusations stung, but they were not without warrant. Her mind turned to Tom. She did act differently when he was around. He made her feel young and carefree, and he was without judgment and constant criticism. But Tom was not her suitor, Jake was, and she'd managed to make him angrier than she'd ever seen him.

"In the future, I will expect you to act in a respectable manner, Mae. There will be no more playing in the snow, and no more time spent alone with Curtis. Do we have an understanding?"

"Yes," she murmured.

"Very well." He crossed the floor and took her by the shoulders. "I have given this careful thought, and I've reached a solution I feel is best for all concerned."

Her heart thumped. Shock — and then relief — filled her. He was going to break their six-year relationship, and she had no one to blame but herself. A sudden giddiness bubbled inside her.

"I am fully aware that women expect, shall we say, more adequate surroundings, but then I know you're not like most women."

His pinched look gradually faded into a pleasant smile when he let go of her shoulders and reached into his coat pocket to withdraw a small box. Her eyes focused on the object.

"Mae Wilkey." He popped the lid open to reveal a sparkling diamond. Not too big to be gaudy, but not so small to be tasteless. "Will you be my bride?"

Something suddenly blocked her air supply and she couldn't breathe. The room immediately became too hot. Her hair! She looked as though she'd been in a wind storm, and the toe of one of her stockings had a hole in it. Focused on the diamond, she realized this was it, the hour she'd waited six years for, longed for, and dreamed about. The prize in the little box twinkled at her.

Going down on one knee, he gently took her left hand. "This is what we've both wanted for a very long while, darling. We need to start our lives together — to become a real couple. Time is passing, and so is our youth."

Mae's eyes lifted. Not exactly dazzling talk, but true. "It's . . . so sudden."

"Sudden?" He cocked a dark brow. "I would hardly say that after six years this decision is based on an impulse."

"No . . . certainly not an impulse."

"Not that we're old by any measure, but the days have a way of taking flight, and we want to be young enough to enjoy children and grandchildren . . . should we be blessed with little ones."

Her eyes pivoted back to the ring he had removed from the box. "Well, darling? What do you say? Will you make me the happiest man on earth and become my bride?" He held the twinkling diamond at her fingertip.

"I . . ." She searched for the appropriate words. Her gaze fixed on a broken prong.

"There is one loose prong, but I'll have that fixed right away." He slipped the ring on her finger. "There. A perfect fit." He smiled. "It belonged to Mother, you know."

She didn't know. Jake rarely spoke of his

family, who lived in Branch Springs and never came to visit. Mae stared at the ring. It felt foreign and heavy on her finger, but the sincerity in his eyes reminded her of the long years she'd spent in pursuit of this moment. Most had been good years, years of memories and envisioning a future together. Jake wasn't the most exciting mate, and she'd suspected as much long before Tom Curtis ever walked into her life, but he was solid and dependable. Jeremy and Pauline's future would be assured. If she married Jake, she could quit her job at the post office and focus on her brother and Pauline's needs.

And it wasn't as though anyone else stood in the wing waiting to claim her hand in marriage. An image of Tom fleetingly skipped through her mind, but she crushed the fairy-tale thought. In a matter of days he would be gone and she would still be in Dwadlo. Lifting her eyes, she smiled. "I would be honored to marry you, Jake." The affirmation neither sounded nor felt the way she'd pictured it would. She didn't squeal with joy or swoon with relief, but then she was close to thirty. A woman couldn't wait forever, especially not in North Dakota. She accepted God's plan for her life. Most likely the path He'd chosen for her was far better than the one she'd started to envision.

Squeezing his hand, she said softly, "The ring is lovely."

Rising, Jake gave his vest a satisfied pat. "Now that we've dispensed with that matter, there's no hurry to set a date is there? We have the rest of our lives, and should we delay a few more years and having children becomes less likely, we'll deal with the matter when the time comes."

"No hurry." She surprised herself with her willingness to agree with him. Planning a wedding took time, time she didn't have at the moment.

He pulled her to him and gave her a hug. "I'd like to see you tomorrow night too."

She realized suddenly that she would have to get used to seeing him more often now that they were betrothed. She studied the ring and was glad he couldn't see the disappointed look on her face, or how she frowned at the broken prong that stood out like a sore thumb.

"Well?" he said, releasing her.

"Well what?"

"Tomorrow night?"

"Oh, yes. Tomorrow would be fine." Looking at him now, she wondered how strange it was that a meticulous man like Jake wouldn't have repaired the ring before he proposed. But at least he had asked her to be his wife.

TWENTY-THREE

Mae sat on the cracker barrel and laughed. Word of her engagement had spread faster than fleas. All of Dwadlo had heard the news: Poor Mae had finally caught her man at last, and she had a ring on her finger.

She held the diamond up to the morning light and admired the setting. It was pretty enough — impressive yet tasteful. The ragged prong was a bit of a distraction, and the jewelry felt heavy on her hand, but Jake had given it to her.

She knew something was very wrong with her engagement, and it was important. She'd waited. What was she fretting about? She'd waited six long years for this celebration, yet she wasn't leaping for joy or standing on the porch shouting the news to anyone who would listen: "Mae Wilkey is engaged to be married!"

She could finally take her mother's wedding dress out of the trunk and try on the fine silky material, something she had never done. She wanted the excitement of the anticipated day to be new, fresh, and totally her own experience.

The door opened and she glanced up, smiling when she saw Tom. The wind slammed the screen shut. Sliding off the barrel, she walked to the cage, her stomach slightly edgy. Had he also heard the news? "Good morning."

Nodding, he went to the root beer barrel, where only ice chunks floated. He'd heard. His cool demeanor and the way his lips pulled up at the corners confirmed her belief.

"Sorry. I'm afraid the root beer is gone, but we have plenty of sarsaparilla."

The hunk of cold metal around her third finger itched. Swallowing, she stepped to the counter, unconsciously fussing with her hair. The edge of the stone's setting caught in her thick tresses, and she discreetly tried to tug it free, but she only succeeded in getting it more tangled.

"Not today."

He went to the back of the store, and she heard him rummaging through the nail bin. Her fingers worked to loosen the ring's firm grip. Drats. Stuck tight as a miser. She heard him return and she straightened. Tom paused at the counter, setting down a sack of nails.

She met his gaze. "I'm sorry, but could you . . . help me? One of the prongs is caught in my hair." She went around the counter and stood before him. After grunting as though she were a worrisome child, he set to work trying to loosen the ring's hold.

"I've heard of nooses around the neck, but never one caught in the hair."

"That isn't funny. It not a noose; it's a ring."

Noose? Ring? Anchor might be more appropriate, because it felt like a lead weight. She clamped her lips closed to make sure the impertinent thought didn't escape. The ring was lovely. Her life was perfect. She had everything she'd ever wished for — didn't she?

"Ouch! Is it budging?"

"It's getting more snarled. We're going to have to cut it out."

"Cut my hair?"

"Do you have a better solution?"

She kept an eye on the front window. If Jake came in and caught her with Tom like this . . . well, his patience did have limits. She'd just barely managed to soothe his accusations last night. Dragging Tom with her, she returned to the cage and picked up a pair of scissors. "Please don't cut more than necessary."

Snipping the scissors sharply a few times, he picked up a handful of her hair and pretended to slash a huge hunk. She moaned.

"Relax."

He carefully snipped the ring loose with a distinct twinkle in his eyes. Being a hair's breadth away from him, she could smell his fresh, clean outdoor scent. An inappropriate ripple raced up her spine.

"Shall I save the hair for Jake's memory book?"

"That won't be necessary." She took the lock and pitched it into the wicker wastebasket.

"So." He leaned against her desk, apparently in a better mood than when he first came in the store. "When's the big event?"

Jake's earlier words floated through her mind. *"There's no hurry to set a date is there? We have the rest of our lives, and should we delay a few more years and having children becomes less likely, we'll deal with the matter when the time comes."*

"We haven't set a date yet."

"Why doesn't that surprise me?" Apparently changing his mind, he grabbed a

279

bottle of sarsaparilla.

She eased around him, well aware he was much too close for comfort. She liked it when they were close enough for her to see the smile lines around his eyes. Liked it far too much for a woman about to marry another man. She paused and let the words sink in. She was engaged to Jake. Formally engaged.

He set a bottle of sarsaparilla on the counter next to the sack of nails. "I'll take a hunk of cheese and some crackers as well."

"This is your lunch?" She stepped to fill the order, relieved he was taking the news of her engagement in stride. He had seemed a bit miffed when he arrived, but that was likely due to problems on the site and not at all with his feelings about her.

"Lunch and supper. I only left the site to send a wire."

"Sure." She wrapped the cheese in heavy white paper and added a pickle, on the house. His vegetable for the day. After wiping her hands on her apron, she stepped into the cage. "To the railroad?"

"Yes. Ask Letterman if he sent the right track yet, or has he got his head up his nose? Get me temporary track and in a hurry if he wants that rail fixed by Wednesday."

She wrote,

PLEASE SEND PROPER TRACK STOP
WORK PROCEEDING ON TIME BUT IN
DIRE NEED OF EXPEDIENCY STOP

"Anything else?"

"Tell him to get off his duff and get the order right! I can't fix the track without the proper material. Do they have a bunch of idiots working there?"

She added,

HAVE A NICE DAY STOP

"Anything else?"

"No." He shelled a peanut and tossed the carcass on the floor. "I don't know how I'm expected to build track without the right material," he grumbled.

"Got it." She took the piece of paper and stepped to the telegraph machine. She was so attuned to the sound of the dots and dashes that she could decipher incoming and outgoing messages from across the room.

"Trouble on the site?"

"The usual stuff. Material isn't right. Weather-related problems. People disgruntled because they can't get their mail." He glanced at the empty cooler. "Or root beer."

"No, but it's not so bad." She finished sending the message and turned to console him, but through the window she caught sight of Pauline.

"Oh, dear."

"What?" He stepped up beside her and looked across the street.

"Pauline's in her robe, and it looks as though she's about to burn something."

The wind was hiking the robe's fancy material higher up the woman's spindly legs. Mae focused on the small container sitting on the ground. "Oh, Tom! She has a kerosene can!" No matter how many times she warned Pauline about burning things with flammable liquid, she couldn't break her of the habit.

Tom was out the front door and running before Mae finished speaking. Grabbing the "Closed" sign, Mae hung it on the door, reached for her cloak, and followed him. Wind gusts loosened her hair further, and her cheeks stung from the biting cold. Her heart raced when Pauline slowly pulled a matchstick from the pocket of her robe.

"Pauline! Hold up!" Tom shouted. "Don't light that!"

The old woman was hard of hearing, and the wind carried his voice in the opposite direction anyway, so it was impossible for her to hear Tom's plea. Pausing before the barrel, she struck the match. Mae froze in her track. Pauline was acting as though this were a calm spring day!

Tom arrived just in time to block the move. "Don't do that. The wind's too high to burn today."

"Oh." Pauline glanced around. "Where'd you come from, sonny?" She looked straight at Tom. "They hurt my feet, so I have to burn them." She touched Tom's arm with her hand. "I'm only burning shoes."

A flood of barking dogs arrived, nipping at Tom's pant legs. "Let me take care of this for you another time."

A breathless Mae arrived and wrapped her cloak around the elderly woman. "Pauline, you shouldn't be outside today. I told you I'd burn those shoes."

"Fiddlesticks. I'm not helpless. I can burn them myself."

Mae glanced at Tom. "Is it safe to burn old shoes?"

"I suppose it wouldn't hurt. But right now?"

Pauline took another match from her pocket. "Yes, now."

He peered in the barrel and saw one pair of shoes. He looked up. "Well, if it has to be now, stand back and I'll light the fire."

Mae backed away and Pauline obediently went with her. Moving the kerosene can well out of the way, Tom struck a match and tossed it into the barrel. A flash — and then a roaring *whoosh* erupted. Yelping dogs scattered, and Tom staggered backward, throwing up a protective arm as flames from the barrel shot ten feet high.

"Oh my!" Heat seared Mae's face. "Pauline, you didn't already put kerosene on the shoes, did you?" She'd only been carrying the can when Mae spotted her.

Pauline nodded. "I emptied one can and went back for another. I figured it'd take one can for each shoe."

Mae focused on Tom, who dropped and rolled in the snow. She must have spotted Pauline when she was returning with the second can. After this experience, Tom would surely rue the day he came to Dwadlo. She bent to stare at him. "Are you all right?"

"I'll be fine." Sitting up, he smothered the last bit of flame on his clothing. "Take care of Pauline, Mae. I'll meet you back at the store."

Poor Tom. She took Pauline into her house and quickly settled her before hurrying back to the store. When she entered, she found Tom perched on the barrel she'd sat on earlier.

"Just look at you! It's a wonder you weren't killed." Mae disappeared behind the counter to fetch a clean cloth, a pitcher of water, and some ointment, and then she walked back to Tom. She wet the cloth and carefully washed the soot off his face, looking for wounds as she wiped his brow, nose, cheeks, and chin.

"How bad is it?"

"Well, your eyebrows and lashes will grow back, and so will the front of your hair." She shook her head. "You may have to wear it short for a while."

"Great. How many cans did she dump on that fire?"

"Only one full one. She was coming back with the second one when I saw her. Hold still."

He gritted his teeth while she finished wiping off his face. "Your skin is red from heat exposure, but fortunately you're not badly burned."

Tom looked down at his clothes and pointed to the holes in his jacket. "You call this lucky?"

"I am so sorry. I've warned her at least a hundred times not to burn things, especially when it's windy." Mae pitched the dirty cloth on the counter and applied ointment to his face. Then she brushed the singed fabric, some of it falling to the floor like paper. "I'll get you a new coat."

"It's fine. There are only a few holes in it."

"No. I'll get you a new jacket. We received a shipment in before the train derailed."

Pushing away from her, he stood. "I have another coat, Mae. Where are my cheese and crackers?"

She wrapped up the crackers and thrust the two packages into his hand. As he carefully put his hat on his head, she held back a chuckle. He looked funny with singed brows and lashes. Then she sobered. He could have been seriously hurt. "I hope the rest of your day is more agreeable."

She winced when he slammed the front door on his way out. Well, at least she had been pleasant. She started back to work but couldn't get him off her mind. *Thank You, Lord, for preventing Tom from being badly burned.*

The door opened and Pauline came in. Dressed in a warm coat and boots, she walked to the pickle barrel and helped herself.

"Everything fine now?" Mae was pleased the woman was finally dressed properly for the time of year.

286

"Fine as frog hairs." She bit into the pickle. "I was sitting over there thinking about my kin."

Nodding, Mae said softly, "Tom's a good man."

"He is, isn't he? I'd never have gotten that pen built if it wasn't for you two."

Smiling, Mae made a notation in her postal record. "I just hope you learned your lesson not to burn on windy days."

Crunching on her pickle, Pauline made a sour face that made Mae want to laugh.

"Yes . . . a good man. Can I tell you something that might upset you?"

"Of course." Mae closed the book and went to join her. "What would you like to tell me?"

"Well, like I said, I was sitting over at my house and thinking real hard, and it suddenly came like a light in the night."

"What came to you?"

"Tom."

"Tom stopped by?" Unlikely, since he was a tad bit hot under the collar when he had left the store earlier.

"No, he didn't stop by. I meant that I suddenly remembered him."

"You do!" Mae sprang to her feet. "That's wonderful! Which side — do you recall?

Does he belong on your mother's or father's side?"

"Neither one."

Mae's heart nearly stopped beating. "That isn't possible, Pauline. He has to belong to one side or the other."

"No, he doesn't. Just like I told him and you, I don't have kin. Tom's that young scoundrel who was with the railroad official nosing around years back. The one who wanted to buy up my property and turn it into a train station."

TWENTY-FOUR

Sinking to the bench, Mae tried to absorb the stunning revelation. Tom wasn't Pauline's kin? He'd made the long trip to Dwadlo, suffered numerous indignities, not to mention he didn't have many eyelashes left, just to pacify both her and Pauline when all along he'd been right? Or was the old woman in another world again? *Oh, please, let that be the explanation.* "Pauline? What day is this?"

"Friday."

"When were you born?"

"September 7, 1800."

Bending closer, Mae asked, "What did you have for breakfast this morning?"

"Two eggs and turnip greens."

She took a deep breath. Pauline's eccentric eating habits put a kink in the questioning. It was quite possible she'd eaten turnip greens and eggs for breakfast. "Oh, Pauline."

The old woman nodded. "Thought this might put a crook in your bustle."

Crook in her bustle? The news would blow her bustle sky-high if she'd been wearing one. How could she tell Tom about the mistake? How could she not? He'd invested nearly two weeks of his time in Dwadlo, North Dakota, and for what? He'd endured Dale's difficult company for twelve long nights, fought off a pack of dogs daily, joined with people he didn't know to lay temporary track . . . But if what Pauline said was true, why hadn't he recognized her? Or, for that matter, the town?

The elderly woman finished the pickle and licked her fingers. "It's a real shame he ain't kin. I like that feller. He growed up good. Must have come from fine stock — even if he does work for the railroad. I could overlook that." She spotted the ring on Mae's third finger. "Jake finally proposed?"

Absently nodding, Mae still sat in stunned silence.

"Well, I like him too. He's about as exciting as watching grass grow, but he's a good man." She stood up. "Not as good as Tom, but then I guess that's water over the dam."

The door closed a moment later, and Mae slumped to her side on the bench. Staring at the ceiling, she let the news penetrate.

Tom Curtis had been right. Pauline wasn't his kin. How was she supposed to tell him Pauline now knew the truth without looking like an utter fool? The telegraph machine came to life, and she slowly got up off the bench and walked over to it, deciphering the erratic clicks.

RAIL TO ARRIVE THIS AFTERNOON STOP TRACK MUST NOW BE COMPLETED BY TUESDAY STOP CAN YOU SMELL TWO THOUSAND HERRING STOP

Tuesday? Wednesday would have been hard short of a miracle, but Tom couldn't possibly meet the new deadline. Drat that Joanne and her fancy wedding. Thunder rolled in the distance. *Lord, please, not thunder snow again.* Mae grabbed the telegram and then slipped on her heavy cloak. Tom needed more help than he had. Picking up the "Closed" sign again, she hung it on the door, locked up, and hurried down the steps. A stiff north wind caught her wrap, and she drew it closer around her. With each adventurous soul she passed, she paused to beg for their assistance in getting the track laid.

Mr. Mango drew his ear horn into place. "Eh?"

"Can you possibly help at the wreck site? Anything would be of benefit!" she yelled above the rising wind.

"Eh?" He bent closer.

"Go tell everyone who can spare a moment to come help!"

"Milk?"

"HELP! THE TRACK HAS TO BE FINISHED BY TUESDAY! JOANNE NEEDS HER HERRING!"

"I KNOW MY HEARING'S NOT WORTH A HOOT!"

"HERRING. FISH! FOR JOANNE'S WEDDING!"

He looked at her as though she was the one with the hearing impairment. "Don't know as I could fish in this weather, but I'll wander down that way."

"GO TO THE WRECK SITE, MR. MANGO! AND PLEASE TAKE ANYONE YOU SEE WITH YOU. THIS IS AN EMERGENCY!"

Nodding, he braced his spindly frame against a heavy gust and set off. Mae continued, knocking on every door she came to and begging for help along the way. If the new track would be here by this afternoon, and enough women could help, they might make the Tuesday deadline. She owed Tom that much — at least that much.

Arriving at the site, she took stock of the dogs tied everywhere she looked. Jeremy was huddled deep in his coat, the familiar rope strips tied around his waist. Dogs yapped and strained to the ends of their leashes when her small party arrived. Seven women had agreed to drop what they were doing and leave their older children to cook the evening meal and care for their younger siblings in order to work.

Taking hold of one another's hands, they formed a circle and Mae led them in prayer. "Gracious Father, permit our hands and bodies to do men's work. Our flesh is willing to help, and we pray for Your blessing on the enormous task set before us."

The dark winter clouds held off, offering an occasional snowflake as a reminder that a blizzard could happen at any time. It was still winter in Dwadlo.

Mae caught Tom's eye as the recruited women approached him. He left the salvage area and walked over to her. She handed him the telegram, saying, "We're here to help."

He scanned the message and his jaw firmed. "They have to be kidding! We haven't even started laying track yet. Wednesday was going to be hard enough, but this will be close to impossible."

"I know, but Joanne's herring is in danger of spoiling."

Wadding the paper in his hand, he grimaced. "I have a pack of edgy travelers needing rail service, but my job is to get the rail down so Joanne Small can have two thousand herring for her wedding reception?"

The plan did sound impractical. Mae stepped closer in order to be heard above the whistling wind. "I thought you'd need extra help, so I brought a few friends with me." She watched Tom's gaze move to the small huddle of women, shivering in the blustery cold front.

"That's my new crew?"

She nodded. "I can drive a spike. We all can."

His gaze shifted back to the pitiful sight of shivering women. "Really."

"Well, they say they can. Actually, we've never been called to do such a thing, but I'm sure we can help if you tell us what to do."

Tom pulled the collar of his coat up higher. "If the shipment is here late afternoon, I'd appreciate all the help I can get for the night, but in order for you ladies to survive the cold you need to have on warmer clothes. Some of your husband's long-johns and trousers would work. Thick socks for your feet in sturdy boots. When it's time, I'll put you all to work."

"Thank you." Mae flashed a smile and then sobered. She had to tell him about Pauline's revelation. But timing was everything, wasn't it? Any fool could see that he'd had all the bad news he needed today. She'd tell him later. The minute she returned to the site this evening she would take him aside and clear the air. She wouldn't mislead him another day. He'd been kind beyond words, but his duty in Dwadlo was over, as far as Pauline was concerned.

And her duty was clear. She and Jake would care for Pauline until the Lord took her home.

Late that afternoon Mae opened the trunk where she stored Pa's clothing and located the needed items. The engagement ring caught her eye and she took it off, placing it carefully in her top dresser drawer. Nailing spikes might further damage the heirloom, and she couldn't risk that. She quickly changed her clothes and refastened her hair in a tight knot.

As the last of the hairpins went in, she heard Jake's buggy pull up and her breath caught. She'd forgotten she'd agreed to see him again tonight. She whirled in a circle. Jeremy was still out at the site working with Tom, carrying supplies to the men, so there was no pot of bubbling stew or chicken and dumplings on the stove. She hurried to answer Jake's knock at the door. Her fiancé's eyes coolly swept her masculine attire.

"Mae?"

"Oh, Jake." She moved aside to allow him to step into the room's warmth. "I'm sorry. It completely slipped my mind that you were coming tonight."

Removing his hat, he dusted a light coating of snow off the brim. "You're having more than your fair share of memory loss these days. I went by Dale's first and you weren't there, so I assumed you were here."

A blush crept up her neck as she fussed with the front of her father's shirt. "I'm sorry. It's been a rather hectic week."

"And that would explain your choice of dress?"

"I was on my way to help at the work site. The track must be finished by Tuesday —"

He squinted at her. "The work site?"

"Where they're laying track, Jake. Joanne Small's herring can't arrive until it's repaired."

"Herring?"

"Yes, herring for her wedding, and time is

of the essence —"

"I don't care about any debutante's wedding."

No, all he cared about was that chicken and dumplings weren't sitting on the table waiting for him. Couldn't he see, as a concerned citizen, that he should pitch in and help? His workload couldn't be that heavy. Removing his cashmere coat, he draped it over the back of the sofa, carefully smoothing the creases.

"Then it's fortunate I arrived when I did. Run along and change your clothing. Surely you can find something for us to eat." He walked to his usual chair in front of the fireplace and sat down, crossing one well-creased pant leg over the other.

Mae turned and went toward the bedroom, resentment churning in the pit of her stomach. She didn't want to spend the evening eating and then watching Jake doze. She wanted to be in the middle of the action. Plus, it was the least she could do after asking the other women to drop their responsibilities to help with the work. And she had to tell Tom the truth about Pauline. Until the words were out of her mouth and off her conscience, she couldn't rest.

An ache started to wind tentacles around her heart. Tom would be gone as early as next Thursday. She wasn't certain why that knowledge hurt so badly, but she was torn. Jake should be her concern, not Tom.

Forgive me, Father. You've given me a wise and patient man. Help me to appreciate Jake's good qualities more, because he has them. Anyone would testify that he is usually the first to help in times of trouble, so I can't understand why he's turned a blind eye to this dilemma.

Actually she knew why. Tom threatened Jake's security, and Jake didn't like the feeling, but he had no valid concerns. Tom had been a perfect gentleman, but his personality differed vastly from Jake's serious demeanor. Jake needed to bend, and Tom needed to settle down.

She returned to Jake. "I think we should both go to the work site and help. I'll pack some sandwiches, and there's coffee there."

His humorless chuckle rankled her.

"In this weather? You're out of your mind."

"It's cold, Jake, but we can dress warmly."

"No, thank you. Run along now, Mae. I'm hungry. A nice T-bone will do — with a few boiled potatoes."

Turning around, Mae started a second time toward the bedroom to change her clothing, anger working its way up her throat until she couldn't breathe. This wasn't fair. He could relent for once and drop his snobbish attitude. She would enjoy a nice thick steak and potatoes too, but she'd promised her friends and Tom that she would help. Closing the bedroom door with a snap, she yanked off the heavy coat and began to unbutton her shirt. But as fast as she undid the buttons, she refastened them.

The other women would be waiting for her. Women whose husbands had worked tirelessly since the accident. They'd been living on cold sandwiches and pots of black coffee. How dare Jake make her cook while others served in a time of need!

Her hands paused, and she focused on the window. If Jake was hungry, the fire in the stove was hot. He could cook his own steak.

Putting the heavy coat back on, she picked up the lantern, tiptoed to the window, and slowly eased it open. Frigid air whipped the thin curtains against the sill.

In a flash she'd gone through the opening, closed the window, and struck off for Pauline's house. Surely she would have something to make sandwiches out of.

The older woman barely cracked the door open when Mae knocked. "It's me, Pauline." Mae glanced across the way and saw that her house was still quiet. Jake wasn't aware yet that she'd left. "Let me in." The door opened wider and she slipped inside.

"What's going on?" Pauline asked as she shut the door.

"I need to make a few sandwiches."

"I have egg salad."

Mae's stomach churned. She'd eaten Pauline's egg salad before, but it would have to do. "Fine. I need three sandwiches. Let's make them large ones."

The women set to work. A few minutes later, Mae eased out the front door and set off for the work site carrying a picnic basket containing the sandwiches, two apples, and two pieces of raisin pie. Light snow sifted down in flakes so tiny she couldn't decide if she was walking through snow or mist. Either way, the weather was cold and miserable.

However, work continued full force when she arrived at the lantern-lit site. Men and women worked side by side. Husband and wife, brother and sister. The heartwarming picture affected Mae deeply, and she blinked back uncharacteristic tears. She was proud of her town, proud of Dwadlo's close community ties. Through watery eyes she spotted Tom standing knee-deep in muddy snow, inspecting heavy creosote ties. His frosty breath created white vapors as he called out orders to the crew. The very way he took command — his self-assurance without an air of superiority, his gentle but firm way of dealing with people — did something to her heart.

God, if You sent him here for a purpose, why now? What am I supposed to do? I love Jake . . . Her thoughts stalled. Did she? Did she really love Jake? If she wanted a good home for Jeremy and Pauline, then yes, she loved Jake enough to marry him, but if she wanted to wake up each morning to warm kisses and the giddy expectancy of a new day with a man who made her feel young and invincible, then marrying Jake would be merely settling.

Marrying him would be forfeiting an exciting, loved-filled life for one that would be lived his way. Everything would be about Jake. Would that mean that Mae Wilkey would cease to exist? She'd be only the lawyer's wife, never a woman with her own mind or thoughts again. It would be so much less than she wanted — or deserved.

The answer was suddenly clear. She loved Jake, but not the way she should. The mutual affection they shared was good, and it might last a lifetime, yet did she want to settle for a lifelong friendship when it was

deep love and affection she longed for?
Would that be fair to Jake or herself?

Twenty-Five

Her unsettling thoughts lay heavy in Mae's heart as she set the wicker basket on a makeshift table. She walked over to Fisk and asked, "Where do I start?"

Minutes turned into hours. The sounds of steel hitting steel filled the snowy night air. Lil made a steady rotation with the coffee pot, serving up the black steaming liquid by the gallons. Mae watched her friend pause in front of Fisk.

"I suppose you want another cup. It's your fifth."

"Just fill the cup, Lil. I don't need you keeping track of how much coffee I drink. It's none of your doin'."

Mae laughed to herself when Lil silently mimicked his words. Fisk turned and stared at her. "You say something?"

"No, sir. Just pouring your coffee." Lil tipped the pot and filled the cup to the rim.

He eyed the exaggerated level. "You did

that on purpose. I can't pick up the cup without spilling it."

"I did?" She tipped the pot and added a few more drops.

When Fisk sprang to his feet, Mae intervened. "Children. Must I send you to your rooms?"

"Be fine with me." Lil glanced at Mae. "I'm freezing my socks off out here." She moved on, politely filling all the workers' cups to the proper level.

Ever so slowly, the tracks began to take shape.

Close to three in the morning, Mae took a break. Her back ached from bending, and she couldn't feel her hands or feet anymore. She found the picnic basket and hunted Tom down. He needed to stop and eat.

"There's still a lot of track to finish before Tuesday." Even so, he followed her to the locomotive.

"Folks have to eat."

Tom had set the shifts to four-hour periods because of the extreme cold. Mae had taken a break earlier, but she knew he hadn't. He'd been working almost twenty-four hours straight. The effort was going around the clock. While some men worked, others would sleep so the work never ceased.

"I'm almost too cold to be hungry." He found a place to sit and motioned for her to join him. She unwrapped a sandwich and handed it to him. He took a bite, pulled the sandwich back, studied it, and then brought it again to his mouth.

"What's wrong? Isn't it good?" She probably should have warned him Pauline made the sandwiches, especially as she tended to get her ingredients mixed up.

"It's okay."

Mae bit into her sandwich, pleasantly pleased with the taste. Pauline had done a good job this time. The eggs actually looked and tasted like something that came from a hen.

"In fact, it's good," he amended, wolfing the first half down.

Eating in companionable silence, Mae gave in to exhaustion. She wanted to tell him about Pauline's shattering revelation, but words failed her. Lack of sleep and bone-numbing cold stole her courage. Her life had been so simple a week and a half ago. Impregnable. Contented. She studied Tom's features from the corner of her eye. Why him? Why had he come along now? A couple of years ago she could have done something about her need for him. Why was the need suddenly eating her alive?

"Mae?"

Startled, she focused on her half-eaten meal. "Yes?"

"I'll be leaving Thursday."

Hammering noises faded into the icy distance and silence settled around her. There was a strange ringing in her ears, and her stomach suddenly felt sick. "I thought as much." When he turned to focus on her, she intentionally avoided his eyes. She couldn't cry in front of him, not when she had accepted another man's ring. Her empty finger reminded her of the token of Jake's love that she'd left in the dresser drawer.

She couldn't go back on her answer to Jake. Her father taught her that a person's word was their honor, yet marrying one man and being in love with another hardly seemed honorable.

Would she do God a disservice by carrying on the charade? Wasn't it possible that once Tom left she'd settle down and realize that what she was starting to feel for him was purely fascination? New man in town. Single man from a big city. Warm, fun to be around. Sighing, she looked at his handsome face and admitted softly, "I'll miss you."

"I'll miss you too."

His response came back so quietly she barely heard the words that washed over her. Jake was the only man who'd ever courted her. She didn't know this frenzied feeling that raced through her blood like lightning had even existed until now. And she had to ruin the moment. He needed to know he was right, that though her intentions were pure, she'd brought him here needlessly.

His voice broke through her thoughts. "You think Jake will marry you soon?"

Surprised by the question, she sat up straighter. Did she think Jake would marry her soon? Though not intended, he made it sound like a kindhearted concession. Tom never spoke about Jake unless he was picking on her. "I don't know. As I told you before, Jake wants to take a little time —"

"That doesn't concern you?"

"I thought it would." She shook her head. "Oddly enough, I'm also in no hurry to marry."

"To marry — or to marry Jake?"

Anger flared. "Why would you ask me such a thing?" She both liked and disliked his unpredictable nature. Even if the unthinkable would happen, and he would express feelings for her, they'd make a terrible couple. She wasn't proud of her stubborn side, and he sure had his own mule-headed moments. They would be Fisk and Lil all over again. But it didn't really matter. He was leaving and she wasn't. Why beat the subject to death?

"Why can't you answer me?"

"Because . . . it's obvious. I've waited six long years for that man to propose."

"And now that he finally got around to it, you feel you've reached your goal — but wait. Is marrying Jake still your goal?"

Her head whirled from the interrogation. She was relentlessly pursuing the same idiotic questions, but he had no right to doubt her intentions. He would get on a train Thursday morning and be out of her life with a turn of wheels, while she would remain here and marry a good, solid provider.

It seemed she was more in love with the idea of marriage than marrying Jake and loving him as a husband. Who made the better choice? Tom would go home to a small room in a house that wasn't his. She would marry Jake, and eventually they would build the nicest, biggest home in town — which wouldn't take much. Two stories would be a mansion in Dwadlo. Hopes of Tom remaining here, marrying her, and forming a family with her — a loving, caring, and devoted family that included Jeremy and Pauline — vanished like her breath in the cold air.

"Tom, are you asking me not to marry Jake?" There, she'd put the problem — if one existed — back on him.

Resting his head on the back of the locomotive, he answered with his eyes shut. "What if I am?"

"*Are* you?" Mae held her breath.

He sat up straight and opened his eyes. "I can't ask you not to marry Jake, Mae. You accepted his proposal and his ring. I was just wondering if that's still your goal in life."

She didn't know how to answer. She'd never been more confused. What was her goal? At the moment she had no idea. She remained silent.

"That's all the answer I need. I guess right now all we have left to talk about is Pauline. I don't plan to desert her. I suppose after all that I'll have to take her to Chicago with me. You, Jake, and Jeremy can have your lives here in Dwadlo. As badly as I hate to say this, Jake's all right. He'll take care of you and Jeremy and provide everything you'll ever need. I'll warn you right now that he'll get rid of the dogs and cats, but I suppose you can live with that even though it will upset Pauline."

His concessions offered little consolation. She knew Jake was basically a decent man. Yet she also suspected he would dispose of the animals swiftly. Why had it taken a silly ring to bring out her true feelings? She met Tom's gaze. "I know you would never desert Pauline. You've been good to her, Tom. So very good, and I thank you for that from the bottom of my heart."

"Isn't that what kin does? Takes care of one another?"

"About that —"

"Tom!" Fisk yelled. "We got a problem over here!"

Setting his hat more firmly on his head, he dumped the remains of his coffee into the snow and then rose to his feet. "It'll be a miracle if we get this track down by the deadline."

Then he was gone. She hadn't had time to tell him about Pauline. A missed opportunity, but perhaps a mixed blessing. For the remainder of the night, he'd still look upon her kindly.

Darkness gradually faded into a cold dawn. Tom sent the late shift home to sleep, and a fresh crew set to work. In the daylight it was easy to see obvious progress, which boosted morale, and the workers sang as they worked.

Mae returned to town and unlocked, the store around seven. Since the accident her whole schedule had been off. The woodstove that sat in the corner burned bright, so Dale must have come back to stoke it and make the pot of coffee that scented the air. She paused and warmed her hands and feet. The night at the site was the coldest she'd ever spent. As tired as she was, she thought she'd be able to accommodate the few customers expected today, as most everyone was either asleep from the night shift or working at the site.

The telegraph machine started to click. She ran around the counter and into the cage to receive the message.

SENDING TRAIN EARLY STOP HERRING MUST BE THERE ON TIME STOP WILL WAIT AT TEMPORARY SITE STOP

Shaking her head, she walked to the machine and wrote down the message. Poor Tom. The railroad wouldn't let up on him. He was working as hard and as fast he could.

She turned when the front door opened and saw that Tom was there. Striding to the stove, he warmed his hands. She shoved the telegram into her pocket, grabbed two clean mugs, and joined him. "A wire just came in for you." She set the mugs down and poured fresh coffee into them.

He picked one up, frowning. "From the railroad, I'm sure."

"I'm afraid so." She removed the piece of paper from her pocket and handed it to him.

He scanned the message, his eyes narrowing. "They can't be serious."

"Seems they don't know what to do with the herring."

"Clive is getting nervous. He doesn't want to be stuck with all that fish."

"You can't blame him." She took a sip of her coffee and watched him as he mulled over what she'd said.

"True, but as hard as we've worked, we still won't have that rail laid until late Wednesday evening."

She wrapped her hands around the warm mug. "Then there's nothing to worry about. We'll post a notice saying that the station will reopen no later than Thursday morning. The herring can be delivered, you can return to your job in Chicago, and I —"

"Will marry Jake."

Twenty-Six

Mae set her cup on a stool beside the stove where it would stay warm. "If you'll excuse me, I need to talk to Jeremy and then get back to work."

"Whoa." Tom stopped her. "You're not going back to work until you've had some rest."

"But there's still so much to do," she protested when he took her arm and pointed her to Dale's quarters in the back.

"Get some sleep, Mae. I'll be back around two and you can spell me."

She doubted his intent. He would work until he dropped. "Only if you promise to rest while I work."

"I promise."

Turning back to argue with him, she met his broad chest. A firm, unyielding wall that smelled of creosote and cold air. He put his hands on her arms to steady her. Slowly lifting her eyes, she locked gazes with him. For a moment the air left her lungs. He was so . . . Tom. So real. Butterflies leaped with joy in her stomach. What if he were the one God intended for her? What if she allowed a young girl's fantasy to sway the future? His gaze refused to leave hers. The store's warmth threatened to overcome her.

They were still locked in a silent duel when Jeremy appeared, pulling on his coat. Stepping back quickly, Mae murmured, "I'll put on a pot of stew before I lay down, Jeremy."

"Okay." The boy grinned. "Hello, Tom Curtis."

Nodding, Tom returned a greeting.

"Can I walk to work with you?" Jeremy patted the hemp tied to his waist. "First, though, I'll have to cut more rope."

Jeremy opened the door and Tom started to follow him out.

"Tom?" Mae watched him turn toward her and her breath caught in her throat. "Before you go, could I speak with you?" Suddenly she felt as though not another minute could pass without her telling him about Pauline.

"Jeremy, you get the rope and I'll catch up with you." Nodding, the boy closed the door. Tom turned to her. "What is it?"

Oh, dear God, grant me the strength to do

this. "There's something that you need to know."

"Okay. Shoot."

"It's about Pauline —"

He sighed. "Can't it wait, Mae? One crisis at a time, if you don't mind."

"No, it can't wait, and didn't you say the only thing we had left to talk about was Pauline?"

"Fine. What is it you need to tell me?"

"You know when you insisted — still insist — that Pauline isn't your kin?"

His nod did little to calm her.

"Well . . . you're correct."

His ruddy features turned vacant and his eyes registered a question.

"That's right, Tom. She's not your aunt. She had a rare lucid moment yesterday, and she recalled exactly how your name and address happened to be written on a piece of paper in her desk drawer. The piece I found and mistakenly assumed from its presence that you were kin."

She waited for him to say something . . . anything. Instead he stood straight, his gaze on her. His features held a totally surprised expression, but she wasn't sure if he wanted to celebrate or strangle her.

"I'm so sorry. I can't justify my mistake. I should have investigated further, but I was desperate —"

"Mae, I know that. Just tell me what she remembered."

"It appears that you were here as a boy. You came with the railroad official who was sent to purchase Pauline's property some years back." Relief left her like air from a pricked balloon. There. He knew, and he couldn't flee this moment because he had to finish the train track or be stuck with a bunch of herring neither he nor the railroad wanted.

It seemed every word struck him like a blunt force. She watched the play of emotions cross his features. Uncertainty. Disbelief. Then the one she feared most. Disdain.

"You brought me all the way here to take care of a woman I didn't know? Someone I had never laid eyes on?"

"Well, that's not true. You had met her. Don't you remember?"

"No, I don't remember!" He shook his head. "Honestly, if I did, do you think I'd have stuck around here, fought off dogs and cats, rode the countryside looking for a home for my 'aunt,' put up with Dale day and night, night and day —" His tone took an ominous drop. "Singed off my eyebrows and hair trying to prevent a woman I didn't know from harm?"

"I . . . think you would." She nodded, her fear dissipating. He was furious, and he had every right to be, but truthfully he was as much to blame as she was. "Are you telling me that *nothing* ever looked familiar to you? Not a single tree, bush, or house? When you apparently walked this woman's property line, helped survey the town — even witnessed when that railroad man bought other property from one of Dwadlo's citizens?"

A light flashed in his eyes. Was it recognition? Mae could only hope Pauline was right in her recollection of what had happened all those years ago.

"Wait . . . that empty building across from the railroad station, did that used to be a saloon?"

"Yes."

"I remember." He smiled. "I remember!"

Her heart soared when he picked her up and twirled her around. She matched his laughter and didn't want the moment to end, but seconds later he set her feet back on the floor.

"I thought there was something familiar when I stepped off the train, but I have seen so many places I ignored the feeling. I was just a kid when we came here. My boss was the official who did all the negotiating. I was here to run his errands, take care of his horse, and get his drinks when he wanted them. The room where we stayed was in the back of that saloon."

"Then how did your name get on that paper in her desk?"

"The old man gave it to her so she could contact me if she changed her mind. He didn't want to have to deal with her. Mae, I want you to know that not for a minute have I been certain that Pauline was kin. As a matter of fact, I never believed she was my aunt."

"Then why did you stay?" The answer begged for more than a simple "Because you asked." Was he good enough to interrupt his life for a complete stranger, or was there something more?

Red-faced, he shrugged and turned away. Why was he upset all of a sudden? Crossing her arms, she waited, aware that somehow she had put him on the defense.

"If you don't know, I'm not going to tell you." Turning on his heel, he walked out, slamming the door behind him.

"What's eatin' him?" Lil asked, reaching in the peanut barrel and watching as Tom stalked off down the street. "He 'bout blew me off my feet when I came in."

"He's upset. And he has good reason to be."

"Track work going too slow?"

"No. Pauline isn't his kin." If she read what Tom had said correctly, she was the reason he'd stayed, but she couldn't tell Lil that. Then again, she could be wrong. He hadn't exactly given her his reason in so many words.

Lil spit out a shell. "Say that again?"

"She's not his kin." Sinking to the bench, Mae bit her lower lip. "I've done a terrible thing, Lil. I brought him here under false pretense."

"How so?"

"I made him believe Pauline was family and he had to assume her care. So he made the trip to Dwadlo."

"And what did he say when he met her?"

"That she wasn't related to him."

"So he knew. What's your point?"

"I kept insisting that she was his aunt and he kept denying it. I thought I had finally convinced him. I made him feel so obligated that he could do nothing less than find the poor woman a home."

"Which he hasn't."

"Not for not trying. He's searched high and low, but he can't perform a miracle. He even agreed to take her back to Chicago with him."

Lil shelled another peanut. "That's your trouble, Mae. So you made a mistake. It's not the end of the world. You were doing a good deed and so was he. Regardless of whether she's either one of your kin, she's old and on her own. Someone has to take care of her."

"Someone will." Mae sighed. "Jake and I will take her in."

"You think?"

"Of course I think," Mae snapped. Lil's tone suggested she knew Jake would object, which he would, but that would be a condition to marrying Mae. Truth be known, Pauline was too old to go to Chicago. Mae wondered what she had been thinking when she'd suggested it in the first place.

"My dear Mae, friend of my heart — you don't know men."

"And you do?"

"I shore do. Like the back of my chapped hand."

"You think pouring a man's coffee cup to the brim so that he can't drink it without spilling it is gaining you favor in Fisk's eyes?"

"No, nothing will make me look good in his eyes, but it gives me great pleasure to annoy him."

"That's your basis for a strong marriage? Annoyance?"

"Me annoying that man has nothing to do with marriage. Life is what it is. I don't make the rules."

"Lil." Mae shook her head. "You should seriously have a stern talk with yourself."

"I have and I don't like the company. I see a hog farmer getting older and fatter every year. I'm losing my youth, Mae. My skin ain't soft no more, my hair don't shine like fire in the sunlight, my steps are slower, and when I look at myself in the looking glass, I'm not sure where the ol' spit-and-fire Lil went."

"She's still here, feisty as ever." Mae leaned toward her friend and hugged her neck. "You're not an old hog farmer. You're a lovely woman who could do with more frequent baths. Your hair still shines if it doesn't have dirt and other things in it, which it does more often than not. You're not as thin as a candlestick, but you're far from fat. You'd give a person the shirt off your back, you know your Bible, though you don't practice your knowledge half as often as you should, and you are a good person." She refused to mention housekeeping, cooking, and choice of dress. She'd stick with the positive. "Any man should be proud to have you."

"I eat too much of my product."

Laughing, Mae marched her over to the new dresses. "Perhaps if you tried a little harder and bought this." She picked up a pretty blue dress. "Fisk might open his eyes and see a loving woman instead of a shrill who threatens his manhood."

"You think so?" Lil eyed the dress thoughtfully and then turned. "Humph! That's about as likely as Fisk getting to drive a locomotive someday."

"God has given you faith, Lil. Now use it." It wasn't that hard to figure out when it came to someone else's life, so why was she having such a hard time with her own?

TWENTY-SEVEN

The sound of the clicking telegraph machine woke Mae from a sound sleep. She hurriedly sat up and realized she'd been so exhausted that she'd fallen asleep on the bench in the store. Her joints, stiff from lying on a hard surface for too long, forced her to move, and she managed to get to the cage in time to transcribe the incoming message. Her heart jumped into her throat at the words.

RUNAWAY TRAIN HEADED FOR DWADLO STOP FULL SPEED STOP TROTTLE STUCK STOP

She had to get the message to Tom immediately! Grabbing her cloak, she flew out the door and ran toward the work site, telegram in hand.

Though her boots skimmed over the snow-covered ground and she could barely catch her breath, she tried to run faster. The town of Dwadlo and its residents' lives depended on her. Cold air burning her lungs, she pushed on until she finally she had to slow down.

As the workers came into view she picked up her pace once again. When she thought she was within ear shot she yelled, "Tom! Tom!" He glanced up and she waved the piece of paper. In the blink of an eye she stumbled and felt her ankle twist. Pain shot up her left leg and the next instant she was lying in the snow. Footsteps approached and she looked up to see Tom.

He knelt down beside her and pulled her into his arms. "Mae, are you all right?"

"My ankle. I twisted it."

"Okay, just relax. Can you move it?"

She wiggled it around. "Yes. I don't think it's broken."

"Can you stand on it?"

"I think so." She felt that with his help, she might be able to do anything. He assisted her to a standing position, and she gingerly tried to apply weight to the injury. "Ouch!"

He picked her up in his arms and carried her back to the work site. "What in the name of good sense are you doing running out here like that, anyway?" He sat her on the back of a wagon.

She handed him the scrunched-up piece of paper. "There's a runaway train." The color drained from his face as she watched him read the message.

"Lord, have mercy on us." He met her gaze. "I'll have someone take you back to town while I try to figure out what we need to do next."

Two hours passed. Safe and warm in the store again, Mae hobbled back and forth, pacing the floor and sending worried glances at the lengthening shadows. Her ankle throbbed like the dickens. She knew she should sit down and put up her foot, but she was too restless. Time was growing short. Would Tom be able to stop the train? Had he decided to ride the distance on horseback to meet it? Had he left already? She wanted to speak with him one last time and watch the way his eyes crinkled at the corners. If something happened to him, she might never see him again.

Tears rolled down her cheeks. She wanted to pray, but she didn't know what to ask God for at the moment. Anything was better than nothing. *Dear God, please protect Dwadlo from harm, and please keep Tom safe as well. He has a special place in my heart and always will.*

Her eye caught Fisk riding past the store. Flinging open the front door, she called, "Fisk!" He trotted on and her heart sank. Placing two fingertips to her lips, she whistled. The shrill sound carried and he pulled back on the reins. Reining his horse around, he headed back to the store. "Miss Mae?"

"I need a ride out to the work site. I need to see Tom." His eyes traveled to her stocking feet and coatless attire. "Give me a second to put my coat and boots on."

"It's mighty cold, ma'am, and there's not a thing you can do. You'd best be packing up a few things and getting ready to move your valuables to safety."

"Where's Tom?"

"I'm not sure where he is at the moment. When I left he was making his plan."

Expectancy filled her heart. "Then he has one?"

"He didn't at the time. It's mighty hard to stop an object that size when she has a will of her own."

"Please wait for me, Fisk." He nodded and she limped back into the store, gingerly put on her boots, and wrapped her cloak tightly around her. She hurried as fast as she could down the steps to where he waited. "You'll have to help me up." The wind squalled like an unruly child.

He extended a gloved hand and effortlessly lifted her. "Tom's not gonna like this."

"I know, but there's not much he can do to stop me."

"Yeah, well he's getting used to things going wrong around here."

"You're a good friend, Fisk." She settled behind him. "I'm ready." Ready? No one could possibly be ready for an event that might change everything forever. A second derailment was unthinkable. This time all could be lost.

Mae was amazed when she spotted the workers feverishly laying track. Esau lumbered through the crowd carrying heavy rail with Lil on his back. Elation surged. The needed track appeared to be close to completion, but not close enough. She spotted Tom's black-and-red checked coat and waved.

Pitching some tools aside, he went to meet her. "What are you doing here?" He helped her off the back of the horse. "Why are you on that ankle?"

"It's better." He had a questioning look on his face, and she longed to touch his cheek. "I'm sorry. I couldn't sit still another moment longer." Her gaze took in the heightened activity. "Are we going to make it?"

Shaking his head, he stepped back. "No. Dwadlo folks would have made the Tuesday deadline. They are loyal, hardworking people, but no one planned on a runaway. I'm not sure how far out it is, but I need to get there fast. Let's hope God has heard everyone's prayers and I can get the valve working." He turned and spotted Fisk. "You ready?"

Fisk nodded. "I hope you don't expect me to be jumpin' on a runaway." He shook his head, looking at the horse stomping in the snow beside them. "Tom, you're gonna need something faster than that animal. I'll be right back." He rode off.

Tom turned and focused on Mae, putting his arm around her shoulder. "If that throttle stays stuck, she'll plough right through Dwadlo."

The situation was hard to digest. She feared Tom would give his life to save the town. The man was doomed either way he turned. Even with his arm around her, she trembled. So many thoughts raced through her mind. In a matter of minutes Dwadlo could be changed forever. Her life would change.

He dropped his arm from her shoulder, reached out, and took both her gloved hands. "Don't go soft on me now, Mae. I need you."

"But the people . . . do they fully realize . . ." His hands squeezed hers to reassure her, but his gesture did little good. She was still shaking and not from the cold.

"They do. I broke the news and they understand the consequences." Tom glanced up and down the unfinished track. "But most haven't lost hope. I'll do everything in my power to stop the train. In the meantime I need you to gather the folks and get them to a place of safety. Take this horse." Tom handed Mae the reins.

"Take them where?"

"Move them to the river. Even if the train plows through the town, it won't reach that distance. Have Jeremy take the animals from Pauline's and move them to safety. When you're through, there shouldn't be a person or creature within a mile of Dwadlo."

Mae thought of the near frozen river and shivered. He reached up to tuck her coat collar closer. "I hate to ask this of you, but I know I can trust you to get this done."

Their gazes met and held for a moment, and then everything blurred as tears welled in Mae's eyes. "I'm terrified, Tom."

"You have every right to be. I'm scared too." He briefly squeezed her hands again. "Once you get the folks to shelter, have Dale hold a prayer meeting. God's in charge, but I want to make sure He has His full eye on us right now." He turned toward the workers. "Listen up! Mae knows what to do, so follow her. I'm going to go try to stop the train. Understood?"

Mae watched everyone nod their agreement. Could she do this? It wasn't a question. She had to.

Fisk rode up with another horse. "Thanks." Tom reached for the reins. "Ready?"

"Ready as I'll ever be."

Mae reached out, longing to catch Tom's hand one final time, but he was off. He had the weight of the world on his shoulders right now, and his thoughts were on everyone's safety. Her growing feelings for the man made her aware that the ring on her third finger pinched beneath her glove. Against the driving wind she huddled deeper into her cloak, and for what quite possibly could be the last time, she watched him ride off into the distance.

Snow started to fall when Tom urged the mare to a gallop. They had gone one, two, then five miles before he spotted the target and mentally groaned. Fisk came up beside him. The train was running full steam, wooden boxcars swaying on the rail and snow flying in all directions as the runaway plowed its way toward town. A red handkerchief appeared from the engine cab as the driver flagged them. Turning their horses and reaching full gallop, they managed to get close enough to hear the engineer's frantic shouts.

"I can't slow her down, Tom! She had a full firebox when the throttle stuck!"

Keeping pace with the steaming monstrosity, Tom shouted, "Okay, Henry. We're coming aboard!"

Nodding, the engineer turned and yelled to the fireman. "Help 'em up!"

"I'll go first," Tom called to Fisk. "You stay back and board as soon as I'm clear."

Fisk indicated he got the message. Tom's horse raced closer to the steaming machine, and he prepared to make the switch from animal to locomotive. He'd only done this once before, when he was young and dumb. Now he was fully aware he was wagering his life. One bad move and it would all be over.

Waiting for the exact moment, he reached and latched onto the fireman's hand. With his other hand he managed to grab a bar bolted on the outside of the engine. Now. He pushed out of the saddle and clung on the side of the train, struggling to gain his footing. Finally, he steadied himself and the fireman was able to pull him aboard. He slumped to the floor and silently thanked God for his life.

Seconds later the man also had Fisk safely aboard, and Tom knelt before the faulty valve to examine the problem. He tried to work the stuck lever, but it refused to budge.

Fisk shook hands with the engineer and introduced himself. "Thank you, sir, Fisk Jester. Dwadlo's blacksmith."

The engineer nodded. "I shore hope you can do something. The town's coming right up, isn't it?"

"In a few miles."

"Fisk!" Tom yelled.

"Yes?"

"You've always wanted to drive a locomotive, haven't you?" If Tom had learned anything this past couple of weeks, it was the fact that it was Fisk Jester's sole dream to drive one of these steaming rigs.

"Yes, but —"

"Henry, show Fisk the basics and then come help me." Tom focused on the stubborn lever. "We have about three minutes to stop this thing."

Mae drew a deep breath. "Everybody move! Go home, get your loved ones, neighbors, and anyone else you see and head to the river!"

Shovels, rakes, and hammers hit the ground as folks took off running. Nudging the horse over to her little brother, who sat with the tied dogs, she called, "Jeremy, you need to take all of Pauline's animals to the river!"

He shot off the rock and hemp flew. She watched the last of the workers gather their belongings. When she was confident the site was clear, she closed her eyes. *Please, God. Help Tom. Help the town.* She touched the gelding with her heels and galloped off, heading for Pauline's. She had to get the older woman bundled tightly for the cold wait by the frozen water.

As she rode past Jake's office she saw a light in his window. He had to be warned. She stopped at the railing and eased out of the saddle, pain shooting through her left ankle when she applied her weight on it. The few stairs to his office seemed like fifty. Jake glanced up when he saw her standing in the doorway.

"Hello, dear. I didn't expect to see you

today, especially after you snuck out on me last night."

He had a good reason to frown at her, but she couldn't worry about that now. "I came to warn you that a runaway train is headed toward town. Tom said to move everyone, including animals, to the river for protection."

He chuckled. "Curtis is quite a dramatic fellow, isn't he?"

She swallowed a spurt of anger. "This has nothing to do with Tom Curtis. The train's throttle valve is stuck. If Tom and Fisk can't fix it, it will come right through town. It's possible . . ." She couldn't bear the thought of the destruction it might bring. "Jake, the entire town could be destroyed."

"Of course it will stop. It's the end of the line."

"Yes, it is. Either way."

"You're talking in circles, Mae."

"Do you not have ears?"

He stiffened. "There's no need for sarcasm. I understand that the throttle is stuck, but Tom's the big railroad official. He'll get the train stopped before it tears through town."

"Tom isn't God."

"Oh, really." He bent to flick a speck of dust off his desk. "That's news. You've certainly been acting as though he were."

Precious seconds were flying by. If Jake wanted to risk his life on the hope that Tom could perform miracles, he could but she wasn't going to. And she wasn't going to marry this man. He wasn't the childhood Jake she'd known and fallen in love with so many years ago. They'd both changed. Their values were different now, as were their hopes and dreams. Removing her gloves, she took the ring off and laid it on the desk.

His eyes focused on it. "Mae . . . you can't be serious. After all these years, years of nagging me for a ring . . ."

"I'm leaving now. I wish you would come with me, but if you don't I'll understand. You're a grown man capable of making decisions."

Shoving back from the desk, he muttered, "Oh, for heaven's sake. I'll go to the river. But I'm telling you that this will all turn out to be a farce. Let me guess. The whole town is in a panic, which your Mr. Curtis excels at accomplishing. I'll be glad when he's gone."

Mae ignored the man, who was wrong about Tom and about so many other things. The only thing Jake proved to her with this display of temper was that he couldn't think of anything, or anyone, other than himself.

TWENTY-EIGHT

Fisk's rapturous grin rivaled the wide Missouri. He sat in the engineer's seat, pulling the whistle cord as the engine barreled across barren hillsides. Snow was falling in earnest now, but neither the weather nor the crisis could cast a pall on the man's delight. And that delight was stepping on Tom's last nerve.

"WHOOOO EEEE!" A whistle pierced the air. "Run, baby, run!"

"Fisk! Knock it off up there! We have a disaster here and you're acting like a kid." Tom couldn't take any more.

"You're right, Tom, I'm sorry."

Sweat trickled down Tom's temples. The stupid throttle refused to budge. He reached for a wrench and pounded the stubborn lever. "How much time left, Henry?"

The engineer consulted a pocket watch. "Maybe two minutes."

Tom whacked the medal. "Come on!"

The engine raced through the winter countryside, steam bellowing high and snow flying off the track in giant waves. Boxcars were whipping behind the out-of-control engine.

The fireman mopped his soot-covered face with a dirty rag. "Curtis, I wouldn't buy anymore of that thar wood you fellers been gettin'. It jest burns too long and too hot."

Grimacing, Tom twisted the wrench, using brute force. "That's . . . the whole . . . idea."

Turning, Fisk yelled over his shoulder. "Town's coming up!"

Time was running out. "Henry, go take your place. Fisk, get over here and help me." The man's added strength might be the key. "Sound the whistle first, Fisk, to let the folks know we're close!" He prayed everyone was away from town by now. Veins stood out when Tom bore down with every ounce of strength he possessed.

"Pauline!" Mae pounded on her neighbor's front door. "Come quick! We have to move to safety!"

Moments passed. "Pauline!" Trying the door handle, Mae discovered that it was unlocked. She stepped inside the small house. "Pauline?" She limped inside, her gaze sweeping the rooms. "Pauline?" The outhouse. She must be in the necessary.

Outside she braced against the howling wind and walked to the small building. Rapping soundly, she called, "Pauline?"

A startled voice answered. "What?"

"Come quickly. Tom is trying to stop a runaway train, but he wants the town cleared."

"What? Why?"

"There's no time to explain! Come out! We have to join the others at the river."

"All right. Hold on." Rustling sounds came from behind the door. Seconds passed.

"Pauline?"

An eyeball appeared in the crescent moon carved in the door. "What?"

"Are you coming?"

"You go on. It'll take me a minute to get my britches on."

Surely she hadn't stripped out of her clothing, cold as it was. "Just hurry!" Mae anxiously waited. A train horn shrilled in the distance.

Precious minutes ticked by as folks streamed from the small town and hurried to the river. "We have to move now, Pauline!" The moment the words left her mouth she heard the unmistakable sounds of a lightning-fast train approaching. She could even see the steam rising high in the sky and knew it was close to where the track was missing. No, it was closer than that. Suddenly an ear-splitting upheaval overtook her and she saw the locomotive enter the town itself.

Lumber and debris flew into the air as the train plowed a path through buildings. The entire town was being turned into kindling. The ground beneath Mae's feet shook and shuddered as though the mighty hand of God picked up Dwadlo and gave it a good shaking. The deafening roar was overwhelming.

The outhouse door flew open and a wild-eyed Pauline stood with her bloomers down around her spindly legs. "I can go like this."

Jerking up the woman's undergarments, Mae took her hand and as fast as possible, with the old woman in tow and an injured ankle, she hobbled across Pauline's property toward safety.

The screeching and banging noises were so loud they hurt her ears. She didn't look back.

They managed to reach the river unharmed, relieved to see their friends and neighbors huddled together, just as scared as they were. No longer able to see what was happening, the sounds echoed and seemed to go on forever.

Armageddon had surely come, fearful whispers declared.

Frantic, Mae searched for Jeremy among the near hysterical mass of people. After handing Pauline off to a visibly shaken couple, Mae threaded her way through the crowd, shouting her brother's name. An older man stopped her, pointing toward the river. "He went after one of the dogs, Mae."

Full-blown terror closed her throat as she made her way closer to the frozen water. "Jeremy!" The wind caught the name and carried it back to her. Snowflakes increased in size, and a biting wind whipped up drifts of snow on the frozen portions of water. Further down the path, she called again. And again. Finally, the wind carried back the young boy's response.

"Over here, Mae!"

Hobbling faster, she veered away from the bank and followed the sound through frozen undergrowth. "Jeremy?"

"Down here!"

Easing closer to a drop-off, Mae peered over the edge. "What are you doing down there?"

Shrugging his shoulders, the boy said, "I

was looking for Seven. I found him here, but when I crawled down to get him he got out. He's fast, Mae." He looked up at his sister. "Now I can't get out. It's too slippery."

"Okay." She glanced around for a long branch. "I'll find a stick and help you up. Pull your hat down closer to your ears so they'll stay warm."

"I'm sorry, Mae."

"It's okay, Jeremy. I know Seven is feisty." Her mind worked to overcome paralyzing fear, and she suddenly realized everything was quiet. That meant the runaway had stopped. What damage had it done to their community, and where was Tom? Had he been in the train when it derailed? Was he at this moment lying dead somewhere? A tight fist of fear squeezed her stomach as she picked up a sturdy limb. The weather was worsening. Heavy snow fell in clumps like cotton. Returning to the edge, she called, "I'm going to have to climb down a ways so you can get hold of this."

"Be careful. It's slippery."

She started to ease her body slowly into the ravine. She'd only moved a short distance when her left boot encountered a patch of ice. Pain shot through her injured ankle, and she bit back a cry. She bumped the rest of the way down on her backside. Landing at the bottom, she saw stars.

"Uh-oh. Mae, are you okay?"

"Yes." Dusting off her hands, she sat trying to collect her thoughts. Someone would come along soon. People had watched her leave in search of her brother. Pauline — *Oh, please be in your right mind at this moment and send someone to look for us.*

Drawing the shivering boy to her side, the two huddled together to keep warm.

"What was that noise, Mae?"

"The train — it derailed." She closed her eyes and prayed that some of Dwadlo was spared. From the destruction she'd heard, she had her doubts.

"Again?"

Nodding, she sighed. "A different one this time, and closer to town." In many ways Pauline was right. Railroad service was both a blessing and a curse, and certainly their recent troubles were costing the railway a small fortune.

"Is Tom Curtis safe?"

Funny how he hadn't asked about Jake first. "I don't know, Jeremy. He and Fisk left to try to stop the train." She blinked back sudden hot tears as the noise and earlier confusion came back to haunt her. Nobody inside that locomotive could have survived the crash, could they? "I don't know if he was on the train when it came through Dwadlo."

"He wasn't. He would have jumped off before then."

"Perhaps." He was a dedicated railroad man, but she hoped what Jeremy said was true. She could picture him frantically trying to fix the throttle even as time ran out.

"Mae." Jeremy straightened. "I don't think you should marry Jake. I think you should marry Tom Curtis."

Pulling him back into her arms, she smiled. Maybe her brother was right. "Tom hasn't asked."

"He might — if you weren't going to marry Jake."

"You don't like Jake?"

"I like him well enough, but I like Tom Curtis better. He's different in a nice way. He treats me like a man — gives me men's jobs. Jake treats me like a baby. Sometimes like a stupid baby."

A male voice called from the distance, the wind making it hard to hear. "Mae!"

Struggling to her feet, Mae pressed against the hillside. "Down here!" Tom? Relief rendered her weak. He was alive!

"I'm coming!"

Turning around, she leaned against the

wall of dirt. "It's him. He made it." Giddiness snatched away her breath. *Thank You, God. Thank You, God . . .*

"Yea!" Jeremy yelled.

Yes, yea. Double, triple yea. They heard heavy footsteps making their way to the incline. Cold — so very cold. Mae's teeth chattered.

"There you are. Thank God."

She lifted half-frozen lids to see . . . Jake? Her heart threatened to stop. Not Tom. Jake. She swallowed back disappointment. "H-how did you find us?"

"Someone said you and Jeremy were chasing one of the mutts and I came to investigate. Why are you in the ravine?"

Because I like it here, she wanted to scream. "I . . . can you just get us out, Jake? I'll explain later."

"Of course." His gaze wandered the site as he buttoned up tighter. "What should I do?"

"Get a long stick." She paused and thought about what had just happened to her. "Forget it. You'll need to do something else."

"Okay. Shall I go back for help?"

"That isn't necessary. If you'll climb down a bit I can grab onto your hand."

His eyes scanned the rugged terrain. "I

don't know about climbing, Mae. And I'm wearing new oxfords. There's no need to scuff them. Perhaps if I lean close and extend a hand?"

Mae gauged the distance he would need to achieve to pull her up and shook her head. "That won't work. You'll have to come down here and hoist us up."

"What if I become trapped after you get out?"

"You won't be in here for long. I'll go get other men to come and help you."

"Why don't I do that now?"

"He doesn't want to come down here." Jeremy stated the obvious under his breath. "Tom Curtis would."

Leave it to a young person to speak the truth even if it hurt. "Shush." She turned back to Jake. "I've wrenched my ankle. Please climb down halfway and help me out of here."

"Oh, darling." He shook his head. "I was worried. I feared you hadn't made it to the river."

Great. Now he was going to act as if he were concerned. Was he serious? All she wanted was to get out of this hole. "Thank you for your concern, Jake. Just step on those large roots — there, in the center. They should hold your weight."

"You know what a mistake you've made."

It wasn't a question. It was a rather forceful statement. "Yes. I should have gone for help instead of trying to rescue Jeremy alone."

"No. You surely realized the moment you left my office that breaking our engagement isn't the answer. I've thought about your accusations, and you're right. I have neglected you of late, and I'm deeply sorry. When I get you out of there, I'm going to put that ring back on your finger, Mae Wilkey, and we're going to forget about all this nonsense."

She glanced at her little brother. He shouldn't be hearing this. "It's not nonsense, Jake, but now is certainly not the time to have this discussion." She looked up and saw that he was glaring down at her.

"Clearly there's a misunderstanding between us. I've loved you for as long as I can remember. We can't let an inconsequential tiff destroy what we've enjoyed for years." His tone turned pleading. "Mae, I promise to be a dutiful husband. I'll give you material possessions beyond your wildest expectations. The finest clothing. Jewelry. Travel. Name your desire."

"Get me out of here." She heard him groan. "I don't want to marry a bank account, Jake. I have a job."

"I only meant that my practice is thriving and you'll want for nothing."

Mae fell silent. Her ankle ached like blue blazes, and she'd give her nose for a cup of hot coffee. His words registered. Business was thriving these days? He'd failed to mention that. "Jake, it's freezing down here. Are you going to help us up or are you not?"

"Not until you promise to accept my ring."

"I can't promise that."

Jeremy pressed closer. "What's he talking about, Mae?"

"I'll explain later, Jeremy. Jake, get us out of here!"

TWENTY-NINE

Jake's teasing side definitely chose the wrong time to appear. He wagged his head, becoming even more annoying. Mae wondered what she'd ever seen in him.

"Say you'll be my bride first."

"She don't have to!" Jeremy yelled.

Jake smiled, pulled something out of his pocket, and tossed it at her. "But she will."

Mae's hand quickly covered her younger brother's mouth before he could say anything more. She glanced down and saw the ring she'd given back to Jake in the snow at her feet. Now she was really getting mad. "You can't blackmail me, Jake!"

His tone tightened. "I understand you're under duress, darling, but I'm deadly serious. Promise you'll accept that ring and we'll never mention this again."

A pair of brown eyes appeared at Jake's side. A pink tongue lolled as the missing dog peered over the rim. His tail shot up and he barked when he spotted Jeremy.

Jeremy pushed Mae's hand away and grinned. "Seven!"

"Mae, stop this nonsense. I'm cold too, you know."

Drawing a deep breath, Mae took off her glove, bent down to pick up the ring, and placed it on her finger, knowing full well it wouldn't stay there. She met Jake's gaze and said firmly, "Jake Mallory, I'm going to put this on for the time being, but you had better get someone to save us and do it now or, so help me, when I get out of this hole your life won't be worth a plugged nickel."

He tilted his head back and looked down his nose at her. "Fine. I accept that."

"You'd better accept it, mister, and fast."

Straightening, he took one final sweep of the area. "There's no use ruining a new pair of shoes and getting trapped myself. I'll go for help."

"We'll be here when you get back."

He started off and then turned. "Would you like anything? Perhaps something warm to drink?"

Now he was testing her. Putting her glove back on, she gritted her teeth and spoke through pursed lips. "Just . . . get . . . me . . . out . . . of . . . here! Get Lil — and Esau."

Shock registered on his features. "You

want me to bring that dirty, cumbersome beast down here?"

She wasn't sure whether he was referring to her best friend or the elephant. "Lil can handle him. Go get her."

"I'm sure she and the smelly thing shouldn't be too hard to find —"

"Jake!"

"Don't let Seven get loose," Jeremy called.

The lawyer turned and carefully stepped around a growing snowbank. "Mangy mutt."

"I heard that! He is not a mutt!" Jeremy turned to Mae. "He isn't mangy either."

"Don't worry, honey." Mae sank to the ground again. When he sat beside her, she drew him close. "There's only one mangy mutt around here, and we both know who it is."

Snow and ice continued to fall, deepening drifts. Mae listened to the sounds coming from Dwadlo. Shouts. Chaos. Closing her eyes, she prayed softly, "God, I plead for Your mercy. Stop this relentless weather." *Tom. Where are you?*

"Mae?"

"Yes, Jeremy?"

"Is it true? You don't want to marry Jake?"

Sighing, she gathered him closer. "It's true."

"Why?"

"Because I don't love him. Not the way I should."

"Not the way you love Tom Curtis?"

Drawing back, she looked directly into Jeremy's earnest eyes. "Wherever did you get the idea that I'm in love with him?"

"I figured it out all by myself. You look at him funny. It's true, isn't it?"

"I . . ." She refused to lie to the child. She never had, and she didn't intend to start. But had she been lying to herself? She realized she'd been ignoring what her heart had known all along. She was in love with Tom Curtis. "Tom is never to know of my feelings." She put a hand on each of the young man's cheeks. "That means you can never tell him I love him."

Jeremy reached up, took her hands in his, and pulled them down. He gave her a big grin, like the cat that swallowed the canary. "I don't have to tell him, Mae. I think he already knows and loves you too."

She hugged him again, mainly because she didn't want to see the innocence in his eyes.

He loves you too. The words were like stakes driven in her heart. Why had they waited so long? Why hadn't one or the other reached out to claim what was so obvious?

Jeremy had always been brutally honest.

Leave it up to someone special like him to figure out how adults should act. She could only hope it wasn't too late to make things right.

She heard heavy footsteps crunching through ice and snow again. The earth shook slightly — it had to be Esau.

"Mae, it sounds like Lil and the elephant are coming." Jeremy helped her to her feet again, which felt frozen inside her boots. Lil, perched on top of Esau, came into view.

"We're down here!"

Lil waved. "You in a ditch?"

"Does it look like I'm in a ditch?"

"Don't be smart, missy. I'm your only way out."

It might not be the right time, but she had to know. "Have you heard anything about Tom? And Fisk?"

"Nary a word. I got a look at the town, and it's gone. Fires are burning everywhere. It's a real sight."

Mae's heart sank. Everything was destroyed? Seven stuck his nose over the edge again, whining when he focused on Jeremy.

"How'd you get in there?" Lil called.

"Does it matter? Just get me out!"

"Hold on to your britches." Esau trumpeted as Lil urged the animal closer to the steep drop-off.

"Are you sure no one's seen Tom?" Mae called, aware that Jake was standing off to the side. Despite being upset with him, her heart ached when she saw his betrayed expression. She had never meant to hurt him. The good Lord knew she didn't. They had meant too much to each other over the years, but dreams and hearts change.

Lil shook her head. "Ain't found any remains yet. It's a mess up there. Took out everything — the station, the store — almost every house in town. And what the train didn't get, the fires probably will."

Of course there would be fires with all the woodstoves stoked to their fullest in mid-winter. Pain seared Mae's heart. Deep, agonizing hurt at Dwadlo's loss. And no sign of Tom. She tried to tell herself that his absence didn't mean he hadn't jumped clear when he knew the train couldn't be saved, but she also couldn't be sure he had time to react and survived leaving the train before it crashed.

"I'm going to throw a rope down, and you and Jeremy need to tie it around your waists. Esau will hoist you up."

Nodding, Mae wondered if her freezing hands would be able to grip a rope well enough to tie a knot. A moment later the line slid over the side, and she reached for

Jeremy to tie the twisted hemp around his waist.

"I can hold on," he protested.

"I know you can, but this way we can be absolutely sure." She jerked the knot tight and then called. "Okay, Lil! Be careful. Jeremy's coming up first."

Giving a sharp whistle, Lil spoke. "Back!"

The elephant placed one foot behind him, then another. The rope tightened.

"Again!"

The animal complied and Jeremy slowly rose to the surface, propping his boots against the hillside as he assisted the mammoth beast during the ascent. Within moments the boy emerged at the top, untied the rope, and pitched it back to Mae.

"Are you hurt, Jeremy? Anything broken?" Lil asked.

"I'm all right. Let's get Mae."

Esau lumbered closer to the rim. "Tie on."

Grabbing the rope's end, she tied it around her waist. Drawing a deep breath, Mae called, "Now!"

The line tightened and she slowly started to ascend. She couldn't feel her hands through the heavy gloves. *Please don't let me lose my hold.* Someday she would look back on this horrendous day and know that God had not failed her.

She could only pray that all of the towns-people had made it to the river. Pauline was safe, Jeremy was safe, but was Tom safe too?

She had to find the man who owned her heart.

Mae joined the crowd as they searched through the smoldering ruins. Her breath caught as she stared at the carnage. The Dwadlo she knew no longer existed. The train station was a pile of lumber. The General Store was gone. Shiny pieces of the mail cage were scattered about the area like children's toys. Her house was destroyed.

She frantically searched through the store wreckage, tears rolling down her cheeks. The overturned pickle barrel reeked of vinegar, but the brine was a better smell than the heavy smoke filling the air. Dale's office chair sat atop a heap of rubble with one leg missing. A hundred yards beyond what had once been the town, the engine lay on its side, steam still rolling from its stack. Boxcars lay flattened on their side. The distinct odor of fish mingled with the stench of fire and oil. So much for Joanne Small's happy wedding. So much for life in Dwadlo.

When Mae caught sight of Tom's coat, hanging on a shredded hunk of metal, her heart nearly stopped. Grabbing it, she held the garment to her chest, breathing deeply of his scent. Hot tears rolled down her cheeks, and she slumped onto a pile of rubble.

Pauline came to sit beside her. "You can't know that sonny's not safe. 'Pears to me he's a purty smart man, and so is Fisk. They are not gonna stay aboard a runaway train."

"Tom would." Mae could barely choke out the words. "He would be so involved in fixing the valve that the town would be upon him before he'd give up."

"Well." Pauline sighed. "I could have told 'em something like this would happen, but that young whippersnapper wouldn't listen. If they'd put the station on my land, they could have run the line straight through to Pine Grove, but they were stingy. They refused to pay me what I wanted, so they bought Dale's land instead, and now look what happened. The station sets in a swamp hole. That train had nowhere to go but in the ditch." She shook her head. "That's a pure shame. Guess I'll get what I'm asking now. Might even up the price."

Mae shook her head. Whoever had thought Pauline was a fool had another think coming. Her memory might hinder

her waning years, but the lady still had a
pirate's heart.

THIRTY

Lil approached, wiping her nose with a less-than-clean handkerchief. Apparently, even the tough hog farmer couldn't bear the sight. Mae stood up and hugged her friend. "Oh, Lil. There's nothing left!"

"Don't have a come apart." Lil stiffened, stepping back and squaring her shoulders. "We can rebuild. Weren't no one hurt, so we should be praising instead of grumbling. Accidents happen in a world where everything's changing faster than a cricket's yodel."

Nodding, Mae understood the reasoning. Not so many years ago Dwadlo was nothing but a spot in the road. The town would rebuild — had to rebuild. Homesteaders depended on the community for supplies and mail service. Her eyes scanned the steaming wreckage. Poor Joanne. Her herring now decorated snow drifts and more wreckage than anyone wanted to look at.

Mae looked again down the road into town. If Tom had jumped clear of the train, he'd have had plenty of time to walk back by now. He wouldn't give up until the last moment. But more than an hour had passed since the train derailed, and there was still no sign of him or Fisk. Lil seemed to read her mind.

"He jumped, Mae. Wouldn't you?"

"Yes, but I'm not that dedicated to my work."

"No one's that dedicated." Lil put her hands on her hips. "He jumped, I'm tellin' ya. So did Fisk. They had to."

Nodding, Mae stiffened. "We should ride down the road, Lil. It's possible they are out there lying in a snowbank and freezing to death. Maybe he broke a leg when he jumped. Same with Fisk." She struggled to stand upright. "Have Esau lift me onto his back —"

But the words had no sooner left her mouth when she saw them. Four men striding toward town, three of them with ripped and dirty jackets and one without a coat. Suddenly her ankle didn't hurt at all. With a cry of relief, she took off running toward them. Fisk had a missing boot, and Tom's hair stuck out in all directions. When she lunged at him he caught her in his arms and hugged her so tightly the air left her lungs. Cold lips searched and found each other, and instant warmth flared between them. Mae couldn't get enough of Tom Curtis or the thrill that shot through her when he pulled her closer and deepened the kiss. *Thank You, God!* Tom was alive and well! The thought made the day's horrific events seem petty.

When lack of breath finally made them come up for air, Mae stroked his wind-chapped cheek. "It's . . . it's good to see you, Mr. Curtis."

"Same goes for you, Miss Wilkey. I've been worried half out of my mind about you. I wasn't sure you'd made it to safety."

"We all did. Everyone is accounted for. No lives were lost."

Tom eased her to the ground, his gaze on the devastation, and he groaned. "We lost the town, not to mention another locomotive."

She pressed her fingers against his lips. "But you're alive. That's all that matters." No longer would she hide her true feelings for the man who still held her.

"I hope the railroad sees it that way." Arm in arm, the two started for the rubble after Fisk, the engineer, and fireman.

Lil approached riding Esau. She met the

blacksmith's defiant glare. "What happened to you? You look like you've been hit by a train."

"Ha-ha. My sides are splittin' with laughter," he growled.

"Suppose I cain't offer you a ride?"

His gaze traveled the animal and then rested on a pair of scuffed red boots. "How would I git up there?"

"If'n you're asking to climb aboard, I'll get you up here."

He kept his eyes fixed on the road. "Don't need your help."

"Good enough. How far have you walked?"

His pace slowed and he appeared to rethink the offer. He glanced at his frozen sock and then up at her. "How do I get aboard?"

A shout went up when Esau's long trunk encompassed Fisk's waist and swung the man up onto his back. Mae burst out laughing at the look of fear that crossed the blacksmith's face. Terror softened into a slow grin.

When Esau let go of Fisk, he wrapped his arms around Lil. Mae glanced at Tom. "I don't believe it."

"Neither do I." He laughed and kissed Mae on the cheek. "We have work to do."

With his arm around her to give her sore ankle some support, they walked beside the elephant and listened to Fisk and Lil discussing the situation above them.

"Well now, this ain't half bad," Fisk said. " 'Pears to me like you been trainin' the animal to snag you a man."

Flashing a smug grin, Lil agreed. " 'Pears that way."

Mae bit back her own grin. Maybe blessings came in bunches and love bloomed in winter. Fisk, until now, had refused to ride the animal, but today — well, today was a new beginning not only for her but, God willing, the entire town. Lil glanced down at the fireman and engineer. "How about you two? There's room for all."

The men started backing away, each holding up a protective hand. "Thanks, but no thanks, ma'am," the engineer said. By then the fireman was well on his way down the road.

Mae smiled up at Lil. "You two go on. It looks as though you have a full load to me." After Fisk's wife passed, Mae had wondered if they would get together. This might be just the push they needed.

The entourage slowly walked up Main Street, and Mae felt Tom tense at the sight. Folks milled about, searching through the rubble as they tried to salvage any belongings they could find. Tears of sadness for the material losses were shed, but tears of joy mingled with the knowledge that the good Lord had spared every life.

Tom's tone was sober. "This is worse than I imagined, but there is good news for these folks, besides the fact that there were no injuries or deaths."

"What's that?"

"The railroad will pay for everyone to rebuild. Everything will be brand new."

Mae thought about what he'd said. They could rebuild bigger houses and more businesses. Life might be changed, but that didn't necessarily mean it was all bad.

She continued clinging to him until she spotted Jake standing on the sidelines. Her conscience hurt. He must have seen her passionate reaction to finding Tom. She had embarrassed Jake in front of friends and clients. Squeezing Tom's hand, she whispered, "I'll be back in a minute."

She caught up with the lawyer as he walked to the large elm they had carved their initials in when they were in grade school. Today the branches were torn and broken, fragile and bare, a mute memorial of their childhood love. Her gaze traced the crooked heart with the initials JM and MW scratched in the wood.

Sitting down beside him, Mae huddled deep into her cloak, longing for a way to ease his hurt, and for the first time her situation struck home. She, Jeremy, and Pauline were homeless, and Jake was too, and all they shared would be a faded memory. Crushing reality settled over her. "I'm sorry you witnessed that kiss. I was . . . I was just so relieved to see him."

He didn't look at her but instead fixed his gaze on the falling snow. She couldn't read his expression, but knew she had caused him great pain. His ways were different than hers, but she still remembered long summer afternoons of sunshine and swimming in the creek. Summer nights when they walked and talked about dreams of a future together.

"I've come to ask your forgiveness, Jake."

"For what? Falling in love with another man?"

"For not being completely honest with you. Do you remember the day we met?"

He nodded. "I remember. Fourth grade. My family moved here from Charleston. Father survived the war, and he and mother tired of city life and moved to the area. I'm not sure what brought them to Dwadlo or what eventually led them to Pine Grove."

"Do you recall that we had the same dreams, the same wants in life?"

Leaning back against the tree, he faced her. "I do. You wanted six children and a big garden."

She smiled, recalling carefree days when nothing happened that a warm hug, a couple of cookies, and a glass of cold milk couldn't cure. "You wanted to plant potatoes. That was your dream. Planting potatoes."

"I couldn't get enough of them when I was a kid."

She took his hand. "I think we've both changed."

"I agree. I eat all the potatoes I want at the café now. I've become a successful lawyer. I'd say that I've done quite well for myself."

"I'd say that too, but I'd also say that love is a seed, a very delicate seed that needs watering and nurturing. True affection can't bloom without care. It becomes dormant — or dies. Love blooms most when both parties work to make it a beautiful thing." She eased the burdensome ring off her finger once again and placed it in his hand. "I'm afraid we make terrible gardeners, Jake. We haven't cultivated our love. We permitted it to die."

He took a deep breath. "Yes, I suppose you're right. I've known it for a long time, but I didn't want to face the truth."

She shifted, bracing against the elements. Where would she sleep tonight? How would she keep Pauline and Jeremy warm? "I don't know how or when it happened. I didn't mean to fall in love with Tom. It just happened."

"He shares your devotion?"

She shrugged her shoulders. Their shared kiss was a powerful indication that he didn't think of her as his sister, but he'd never voiced exactly what he thought of her. Of them as a couple. She could be putting too much credence in one kiss from a man who'd just escaped death. Truthfully, he might have kissed a donkey in relief. Rubbing warmth into her arms, she said, "We haven't discussed our feelings, but I think he shares an attraction. Perhaps not with the same hope for a future together, but my woman's intuition tells me that he feels something more than friendship."

Nodding, Jake said softly, "He's in love with you, Mae."

"Do you think so?" Her eyes searched his. "Honestly?"

"I've watched a growing attraction for you from the moment I met him. He looks at you as though you're water to a thirsty man."

She reached out and hugged him. "Thank you! I'd like to believe that."

"Believe it." He leaned his head back, closing his eyes. "I'm a man and I know the look well. He looks at you the way I should have. You're right, Mae. We have changed. We are more like brother and sister. We could never have made each other happy." He opened his eyes and looked at her. "I'm moving to Philadelphia."

"Oh?" His statement came as no big surprise. Jake wasn't meant for Dwadlo; he was destined for the big city. This town didn't inspire his mind or stretch his intellect. She still loved him the way she loved Jeremy, but he needed bright lights and elegant culture. Women would flock to this smart, savvy man, and he deserved someone who would appreciate him for who he was. A good man, but not her man.

"I'll be leaving in the morning. If Fisk has a chance to round up some of his stock, I'll purchase a horse from him."

Leaning back, Mae rested her eyes. A numbness settled over her bones. "I wish you nothing but happiness, Jake."

"Thank you. I wish you the same, Mae. Tom's a good, solid man." He looked her in the eye. "I should have ended our relationship long ago."

She nodded. "I suppose you'll open an office in Philly?"

"Yes. As soon as possible. A new start — that's what I need."

"You're a fine lawyer." She noticed that he didn't ask her about her immediate plans, but then he'd never really cared about what she wanted, and she couldn't have told him anyway. She had no home, no job. Just a boy and Pauline to feed and clothe.

She and Jake could talk about their childhood all afternoon, but their adulthood could be summed up in a few short sentences. It hardly seemed fair, but then sometimes life wasn't fair.

God never intended it to be.

THIRTY-ONE

Dale waded through ankle-deep rubble, shaking his head. When he approached Tom, the man had tears in his eyes. "Everything is gone."

Surprised that he was finally speaking directly to him, Tom nevertheless reached out to steady the pastor. "You can rebuild."

"I'm not worried about material possessions. It's the *memories,* Tom." Dale's eyes swept the devastation. "So many memories of my mother, my childhood. Gone."

"Memories are stored in the heart," Tom reminded him. "Nothing can take those away from you."

The man nodded, tears openly streaming down his cheeks. "Can you sit a spell? I'd like to tell you something."

The invitation was too good to ignore, regardless of circumstances. "Sure." They found comfortable seats by the store's broken steps. For a moment they sat in silence before Dale began.

"I want to thank you, Tom."

"Thank me?" A humorless chuckle escaped him. "What on earth do you have to thank me for?"

"Your goodness." The pastor's eyes softened. "I know that doesn't sound very manly, but the word fits you. You are a good man. I'm aware that I'm a bit eccentric, and I haven't tried hard enough to get to know you. I'm sure you've noticed that I'm basically a shy man. The only time I can find my tongue and express my feelings is in the pulpit. I don't like my personality, but the good Lord saw fit to make me this way, and I'm not in the habit of doubting His work. Casual conversation comes hard for me, even with people I know well. And I guess my mother spoiled me rotten. . . . or so I've heard." He lifted his head and offered an apologetic smile. "I became accustomed to the pampering, but I want you to know that I'm deeply indebted to you for the personal risk you took in trying to save our town."

The man sitting beside him, quietly struggling to express himself, touched Tom. Every man had his flaw. And Dale's could be worse.

"You have a lot of friends here, Dale. Mae thinks the world of you."

370

"She's the daughter I'll never have," he confessed, wiping away his tears with his hand. Tom reached into his back pocket, pulled out a clean handkerchief, and offered it to him.

"I appreciate your thanks, but they're not necessary. I'm sorry your store and home are gone."

"I'll rebuild." He blew his noise loudly. "You?"

Him? Tom didn't know where he'd go or what he'd do. Life was suddenly a big mess. Since coming to Dwadlo and meeting Mae, nothing was the same. He thought he'd had everything all figured out. Work for the railroad until he couldn't board a train anymore.

Maybe God had a different thought.

He reached over and slapped Dale on the back. "What say you and me help these folks get settled for the night?"

Nodding, Dale reached to shake his hand. "I appreciate . . . and love you." He paused to wipe his nose. "It's okay for a man to tell another man that he loves him, isn't it?"

"It's okay for this man." Smiling, Tom firmly shook his hand. "You're a good man, Dale. Don't let yourself ever tell you any different."

■ ■ ■ ■

Returning to the accident site, Mae spotted Tom among a crew of men clearing timber from the railroad station. She supposed they would rebuild the platform first so that once new rail was down the train could arrive with supplies. There would be a massive town rebuilding project, but she was confident the residents of Dwadlo were up for the challenge, and with the grace of God they would succeed.

Straightening, Tom waved her over with a big grin on his face. She carefully picked her way through the rubble to reach him.

"Look!" He bent and lifted a wooden crate. "Root beer and not a single broken bottle!"

Shaking her head, she smiled. "The blessings just keep flowing." What else could she say?

"Hey." He waded through debris to take her arm and move her carefully over the carnage toward the general store. "I have something I want to show you."

"More root beer?"

"Just follow me." They made their way up, over, and through broken boards and shattered glass. They were clear of the train station now, but rubble stood deep in the streets. The General Store sign was upside down in the middle of the road. Dale, with a broom in his hand, quietly swept glass from what remained of the porch steps. In the background, the store and post office were in complete rubble. The gut-wrenching sight pierced her heart. Nothing looked familiar. Canned goods littered the ground. A roll of white butcher paper was caught in bare tree limbs. The barrel that had held ice, sarsaparilla, and root beer had been blown into an empty field. "Come on." He urged her up the store steps and past Dale to where the postal cage once stood. On top of a small wooden box, the telegraph machine sat.

Her jaw dropped. "Oh, how could that be?"

"Can you believe it? It doesn't seem to be damaged — and the line's still up." He stepped to the machine to peck out a message, and her mind absorbed the familiar cadence.

COULDN'T STOP TRAIN STOP LOST ANOTHER LOCOMOTIVE AND CARS STOP NO INJURIES STOP PLAN TO STAY AND HELP REBUILD STOP WILL HAVE THE STATION UP AND RUNNING

WITHIN A MONTH STOP SEND
TWENTY-FIVE TENTS IMMEDIATELY,
PLUS FOOD, CLOTHING, BLANKETS,
AND WORKERS MORE ROOT BEER STOP
AND A WEDDING CAKE STOP

Closing her eyes, she experienced an overwhelming sense of gratitude. It warmed her to her toes. No wonder she loved this man. With all the things on his mind, he had the forethought to order Joanne a wedding cake. "That is so kind, Tom, but Joanne doesn't need a cake. She needed the herring."

"She has her fish." He pointed to what was left of two barrels and the herring that lay everywhere. "Folks can help themselves."

The most miserable night of Mae's life was nearly over. A few folks still had homes and took in as many as they could, but Pauline had refused to be separated from Mae and Jeremy, and so the three of them, Tom, and a pack of dogs and cats huddled around a blazing campfire that drove away the worst of the chill but failed to completely thaw frigid bones. Mae's twisted ankle no longer bothered her; brutal winter weather was the enemy. The citizens of Dwadlo struggled to survive the overnight temperature, praying

374

for dawn's light.

When a weak sun crested the skyline, Mae was thankful they had gathered supplies from the work site. Coffeepots were simmering, and by midmorning the townsfolk had found enough edible food to feed the children. Adults had to wait for the supply train.

By midafternoon they learned the new supply train had arrived safely beyond the wreckage site. A bunch of burly men went to meet it, and soon they were back and unloading from the wagons much-needed supplies: tents, cases of canned goods, blankets, and warm clothing.

Sitting with a group of women, Mae tried to locate Tom. Dogs and cats roamed the site, sniffing out tasty treats left by small children. Jeremy, ropes tied around his waist, struggled to control the animals and keep them away from the crowd.

Tom's eyes caught sight of the woman who filled his heart. When he realized the train was going to wreak havoc on Dwadlo, his only worry had been for Mae, Jeremy, and Pauline. He'd become very fond of the lovely postmistress. No, it was far more than that — he loved her. There, he'd admitted it. He loved Mae Wilkey. Now he had to decide what to do about it.

Actually, he knew exactly what needed to be done. He had to talk to her before he did one thing more. He needed to settle a large part of his life, and it couldn't wait. "Mae."

She turned at the sound of his voice.

"Will you come with me, please? I need your help with something."

He heard the other women telling her they were fine and for her to go with him. She approached him looking more tired than he'd ever seen her. He put his arm around her shoulders, and they began to walk up the street. "How's Pauline?"

Mae sighed. "She's very cold. Are the blankets unloaded yet?"

He nodded toward the large crates stacked on the right. "In there."

"I'll take her one."

"Hold on. I want you to come with me." Folks were forming a crowd, vying for supplies, but he led her away. He was confident someone would look out for the elderly woman.

Walking toward the river, Tom rubbed the kinks from his neck. Mae watched from the corner of her eye, wishing she could do that for him. "Where are we going?" A sharp wind was slicing through her, and she longed for the campfire. She needed to claim a large tent and get it set up before dark. Pauline and Jeremy would stay with her until — until what? She rebuilt her tiny home?

Thank God for C&NW's generosity in financially helping Dwadlo pick up the pieces and put it all back together. She didn't have the funds to rebuild, nor did the other residents. She had a jelly jar she had kept in the cabinet for emergencies, and this was certainly an emergency, but she didn't have nearly enough to build a new home. Besides, she wasn't sure she would even find the jar.

Winking, Tom smiled. "Just follow me. Hold your questions."

She did as she was told, wondering where he could be going when his help was sorely needed in town. Approaching her house — or where her house had once sat, she winced when she saw what remained. Windows had been shattered by flying debris. Broken two-by-fours were lying like matchsticks in the yard. Yet on closer inspection, she realized that even with the massive damage the house might be salvaged. Pausing, Tom verified her thoughts. "It needs a new roof, new windows, and quite a bit of other repair, but we should have you back in your home in just a few weeks."

Sighing, she sagged against him for support. His arms closed around her, and they nestled together against a stiff gust of wind. For a moment the world felt right again. Her gaze strayed to Pauline's place and then her heart broke. Her house appeared to suffer massive damage, and the poor woman barely had enough money for food. Lumber and bits of paper — like bank notes — littered the ground. The bank was gone, as well as Jake's office. Perhaps that was good. He wanted to leave his former life behind. Maybe God had helped him make a clean break.

"What are we doing here, Tom?"

"We're taking stock of our lives."

She glanced up. "*Our* lives?"

"You didn't think the news of your engagement being off wouldn't race through town like wildfire, regardless of the disaster and countless other problems?"

"That was yesterday, and you haven't said a word."

He shrugged. "I've been a little busy. Besides, I didn't feel it was my place to mention it. We really haven't known each other long enough for me to pry into your personal life."

Snuggling closer, she whispered, "I feel I

know you well enough to tell you anything. The length of time we've been acquainted with each other doesn't matter." She'd known Jake forever, and in many ways he was still a stranger.

His hold tightened. "I figured you would tell me when the time was right."

"And you think this is the proper time to discuss my spinsterhood?" She looked away. "I don't know if I'll ever marry. There's so much to do here, I'd never be able to leave."

"Jeremy?"

She nodded and looked up at him. "He's a part of me, Tom. He'll be with me the rest of his life."

"And then there's Pauline."

"There's always Pauline. I am so deeply sorry about the mistake. I should have made certain you were kin before I sent the letter, but I had exhausted all means of finding her family —"

"I've been meaning to mention that. I had lived a carefree bachelor life for years and just received a good promotion — one that would set me up for life. Then your letter came. A month passed, and the second letter turned up."

"You didn't answer. I was afraid the first letter hadn't reached you, so I wrote another one."

"I got both letters, but I thought my men were pulling a joke on me. I knew I didn't have kin in Dwadlo, North Dakota."

"Then why did you respond?"

"Well, there was always the slim chance I could be mistaken. Once both my parents had passed, I didn't keep up with family matters. I had a sister, but she had passed away, so when your second letter came it raised doubts. I thought maybe I did have kin here and just didn't know it."

She shook her head. "I gather the Curtises weren't a close family."

"Not close. Not after I left home. I misled the railroad and told them I was seventeen to get my first job. I was fourteen, but I worked as hard as any man older than me."

"You lied?"

"I misled." His gaze fixed on Pauline's place. "I lied. I'm not proud of it, but I wanted that job so badly I could taste it, Mae. Have you ever wanted anything that badly?"

Her eyes searched his and then she smiled. "Yes." She snuggled deeper into his arms. "I'm glad you're going to stay and help us rebuild."

Pulling slightly away, he studied her. "How do you know I plan to stay?"

"You said so in the telegraph you sent Clive."

"Actually, I'm going to rebuild the station — only this time I'm going to do it right. The railroad will pay Pauline's asking price. If today doesn't prove that C&NW needs that track to run to Pine Grove, then I'll eat my hat."

Smiling, she hugged him. "I'll help you."

"You can't help. You'll be too busy."

"Doing what?"

"Well, here's my plan." His gaze shifted back to Pauline's property. "That's a handsome piece of land. What does she own? Thirty, forty acres?"

"About that."

"It doesn't take thirty or forty acres to lay track and build a decent station."

"No, I wouldn't imagine."

"And I'm thinking that Dwadlo wants to remain small."

"I could use a bit bigger house."

"You can build as large of a house as you want. The way I figure, I'll talk Pauline into selling the railroad enough land to bring the track through her property, but I'll advise her to hold back enough to build a good-sized home — a big one."

"What will Pauline do with a big house? She couldn't manage the little one she had."

"Agreed, but times are changing. Folks can't always take care of their own. I want to put up a place that will house widows and even widowers. Take care of them. Feed them. Give them back a small semblance of life, respect, and care in their old age."

"Goodness, Tom, like one of those places we talked about sending Pauline to? Who could picture such a thing in Dwadlo? Folks take care of kin regardless of the changing times."

"But there are others like Pauline who have no family. I can imagine it. It'll work, Mae, and Pauline will be our first resident. We'll name it the Pauline Wilson Rest Home."

"Rest home!"

"It has a nice ring to it, honey. And it's needed. The world is changing, and we're going to change with it."

"Tom!"

"Mae, face it. When you get to be Pauline's age you're in the way. If you're fortunate to have a Mae Wilkey in your life, you'll do fine, but most folks aren't that lucky. If God allows a man or woman a good long life, eventually everybody they know and love dies. There's no one to take care of these folks. Dwadlo is the kind of town they could spend their last days in peace and —"

"Tom!"

"What?"

"What did you say?"

"I said, most folks —"

She stopped him. "Before that."

"The world is changing?"

"Before that."

Grinning, he said. "Honey. I called you honey, all right? You're not engaged to Jake anymore, and honestly, Mae, I've wanted to call you that for a while . . ." He paused. "Look. You might as well know right now that I'm not good at this sweet talk stuff." He turned toward the General Store. "I have an idea. Come with me."

A few minutes later Mae found herself back at the debris site of the store. "Tom, I'm half frozen, and I really need to claim a tent."

"You have one. I set it aside earlier, along with food, blankets, clothing — everything you need." He shoved a broken counter aside and made his way through the rubble and paused before the telegraph machine, where he typed a message.

If I stay Stop What are the chances of us — you and me Stop You know

Deciphering the code, Mae broke into a grin. He met her gaze expectantly.

"Are you planning to send that?" she asked.

"I just sent it . . . to you."

"Well, as you say, times are changing. Do you want me to tap out my reply?"

Giving her a slow, easy grin, he winked at the woman he loved and said, "I'd rather get the message in person."

Shoving a board aside, she moved to give her answer. Wrapping her arms around his neck, she smiled. "I'd say the chances are as good as they get."

His gaze softened as he pulled her to him. "I might want to stay around a long time, Miss Wilkey. Could be a lifetime."

Kissing him softly, she whispered, "Why, Mr. Curtis, that's what I'm counting on."

DISCUSSION QUESTIONS

1. Mae assumed her life was settled until Tom came along. Has God ever changed your plans (as we say in Missouri) "in the middle of the stream"? Discuss.

2. Mae didn't realize it, but she was settling for something less than love. Can you think of any time in your life when you've settled for something less than you wanted?

3. Did Mae have the right to contact Tom and hand off her problem to him? In small communities the citizens often bond as a family. Did Dwadlo residents have a responsibility to their elderly?

4. Can you think of specific instances in the Bible where God speaks of His family?

What are His instructions for family responsibilities?

5. If you, like Tom, were told you had a distant relative who needed care, how would you respond? Would you answer the call?

6. Dale is a colorful character in *Love Blooms in Winter.* Have you known people with a similar personality? Shy and unable to express thoughts and feelings? How do you react to such a person? Do you make an effort to bring him or her into your circle of friendship? Why or why not?

7. How difficult is it for you to follow 1 John 4:11, "Beloved, if God so loved us, we ought also to love one another"? Was Mae truly trying to help her friend Pauline, or was she trying to make her personal life easier? To what extent does the Lord expect us to closely follow 1 John 4:11, and why do we so often fail in our efforts?

8. Pauline is another lively character in the story. Does anyone in your group have a "Pauline" in his or her life? God tells us to care for the widows and the elderly. To what extent are we commanded to do this?

Are nursing homes an easy way to solve the problem? Discuss the pros and cons of caring for the elderly.

9. Jake loved Mae, and Mae loved Jake, but they had outgrown true affection. Have you experienced this in your own life? Have you witnessed marriages where love has turned to dutiful indifference? Do you think that can happen to God's children if deep love isn't present? If someone came to you with such a problem, how would you advise them?

10. If you could glean one specific personal or spiritual lesson from this story, what would it be?

■ ■ ■ ■

Coming Soon from
Lori Copeland and
Virginia Smith,
Book 1 in Their
Brand-New
Amish of Apple
Grove Series

■ ■ ■ ■

THE HEART'S FRONTIER

CHAPTER ONE

Mid-July, 1881, Apple Grove, Kansas
Nearly the entire Amish district of Apple Grove had turned out to help this morning, all twenty families. Or perhaps they were here to wish Emma Switzer well as she set off for her new home in Troyer, fifty miles away.

From her command post on the porch of the house, Emma's grandmother kept watch over the loading of the gigantic buffet hutch onto the specially reinforced wagon. Her sharp voice sliced through the peaceful morning air.

"Forty years I've had that hutch from my dearly departed husband and not a scratch on it. Jonas, see that you use care!"

If *Maummi*'s expression weren't so fierce, Emma would have laughed at the long-suffering look Papa turned toward his

391

mother. But the force with which *Maummi*'s fingers dug into the flesh on Emma's arm warned that a chuckle would be most ill-suited at the moment. Besides, the dozen or so men straining to heft the heavy hutch from the front porch of their home into the wagon didn't need further distractions. Their faces strained bright red above their beards, and more than one drop of sweat trickled from beneath the broad brims of their identical straw hats.

Emma glanced at the watchers lined up like sparrows on a fence post. She caught sight of her best friend, Katie Beachy, amid the sea of dark dresses and white *kapps*. Katie smiled and smoothed her skirt with a shy gesture. The black fabric looked a little darker and crisper than that of those standing around her, which meant she'd worn her new dress to bid Emma farewell, an honor usually reserved for singings or services or weddings. The garment looked well on her. Emma had helped sew the seams at their last frolic. Of course, Katie's early morning appearance in a new dress probably had less to do with honoring Emma than with the presence of Samuel Miller, the handsome son of the district bishop. With a glance toward Samuel, whose arms bulged against the weight of holding up one end of the hutch, she returned Katie's smile with a conspiratorial wink.

Her gaze slid over other faces in the crowd and snagged on a pair of eyes fixed on her. Amos Beiler didn't bother to turn away but kept his gaze boldly on her face. Nor did he bother to hide his expression, one of longing and lingering hurt. He held infant Joseph in his arms, and a young daughter clutched each of his trouser-clad legs. A wave of guilt washed through Emma, and she hastily turned back toward the oxcart.

From his vantage point up in the wagon bed, Papa held one end of a thick rope looped around the top of the hutch, the other end held by John Yoder. The front edge of the heavy heirloom had been lifted into the wagon with much grunting and groaning, while the rear still rested on the smooth wooden planks of the porch. Two men steadied the oxen heads, and the rest, like Samuel, had gathered around the back end of the hutch. A protective layer of thick quilts lined the wagon bed.

Papa gave the word. "Lift!"

The men moved in silent unity. Bending their knees, their hands grasped for purchase around the bottom edges. As one they drew in a breath, and at Papa's nod raised in unison. Emma's breath caught in her chest, her muscles straining in silent sympathy with the men. The hutch rose until its rear was level with its front, and the men stepped forward. The thick quilts dangling beneath scooted onto the wagon as planned, a protective barrier from damage caused by wood against wood.

The hutch suddenly dipped and slid swiftly to the front. Emma gasped. Apparently the speed caught Papa and John Yoder by surprise too, for the rope around the top went slack. Papa lunged to reach for the nearest corner, and his foot slipped. The wagon creaked and sank lower on its wheels as the hutch settled into place. At the same moment Papa went down on one knee with a loud, "Ummmmph."

"Papa!"

"*Ach!*" *Maummi* pulled away from Emma and rushed toward the oxcart. Heart pounding against her ribcage, Emma followed. Men were already up in the cart to check on Papa, but *Maummi* leaped into the wagon bed with a jump that belied her sixty years, the strings of her *kapp* flying behind her. She applied bony elbows to push her way around the hutch to her son's side.

She came to a halt above him, hands on her hips, and looked down. "Are you hurt?"

Emma reached the side of the wagon in

time to see Papa wince and shake his head. "No. A bruise is all."

"Good." She left him lying there and turned worried eyes toward her beloved hutch. With a gentle touch, she ran loving fingers over the smooth surface and knelt to investigate the corners.

A mock-stern voice behind Emma held the hint of a chuckle. "Trappings only, Marta Switzer. Care you more for a scratch on wood than an injury to your son?"

Emma turned to see Bishop Miller approach. He spared a smile for her as he drew near enough to lean his arms across the wooden side of the wagon and watch the activity inside. Samuel helped Papa to his feet and handed him the broad-brimmed hat that had fallen off. Emma breathed a sigh of relief when he took a ginger step to try out his leg and smiled at the absence of pain.

"My son is fine." *Maummi* waved a hand in his direction, as though in proof. "And so is my hutch. Though my heart may not say the same, such a fright I've had." She placed the hand lightly on her chest, drew a shuddering breath, and wavered on her feet.

Concern for her grandmother propelled Emma toward the back of the wagon. As she climbed up, she called into the house,

"Rebecca, bring a cool cloth for *Maummi*'s head."

The men backed away while Katie and several other women converged on the wagon to help Emma lift *Maummi* down and over to the rocking chair that rested in the shade of the porch, ready to be loaded onto the cart. *Maummi* allowed herself to be lowered into the chair, and then she wilted against the back, her head lolling sideways and arms dangling. A disapproving buzz rumbled among the watching women, but Emma ignored them. Though she knew full well that most of the weakness was feigned for the sake of the bishop and other onlookers, she also knew *Maummi*'s heart tended to beat unevenly in her chest whenever she exerted herself. Yet another reason why she ought to stay behind in Apple Grove, but *Maummi* insisted her place was with Emma, her oldest granddaughter. What she really meant was that she intended to inspect every eligible young Amish man in Troyer and hand-pick her future grandson-in-law.

Aunt Gerda had written to say she anticipated that her only daughter would marry soon, and she'd appreciate having Emma come to help her around the house. She'd also mentioned the abundance of marriageable young men in Troyer, with a suggestion that twenty-year-old Emma was of an age that the news might be welcome. Rebecca had immediately volunteered to go in Emma's place. Though Papa appeared to consider the idea, he decided to send Emma because she was the oldest and therefore would be in need of a husband soonest. *Maummi* insisted on going along in order to *"Keep an eye on this hoard of men Gerda will parade before our Emma."*

As far as Emma was concerned, they should just send *Maummi* on alone and leave her in Apple Grove to wait for her future husband to be delivered to her doorstep.

Rebecca appeared from inside the house with a dripping cloth in hand. A strand of wavy dark hair escaped its pins and fluttered freely beside the strings of her *kapp*. At barely thirteen, Rebecca possessed the rosy cheeks and smooth, high forehead that reminded Emma so sharply of their mother that at times her heart ached.

Rebecca looked at *Maummi*'s dramatic posture, and her eyes rolled upward. She had little patience with *Maummi*'s feigned heart episodes, and she was young enough that she had yet to learn proper restraint in concealing her emotions. Emma awarded her sister with a stern look and held out a hand for the cloth.

With a contrite bob of her head, Rebecca handed it over and dropped to her knees beside the rocking chair. "Are you all right, *Maummi?*"

"*Ach,* I'm fine. I don't think it's my time. Yet."

Emma rang the excess water from the cloth, waved it in the air to cool, and then draped it across the back of *Maummi*'s neck.

"*Danki.*" The elderly woman realized that the men had stopped working in order to watch her, and she waved her hand in a shooing motion. "Place those quilts over my hutch before you load anything else! Mind, Jonas, no scratches."

Papa shook his head, though a smile tugged at his lips. "*Ja,* I remember."

The gray head turned toward Emma. "Granddaughter, see they take proper care."

"I will, *Maummi.*"

Katie joined Emma to oversee the wrapping of the hutch. When Samuel Miller offered a strong arm to help Katie up into the wagon, Emma hid a smile. No doubt she would receive a letter at her new home soon, informing her that a wedding date had been published. Because Samuel was the bishop's son, there was no fear he'd not receive the *Zeungis,* the letter of good standing. Rebecca would be thrilled at the news of a proper wedding in tiny Apple Grove.

But Emma would be far away, in Troyer, and would miss her friend's big day.

Why must I live in Troyer when everything I love is here?

She draped a thick quilt over her end of the hutch and sidled away while Papa secured a rope around it. The faces of her friends and family looked on. They filled the area between the house and the barn, maybe eighty in total. She knew every one, loved every one in her own way. Yes, even Amos Beiler. She sought him out among the crowd and smiled at the two little girls who hovered near his side. Poor, lonely Amos. He was a good father to his motherless family. No doubt he'd make a fine husband, and if she married him, she wouldn't have to move to Troyer. The thought tempted her once again, as it often had over the past several weeks since Papa announced his decision that she would live with Aunt Gerda for a while.

But she knew that if she agreed to become Amos' wife, she'd be settling. True, she'd gain a prosperous farm and a nice house and a trio of well-behaved children, with the promise of more to come. But the fact remained that though there was much to respect about Amos, she didn't love him.

The thought of seeing that moon-shaped face and slightly cross-eyed stare over the table for breakfast, dinner, and supper sent a shiver rippling across her shoulders. Not to mention sharing a marriage bed with him. It was enough to make her throw her apron over her face and run screaming across Papa's cornfield.

He deserves a wife who loves him, she told herself for the hundredth time. Her conscience thus soothed, Emma turned away from his mournful stare.

"That trunk goes in the front," *Maummi* shouted from her chair on the porch. "Emma, show them where."

Emma shrank against the gigantic hutch to give the men room to settle the trunk containing all her belongings. An oiled canvas tarp had been secured over the top to repel any rain they might meet. Inside, atop her dresses, aprons, bonnets, and *kapps*, was a bundle more precious to her than anything else in the wagon. A quilt, expertly and lovingly stitched, nestled within a heavy canvas pouch. Mama had made it with her own hands for Emma's hope chest. The last stitch was bitten off just hours before she closed her eyes and stepped into the arms of her Lord.

Oh, Mama, if you were here you could

convince Papa to let me stay home. I know you could. And now, without you, what will happen to me?

Yet, even in the midst of the dreary thought, a spark of hope flickered in the darkness in Emma's heart. The future yawned before her like an endless Kansas prairie. Wasn't there beauty to be found in the tall, blowing grasses of the open plain? Weren't there cool streams and shady trees to offer respite from the heat of the day? Maybe Troyer would turn out to be an oasis.

"Emma!"

Maummi's sharp tone cut through her musing. She jerked upright. Her grandmother appeared to have recovered from her heart episode. From the vantage point of her chair, she oversaw every movement with a critical eye.

"Yes, ma'am?"

"Mind what I said about that loading, girl. The food carton goes on last. We won't have time to go searching for provisions when we stop at night on the trail."

An approving murmur rose from the women at the wisdom of an organized wagon.

"Yes, ma'am." Emma exchanged a quick grin with Katie and directed the man carrying the carton of canned goods and trail provisions to set his burden aside for now.

A little while later, when all had been loaded and secured under an oiled canvas, the men stood around to admire their handiwork. Samuel even crawled beneath the wagon to check the support struts, and he pronounced everything to be "in apple-pie order."

Emma felt a pluck on her arm. She turned to find Katie at her elbow.

"This is a gift for you." Her friend pushed a small package into her hands. "It's only a soft cloth and some fancy colored threads. I was fixing to stitch you a design, but you're so much better at fine stitchery than I am that I figured you could make something prettier by yourself." She ducked her head. "Think kindly of me when you do."

Warmed by her friend's gesture, Emma pulled her into an embrace. "I will. And I expect a letter from you soon." She let Katie see her glance slide over to Samuel and back with a grin. "Especially when you have something exciting to report."

A becoming blush colored the girl's cheeks. "I will," she promised.

Emma was still going down the line, awarding each woman a farewell hug, when Bishop Miller stepped up to the front of the wagon and motioned for attention.

"Time now to bid Jonas Switzer Godspeed and fair weather for his travels." A kind smile curved his lips when he looked to *Maummi* and then to Emma. "And our prayers go with our sisters Marta and Emma as they make a new home in Troyer."

He bowed his head and closed his eyes, a sign for everyone in the Apple Grove district to follow suit. Emma obeyed, fixing her thoughts on the blue skies overhead and the Almighty's throne beyond. Silence descended, interrupted only by the snorts of oxen and a happy bird in the tall, leafy tree that gave shade over the porch.

What will I find in Troyer? A new home, as the bishop says? A fine Amish husband, as Papa wishes? I pray it be so. And I pray he will be the second son of his father, so he will come home with me to Apple Grove and take over Papa's farm when the time comes.

A female sniffled behind her. Not Katie, but Rebecca. A twist inside Emma's ribcage nearly sent tears to her eyes. Oh, how she would miss her sister when Rebecca left Troyer to return home with Papa. She vowed to make the most of their time together on the trail between here and there.

Bishop Miller ended the prayer with a blessing in High German, his hand on the head of the closest oxen. When the last word fell on the quiet crowd, *Maummi*'s voice sliced through the cool morning air. "Now that we're seen off proper, someone heft me up. We'll be gone before the sun moves another inch across the sky."

Though she'd proved earlier that she could make the leap herself at need, *Maummi* allowed Papa and the bishop to lift her into the wagon. She took her seat in her rocking chair, which was wedged between the covered hutch and one high side of the wagon bed. With a protective pat on the hutch, she settled her sewing basket at her feet and pulled a piece of mending into her lap. No idle hands for *Maummi*. By the time they made Troyer, she'd have all the mending done, and the darning too, and a good start on a new quilt.

Emma spared one more embrace for Katie, steadfastly ignored Amos' mournful stare, and allowed the bishop to help her up onto the bench seat. She scooted over to the far end to make room for Papa, and then Rebecca was lifted up to sit on the other side of him. A snug fit, but they would be okay for the six-day journey to Troyer. Emma settled her black dress and smoothed her apron.

"Now, Jonas, mind you what I said." *Maummi*'s voice from behind their heads sounded a bit shrill in the quiet morning. "You cut a wide path around Hays City. I'll not have my granddaughters witness to the *ufrooish* of those wild *Englischers*."

On the other side of Papa, Rebecca heaved a loud sigh. Emma hid her grin. No doubt Rebecca would love to witness the rowdy riots of wild cowboy *Englischers* in the infamous railroad town of Hays.

Papa mumbled something under his breath that sounded like *"This will be the longest journey of my life,"* but aloud he said, *"Ja, Mader."*

With a flick of the rope, he urged the oxen forward. The wagon creaked and pitched as it rolled on its gigantic wheels. Emma grabbed the side of the bench with one hand and lifted her other hand in a final farewell as her home fell away behind her.

ABOUT THE AUTHOR

Lori Copeland is the author of more than 90 titles, both historical and contemporary fiction. With more than 3 million copies of her books in print, she has developed a loyal following among her rapidly growing fans in the inspirational market. She has been honored with the *Romantic Times* Reviewer's Choice Award, The Holt Medallion, and Walden Books' Best Seller award. In 2000, Lori was inducted into the Missouri Writers Hall of Fame.

Lori lives in the beautiful Ozarks with her husband, Lance, their three children, and five grandchildren.

The employees of Thorndike Press hope you have enjoyed this Large Print book. All our Thorndike, Wheeler, and Kennebec Large Print titles are designed for easy reading, and all our books are made to last. Other Thorndike Press Large Print books are available at your library, through selected bookstores, or directly from us.

For information about titles, please call:
  (800) 223-1244

or visit our Web site at:
  http://gale.cengage.com/thorndike

To share your comments, please write:
  Publisher
  Thorndike Press
  10 Water St., Suite 310
  Waterville, ME 04901